Embraces

Embraces

DARK EROTICA

Edited by Paula Guran

For the Darklings—at least those of legal age

. . .

Special thanks to Marti Hohmann for giving me a chance even if it didn't work out and to Cara Bruce for working it out; Rick Berry for "Kali" and the inspiration and impetus for the title; Thomas S. Roche and M. Christian for guidance and friendship; David J. Schow for honing the edge; Michele Patterson and Jay Sheckley for the faith and support; and John Shirley for keeping me so busy I never have time to worry if I can do it or not.

Contents

Introduction

L onging for more sizzling stories of sexy demon lovers, seductive vampires seething with oral metaphor, kinky succubi ready for nameless sins? Are you slavering to taste the obscene forked kiss of tales that titillate and terrorize?

Well, forget it. If you want unsurprising, comfortable "erotic horror," you've got the wrong book in your hands. Put this book down RIGHT NOW and move on or ship it back before you crack the binding and get fingerprints all over it. Go find *Fangs For The Mammaries XXIV* or some similar tome.

But if you want something a little dangerous, stories that take a chance, and—instead of opting for the safety of the now-accepted subgenre of "erotic horror"—draw blood with writing that goes a step further, an inch deeper than before—read on.

Embraces: Dark Erotica started out (under another title or two) as an anthology from an established erotica publisher that offered writers a chance to explore the dark side with a highly sexual approach. The house editor (a bright, fresh, intelligent female) wanted literate original stories by writers who were not particularly known in the erotica field. The publisher (neither fresh nor female) was primarily concerned that the stories have "enough sex." I wanted a "good anthology." So, I invited writers to stomp on a few boundaries, cross some lines, and create non-traditional cutting edge dark erotica.

[Not that anyone really has a definition of what "cutting edge dark erotica" is, or even what "cutting edge horror" is. (I suppose if we defined it, then it might not be cutting edge anymore?) What we do have is some idea of what cutting edge horror is *not*: it's *generally* not about monsters or black magic or evil incarnate.

It abandons the archetypes of the past; instead it goes into the forbidden zones, attempts the unknown, and sometimes delves into that which is slightly beyond what most of us term reality. When the monsters do creep in, they are offered with originality and new perspective or are a reflection of our knowledge that the real monsters are, after all, us.]

Eventually the stories selected tended to confront and disturb with dark, twisted, and even humorous truth. They were sexy, speculative, literate, surreal, transgressive, obsessive, metaphorical, post modern, satiric, visceral, redemptive, bizarre, transformative, weird, confrontational, edgy, and often indescribable. Some were provocative, some provoked laughter; some touched upon societal horrors and others on personal psychological terrors. They went over the top and under the edge—and they did go all the way.

Everyone was happy. But, as anyone who has anything to do with the world of publishing knows, just having a book commissioned, contracted, accepted, provided with an ISBN, and on the schedule doesn't mean you really have a book. Things happen. I was left with a manuscript of stories that had nowhere to go.

Many months and a few adventures later, another publisher—a bright, fresh, intelligent female herself—knew a Good Thing when she saw it and thus the anthology (after much debate and some adjustments) was reborn as *Embraces: Dark Erotica*.

Over the year or so all of this took I read two stories (and really only two) that were most suitable for this book. One, "Saturnalia" by David J. Schow, appeared in a limited edition anthology, *Subterranean Gallery*, edited by Rich Chizmar and William Schafer; the other, a very short piece, "Homewrecker", from Poppy Z. Brite, appeared in a webzine that the bright, fresh, intelligent female publisher was editing. Few folks, I warranted, had had a chance to read these two gems. After only minimal pleading on my part, both authors graciously allowed me to include these stories. I think we have a happy ending.

During the sixteen months between first writing this introduction and writing the version you now read, I was reminded several times (by folks who had never read this book) that "erotic horror" was dead. Part of the evolution of dark fiction in the last decade or so included a more open examination of the sexual aspects of horror and combining the erotic with the horrific under the label of "erotic horror." But the term erotic horror became somewhat corrupted. Often what was (and is) published under that banner is really "sexually nasty horror"—meat-cleaver maniacs preying on women and having it off with their victims' truncated corpses; or sex-negative "divine retribution for enjoying yourself" plots—have-sex-get-snuffed. These works are horrific and sexual, but they are certainly not erotic. And if that's what erotic horror means, then, let it rest in peace.

Somehow in the rush of bringing the subtextual, metaphoric, and atmospheric sex indigenous to horror to the forefront, the ideas explored became formulaic. The fiction (and the sex) became pretty safe and predictable.

To be effective, both horror and the erotic must continue to find the door to the forbidden, subvert convention, go beyond formula and audience expectation; they should embrace the experimental. There's nothing wrong with comfortable, reliable fiction any more than there's anything wrong with plain old lights-out, missionary-position, straight sex. That may be enough to be enjoyable and satisfying … for some people or for some of the time. But good horror—like good sex—must find ways to go further and have a willingness to push beyond previous limits to remain vital and exciting.

Is this to say that all the stories in *Embraces: Dark Erotica* can be truthfully labeled as erotic? Let's just say that eroticism is in the mind of the reader and when you take a walk on this dark side you might be surprised at your own reactions.

I'm not sure anyone, other than me, is perverted enough to like *every* single story in this anthology any more than any individual can be expected to respond to the complete gamut of sexual stimuli or indulge in every single kink they come across. But then again—we *are* out to push your limits.

Paula Guran
March, 2000

You Give Me Fever
by Nancy Holder

Cold: heatless, sunless, unheated, unwarmed.
Frigid.
Practically shaking with cold; in the mirror, her nipples contracting through her jog bra. House music throbbing, or was it her heartbeat, too fast, much too fast, straining to warm her as she exercised beside sweaty, overheated women? She hadn't even broken a sweat, because she was so cold.

Everything squeezed together and pulled in: pecs, buttocks, all the muscles of her abdomen. She wore a thong leotard over her midthigh tights, and it centered itself between her labia to pull rhythmically over her clit, keeping pulse with the music and the beat of her body. In the old days, that would have been enough for her to have a private little orgasm. But these were not the old days. These were the freezing days.

Glacial, polar, frostbitten. Her name was Jennifer, she was twenty-four, and she had recently left her husband. When seventy-five percent of the marriages in California ended in divorce, it wasn't difficult to explain. Her flimsy reasons were readily accepted.

But here was the truth of it: fucking Brian had been killing her.

Brian: everything a lover must be: broad shoulders and chest, slightly-rounded ass, the glorious length of his cock. That he trimmed his pubic hair endeared him to her; he took his attractiveness seriously. That he worked out (the gym she was aerobicizing in was originally his gym, now gallantly vacated so they wouldn't run into each other) excited her and made her work out to stay in shape, too.

Heat. He had the heat. He put her in heat. He loved sex, and he made her love it, too. Porno movies for both of them. Arty and tasteful erotic magazines. On a hot afternoon, with the Santa Ana winds rushing down the canyons of Los Angeles, he would lick the sweat running between her breasts. He would say, "I wish we were in our bedroom screwing with all the windows open."

Masturbation was an art form, and an audience of one was welcomed. And as she sweated and ground and gasped, waves of heat rolled off her. Her pussy was steam. Her orgasm was a fire storm.

Heat. He loved pleasing her in bed. There existed no more deft lover than Brian. In her ear with his hot, moist breath, his rain forest whispers against her neck as he fanned flames already burning out of control: how much he loved caressing her breasts and sucking on her nipples; roaming over her belly with his pitchfork lips and tongue; sliding his fingers into her melting body. He loved doing it all to her. He loved having it all done to him. Uninhibited, passionate, joyfully lustful.

But it had been killing her.

She hadn't understood it at first. Her sex life before him: okay. Some experimentation, nothing to write home about. She figured she was just one of those women who didn't have a lot of range. So in the beginning she assumed that it made sense to feel as lethargic and drained after the hot, hot sex with Brian. But she was so tired afterwards that sometimes she would fall unconscious; Brian would tap her shoulder gently and say, "Hey, Christy, need a cold shower?"

But it was the fevers that got her. In the beginning, her illnesses were never severe, but her fevers spiked. Aspirin, antibiotics. No cause for alarm. It was the season, it was the sick building she worked in (she was a graphic artist), it was the way things were.

Brian got a new job. He had to travel. At first, it was almost exhilarating, missing him with body and spirit while he was on the road. Heat: They began having phone sex, at which they became very, very good. They tantalized and teased each other to fiery climaxes with words. Your pussy. My cock. Sliding. Thrusting. Holding you as wide open as possible. My mouth around you. Deep-throating you. Shooting into you. Swallowing every drop. Notes and videos, elaborate photographs in corsets and thongs, legs wide open, on all fours, head thrown back, posing with his erection, in handcuffs, tied up with velvet ropes. The pictures taken by Brian's obliging sister.

Noted: the longer and more often he was gone, the better she felt. In all other ways. Sexually, she was frustrated on a short-term basis, but she knew the waiting only made their next lovemaking session all the sweeter. It didn't particularly bother her. The heat was inside her now; she knew how to stay warm, how to stoke the fire.

Then Brian's job duties changed, and he was home all the time. They made love almost constantly.

Fevers, bad ones. High ones. This time the doctor started worrying about brain damage, ordered a CAT scan.

Brian forgot his weight belt at the gym: hernia operation. Sex was out for the near future.

Recovery.

To say that they made the connection immediately would be untrue; it took a long time first for Christy to believe it, and then Brian, when she told him about it. But she really began to die. Her RBC dropped and her immune system went completely out of whack. Night fevers: 103, 104. Higher. Emergency rooms and shaking in tubs of ice, imagining that she sent steam into the cubes, that she was a bar of molten metal that would burn whatever it touched. Except for another bar of molten metal: Brian's tongue. Brian's hands. Brian's cock.

Belief occurred like a simultaneous climax. Brian did everything he could to stay away from her.

Complete recovery. A horrible, unbelievable miracle.

Trips to doctors and therapists (none of whom believed) to confirm, between them, the diagnosis. And after time and desperate experimentation, the prognosis: terminal, if Christy continued to fuck Brian.

Brutal unfairness, to know such ecstasy must be denied. To have believed they had a lifetime ahead to push the envelope, and then to part. They couldn't live together and not have sex. They could barely live in the same town and not have sex, but distance would help. And so, divorce. Awful, shattering dissolution, as it was called: irreconcilable differences.

Six months.

Cold as the dead. As dead as the dead. She had touched a dead person once: her father, at his funeral. Unbelievably cold. The sky outside the church, gray. The rain at the grave site, icy.

This loss equaled the word she could barely speak: frigid. No longer lustful. No desire for sex at all. She tried forcing herself to feel, if not fevered, passionate delirium, then at least a crackle of interest. Movies, books, masturbating with and without her vast array of vibrators, plugs, and dildos, sex with men whom her mind—but not her body—registered as incredibly sexually attractive. No good. Losing Brian: complete and total female castration, replacement of the organs with the ice cubes that had brought her fever down and saved her life.

Worth saving?

In her gym class, perfecting a body wasted on her. A body she had crafted for sex; all the right muscles honed. All could be plucked and stretched like marionette strings for her own pleasure and that of a red hot lover. Brian had loved to push her thighs into the splits, laughing appreciatively at the way she could arch her back at the same time. The positions she could contort herself into, effortlessly. He loved to tell her he saw a little fire burning in her pussy.

All of that, still there, somewhere, in the burning fields of her intense preparation.

Grief extinguished passion. Cold: depressed, uninspired, dispirited.

After two months, she called him.

He had moved on. He had a new woman. Christy heard her laughing in the background while he apologized. Two months without sex: for either of them, the ice block in the center of hell. Certainly not the flames.

. . .

"Check your neighbor! Is she smiling?" the aerobics instructor commanded. An in-class joke: was she smiling, or were her glutes squeezed tight?

Christy didn't give a damn. She was cold. She had been exercising aerobically for forty-eight minutes and she wished she had a sweater.

Then the blonde in front of her turned and smiled at her. Perhaps an actress: taller than Christy, and her long, streaked blonde hair cascaded to her shoulder blades, held back by a black headband. Her clothes, soot black: sports bra, midthigh tights, socks, shoes. Her body: on fire, as they used to say. Not too muscular, very toned. Her bra crisscrossed over a well-proportioned back and the kind of slender-yet-cut arms Christy had always admired on other women. Her hips: flexed and hard. Thighs powerful, but the muscles long and lanky. Flush: red, glowing warm. Christy stumbled over the next step of the routine, which she'd performed flawlessly in at least a dozen previous classes.

For the duration, Christy though she felt not warm but, perhaps, at least less frozen. Wishful thinking?

The class broke up. The blonde strode into the women's locker room. Christy followed a minute or two after. All the shower curtains were drawn, and water sprinkled down on a row of feet with fire-engine-red painted toenails.

Christy's routine: start the sauna on the highest setting, strip, put it all in a locker, drape with a towel, go to the hot box. Today, stealing a glance at her naked body in a mirror. Nothing different, much to please: firm breasts, large nipples, bikini wax. In the hot days, she would have quickly spread her labia apart and stared at the ember-pink interior, the fireworks clit above, flames dancing inside as moisture ran down her thigh. Now, if alone, she would have run her fingers inside the tinderbox just to see if it turned her on, and cried long and hard because it didn't.

She crossed to the sauna and went inside.

Hellishly hot, a dry sauna, and as Christy closed the cedar door behind herself, her face prickled.

Warmth: she sought it like a starving animal seeks prey. The sauna did the best job, although it was inadequate. The icy day of her father's funeral, the icy days of her life without Brian. Death, when the hot blood cooled and all desires fled.

Of a habit, she flicked on the light and stepped into the sauna.

A small object lay in her usual spot. She crossed the small room: a Flame Pearl vibrator, one of her favorites. Good for the pussy, good for the clit, good for the ass. Christy had several of them at home. In the forest fire, they had made her smoke. Now, they did nothing.

She imagined a woman bringing the vibrator into the sauna with her, imagined her nipples contracting, the heat hotter than the sauna. Thought of hips thrusting, of a sweet belly pushing outward, a muffled cry, and a sigh.

She picked up the vibrator and placed it at the head of the shelf, for the owner to find. Lay down and loosened her towel. Soon the heat penetrated her skin, down through her muscles and organs to her numb bones, but at numb bones, stopped. Dozing, then, a cool memory of the comas—the timer set, in no danger of overheating—cruel double entendre, useless thought.

She wondered if the blonde owned a vibrator. Then thoughts slid away, and tears replaced them. Cold, icy tears that soon had her shivering again.

. . .

The next day in class, the blonde was there, standing in front of Christy again. Christy: Voyeur, voyeuse? She smiled at Christy. The flush spread to Christy's upper chest. Nothing more passed between them.

In the sauna, Christy found a box, beautifully wrapped, a card: For C.

The Flame Pearl.

Christy inserted it, wincing at her dryness. Turned it on. Waited for feeling.

Perhaps a slight warming. Perhaps simply a wish.

Treasures, left in the sauna: Six-and-a-half-inch hand-molded dildo of silicone, curved as Brian had been curved; a pair of nipple clamps, which she had always favored. Treasures left for her.

She began to imagine they were from the blonde. She had no idea.

The thought a flicker. A degree.

Beneath her towel in the sauna, she used them. She did not feel the heat but—

—a degree?

. . .

In the heat of the sauna, over the days and the weeks, Christy worked with the toys. An oxymoron, working with toys.

A way to save her life.

In the world: Los Angeles was never cold, but she owned gloves, scarves. Her constant temperature: 96.6. People noticed.

In the sauna. Her temperature: perhaps 97.6. Perhaps.

And then, one day, with the toys and the frustrations and the yearnings:

The blonde, in the doorway of the sauna.

And the blonde said: "There will be heat, there will be light you may die of me."

Ignition.

As she came to Christy naked and searing, the fire a cauterization; Christy took her in her arms and

Ignition.

The blonde in her arms, her nipples hard against Christy's nipples, their navels pressed together. Labia pulled away, clitorises encircled enCirce'd enraptured, warmed, finally warmed, by the rocks of the sauna and heat: passion, rapture, ecstasy of the tongue and the lips and the pussy and the nipples and the ass of the blonde.

Christy could never overheat in the sauna, never doze and die there, at the highest setting. But now: There will be heat there will be light you may die of me.

Grappling, clinging, panting, grasping for the unattainable
the unattainable I thought you were unattainable, heat, you are
inside me now I am so hot.

I am so fevered.

Give me fever.

The blonde pulled gently away.

With a cry, Christy reached for her.

The blonde said: "You nearly died once for passion. Can
you die?"

And suddenly the cold rushed in, from the tip of Christy's
head to the knuckles of her toes. And she thought, One more
moment of that kind of heat, for one moment of heat I would
gladly go to hell.

And the blonde looked at her, and there was something evil
about her smile, and something cruel about her caress, but
Christy didn't care. Her hands were warm.

Then the blonde gave her a harness to wear around her hips.
She gave her an enormous curved dildo to put into the harness.
It was shaped like him, veined like him, it was a model of him.

Christy whispered, "Brian," and the blonde answered back,
"Just so."

The blonde said, "You must stay with me here, in the sauna.
It is the only place for us, the heat of the sauna. If you cannot
do this little thing, I will leave you."

Christy fell on her knees and spread the blonde's labia wide
and murmured, "Give me fever, give me fever."

"You will overheat in this sauna," the blonde said. "You will
be too hot."

"Give me fever."

The blonde sat on the shelf and spread her legs as wide as
possible. Christy drank of her, pushed her tongue into her. She
rubbed her breasts and her nipples and her belly with the melting wax of her.

The melting of her.

The heat.

Burning away: pure desire.

Clit, labia, the molten core. The hottest place.

In the fire, the blonde's mask melted away: beneath the mask, lust was just as beautiful. Hunger, just as perfect.

Talons, claws, eyes that glowed a blistering crimson.

Christy tongued the craters and the pits and the hollows.

"In the morning they will find you dead," the blonde promised Christy. "Incinerated."

The sauna began to burn.

"Your bones will be ash."

Christy's answer was to mount her with the strap-on dildo. To light the match herself.

And the heat was glorious: the heat was what every lover knows: the world, for that high moment of passion. The end of the world, for that peak. Obliteration, for the translation of bone and sinew into speechless, dumb, Orphic mystery. Disaster, tragedy, consequences beyond reckoning. Damnation: exile, curse, excommunication.

For heat, yes.

Burned in the morning, Christy rejoiced. Ash. Yes!

Oh, Brian—one last thought as she thrust as he would have, as she pushed as he would have, as he pleasured as he would have; one memory, one kiss, as the blonde writhed and sobbed. As they both exploded in a whitehot orgasm.

As the sauna went up.

You give me fever.

Saturnalia
by David J. Schow

"So, uh, would you like me to drop my uh pants?" Colin was halfway out of his seat, belt already unbuckled above a growing erection, when his interviewer's wave sat him back down, unexposed.

"I don't need to see it," Valentina Sykes said, looking him straight in the eye. "You would not be here if I held any doubts about your ability to function. Mere function doesn't interest me. Performance is the key word, here."

Valentina gave Colin Freehand—real name, Dex Wilson—the once-over for about the eighth time, scalp to shoes. About now, she thought, he's concocting a mental porn loop in which he figures out how to make all the right sounds while he hammers a woman slightly older than his eldest grandma. She had no doubt she could still teach him a thing or six; he was the eager puppy type, straining to prove how-big, how-long, how-humpable; easy to be hard. His stage name, Freehand, came from the gag about how he could pilot a car, among other things, without using his hands. His abs were ripped, his back marbled with superfluous show off muscle, purest gymsteak. The concerns of his life were his hyperthyroidal sports car (and how soon he could score a flashier one), his daily intake of hydrolyzed soy protein, and how long he could keep his name at the top of the treacherously mercurial adult film biz. Average burnout ceiling for a newcomer was eighteen months to two years—after that, the blur of double penetrations, condomless fucking and sucking, HIV scares, easy access to rock and dust and worse, plus the erosions of casual brutality and even more casual usury, generally caused new meat to run back to Iowa, blow out their brains, or decay into walking ghosts, background players in the flesh trade; no lines except the ones that vanished up their noses.

How simple it would be to make him grovel, thought Valentina. To beg for something he could never have when he's used to getting everything he wants.

"That look you're directing toward me might have been flattering, forty years ago," said Valentina. "You're generally always on the make, aren't you?"

Colin shrugged. Seduction was coded into his DNA factor.

"I think you'd be surprised," she said. "But it's not to be. I didn't bring you here, after culling so many candidates, to give an old lady her jollies by slipping it in and pretending."

"You mean I don't get paid?"

She enjoyed the abrupt alarm in his tone. "You get paid."

"I mean, for you and all, it's kind of an honor, anyway."

"What are you talking about?" She wanted to see if he could form coherent thoughts into sentences, maybe even extrapolate.

"I saw all your movies you made in the fifties," he said, happy to chance onto a subject he could do at least partially on autopilot. "Marilyn Monroe was blowsy, a tart for the masses to idolize. You didn't do the squeaky little-girl voice or stick your thumb in your mouth or play that white-trash sexy schtick. You were beautiful, and you knew it, and you didn't have to advertise. I've always admired that."

She imagined him a few years younger, furiously whacking off to a black and white photo of her on the cover of *Photoplay*. If she wanted him to play with himself right now, in front of her, he'd probably do it. She was seventy-three years old and no one had taken her photograph for nearly a quarter of a century. She could completely unman him, this instant.

Instead she lowered her eyes and said quietly, "Thank you."

Colin was the one, all right; she had selected him well. Now she felt linked to him. Besides, she had always thought Norma Jean was a coddled little tramp, as well.

She handed Colin a photograph of a young woman who had, just the month before, been available to the nation, via newsstand, in a magazine for which she constituted a precedent-setting centerspread.

"Do you think you could make love to her?"

Colin barely glanced. "Yeah, I could fu—" He caught Valentina's look and decided to mind his manners, and not cuss. "Yes."

"Tonight at eight, she's yours."

It took Colin a minute and a half to locate the copy of the overpriced men's mag in his bathroom stack. The monthly gatefold queens of this particular publication were notable for their apparent lack of personal history—they were photo-perfect, gorgeous to a fault, fantasy food for millions of male hetero underachievers ... and they issued, seemingly, from the heartland of America without preamble, backstory or nasty personal habits. They listed their fatuous pastimes and favorite boring movies, all the false assurances of their attainability ...

... to legions of substance-abusing ground-pounders who called themselves men, who bellowed *yee-hah* and wore their baseball caps backwards, who depended on armpit funk (or something) to magnetize the slack-jawed pigs with whom they reproduced.

Damn, thought Colin. Sometimes his job was just too easy. It was fun to do what he was good at.

When Colin paged to the shot of Catherine Ankrum holding the garden hose, he just had to jack off. He shot semen across Catherine's four-color face the way he planned on doing it in real life, soon. She kept on smiling. Practice, practice, practice.

No way this bitch could be so clean, he thought. He wanted to ram into her and force her to tell the truth about what a slut she really was. She'd be licking her own shit off the crown of his dick in no time. Beautiful or not, famous or not, they all looked more or less the same with a cock in their mouth.

Colin napped, showered with antibacterial soap, and showed up in loose, comfy clothing at the appointed time. Ding-dong.

The bedchamber was the color of pale fire.

The bed was mahogany, draped in satin—not silk, as Colin had anticipated. He had nodded once on silk sheets and awakened with his cock-head swollen up like a party favor; something to do with static electricity. He hated silk. It was a cliché. Cotton was washable. Satin would pass.

Two tables with carafes. A vase of cut lilies. That was about it; the room was not tarted up. No mirrors, no rack of whips, no kitsch.

The camera lenses were innocuous, but their sweep covered every corner. He spotted them at about the fifteen-minute mark by his estimate, because he had not worn a watch. His brain was shrieking that it had been at least an hour before his date finally showed.

Catherine Ankrum entered wearing workout clothes and offered Colin a broken little smile. She smelled like coconut oil and her skittish manner kicked Colin's autopilot into overdrive; from now on he could steer.

"It's a little weird," he offered her confidentially. The return spark of fake hope in her eyes was something he never tired of seeing from women who had gotten themselves in too deep.

"My year has kind of sucked," she said, not going into the details of a big heroin tab and a celebrity too slow in materializing. So much for the pre-fab bio.

"Doesn't matter." He took her hand, as if he planned to be kind to her.

She had eyes the color of decaf coffee—they looked strong but wouldn't keep you up. Not contact lenses; that was a point in her favor. Her face had been rebuilt, to lose the peasant nose, and plucked to pattern a genetically-tragic hirsuteness. Her teeth had been straightened enough to leave the inside of her mouth ribbed with scar tissue. Stripped and lubricated, Colin found little to distinguish her. He hated implants, but decided to overlook hers since they weren't as grotesque as they might have been and the shiny slug-skids of surgery were well-concealed. His big dick was bonafide, and the last place he wanted to put it was between two nerve-dead silicone sacs. She had undergone laser tightening and a slight labial tuck, leaving her with what Colin thought of as a too-symmetrical "stripper pussy," but the job was expensively good, and he wouldn't have his nose in it for long. Maybe that was the hole into which her bank had vanished.

Once he had helped her come—she wasn't faking because he could feel the difference—she admitted breathlessly that she had been watching him on the closed circuit monitors before coming into the room. Just watching him walk around, looking for the cameras.

"Did that flip her switch, ole Miss Valentina?" said Colin.

"She was watching, too," said Catherine, as though they weren't wired for sound in this place of intimacy.

"The voyeur thing. She likes to watch."

Colin nearly bolted upright. *She likes to watch, all right — the way you watched HER, in all those black and white antiques of motion picture history.* He squeezed his eyes shut. No way he was going to lose control, here; no way *she* was going to force him to lose control.

He took it out on Catherine after slapping himself erect. He could feel his knob bruising her uterus. Resolve clunked shut in his gut like the bolt of a lock, and when he finally pulled out and creamed her face, she was crying.

"Godammit, I'm *bleeding*, you *fucker!*"

Fucker's right, thought Colin. It's what I do for a living.

The amount of Valentina's check brought Colin back for more. Her smile was wry, bemused. "Everything satisfactory? No fallout?"

"What's next?"

"Not so fast. Savor each moment. Don't let them rush past untasted."

"What do you mean?"

"Like that bit where you confided in her, and turned her on just enough to trust you to mount her one more time, then hurting her when you did it."

Colin performed that little twitch of the head that announced he was guiltlessly at sea. Whatever.

"Come on, Colin, when you told her, *oh, Valentina likes to watch?* That united you both against me—the voyeur—and you immediately exploited that trust, and hurt her." Valentina's eyes held level and gray. "That's a tactic I'd expect from a chess player."

Colin smiled to cover the truth—he did not know what in hell Valentina was talking about. But her money spent excellently.

She snapped her fingers to bring him back. "You were asking what came next?"

A naked brunette is sucking a horse's penis, or trying to. The head of the penis is the size of a cantaloupe, which makes the woman look like a small snake trying to swallow a large egg. Her mouth is wide open as she sort of smears her face around the tip of the erect member. The shaft looks three feet long.

Colin blinked. Looked again. The woman was still naked. Funny, that he wasn't reacting to her nakedness.

The phallus is all there is, as she tries to tame it.

Colin did not notice how nice her breasts were. No implants.

The horse is some kind of muddy chestnut. Its head is out of frame. Its dick dominates the view, obliterating cognizance of virtually any other consideration, and there's suspense, too—not will it go off, but how soon?

Essentially, this was what men and women have joked about for centuries, the legendary big dick, the scepter of supposed male power. All men are supposed to want big dicks the way all women are supposed to want bigger breasts, and anyone who denied this, traditionally, was either lying, or already packing.

The horse ejaculates. The force of it seems to physically shove the woman back, like the kick of a gun. She tries masterfully to field what looks like about half a gallon of jetting Flicka come. She manages a mouthful, the kind that balloons her cheeks. Then she wrenches forward, coughing, live and in real time, nothing edited. Her cupped hands overflow with regurgitated horse jizz.

Colin imagined it to be pretty warm, like gravy.

It gushes from the woman's nose as the cock keeps spurting past her face. Horses, apparently, come as much as they shit.

Colin wondered what this woman sought in a sex partner when she wasn't sucking off stallions for home video. The business end of the horse dick put Colin in mind of a baby's head, and he questioned whether this anonymous mystery woman had ever borne any children. Whether she joked about men with tiny dicks. Whether she liked men at all. He imagined a quick, nonspecific fuckfest in which, to fulfill her hunger, somebody has to shove a baby up her twat.

"Last week I saw one on the Internet where a woman bends over, spreads for the camera, and squeezes out a full Coke can," said Valentina, over Colin's shoulder. "Letting a lens record this sort of thing is not the most dignified road to immortality, is it?"

"What, do I get a lecture, now?"

"It was a rhetorical question." She lowered her eyes in a studied move that made her look bemused. "I apologize."

Somehow Colin did not feel empowered. This time, when he entered the bedchamber, he just sat on the bed. He'd done the tour last time. He felt the lenses, watching him.

He couldn't push Valentina's little Wild West video out of his mind. He kept circling back to the idea that it was not intended as outrageous ... it was meant to overwhelm with inadequacy all who viewed it. Beyond the beery, frat-boy grossout lurked an agenda which humiliated the woman gulping horse come last of all.

For the first time, Colin pondered whether women were repulsed by the taste of his own semen, then whether the women he'd like to fuck *might* be. He had tasted it himself— slippery, alkaline, not as "salty" as bad porn would have you believe. Perhaps his own was a special mix. Perhaps it would seem saltier if he were compelled to chug a tumbler of it. He thought about going down on women he'd known, on women he'd *like* to know. All that glaze and lube was just mucous, basically. You don't think about licking your girlfriend's nose when she has the flu.

Get real, he chided himself. The horse didn't care whether it was being jacked off by a man, a woman, or a milking machine run berserk. The mystery woman had to have been solicited, acquired, and willing to do all this buck-naked, drugs or not. And paid, assuredly. It was not some sniggering plot targeted on his own sexual fears; that required thought, and nobody actually *thought* about this shit—they just went ahead and did it.

"My name is Soliel." The voice whipped Colin's head around; he'd been caught with his alarms off.

The second thing that nailed him was how plain this one looked. No aerobics android, here. She had kept the nose Catherine Ankrum had erased. Her complexion was hit and miss; she was not so much unattractive as undistinguished. She came clad in the sort of junk women wear to hide their bodies when they feel ugly.

Soliel fondled his crotch, unzipped his pants and did her best to suck him up hard. Colin recalled the high school joke about fat chicks; it took him forever to petrify. In his mind, he had to lapse purposefully back toward his reliable autopilot. Pretend he was on a set, fucking Cherry Canyon's honey-hole (or vice-versa); play the game where he strove to hump so long that the crew ran out of film, or, even better, videotape.

Soliel was due for the trick where Colin orgasmed, stayed inside, kept pumping, re-engorged and orgasmed again. Despite his performance she seemed a universe away, enwrapped in her own sensations. Her vagina was capacious and elastic, making sustained friction a problem.

Colin kept thinking about the damned horse, and never managed that second erection.

He was able to locate nine of Valentina Sykes's films in one day, though it required four different video stores, none of them Blockbusters. His mini-marathon had nothing to do with plot and everything to do with characterization. Valentina invariably portrayed strong-willed women who would destroy those around them rather than bend. Love was generally a bad idea that led to destruction. There remained only manipulations of greater or lesser finesse … and, sometimes, a victor, or at least a survivor, usually Valentina.

"I was an actress, Colin … what did you expect to see?"

It was easier to see her face, then, in her face, now. "I don't know; I'm not sure. I want to know what all this makes you feel, I guess."

"You don't know, you're not sure, you guess." Valentina threw back enough straight Polish vodka to keep a tiki lamp going for an hour. "Did you masturbate or not?"

"In the end, yeah. Halfway through *The Stars in Her Eyes*."

"Ah. The corset scene."

"It's the most naked you ever got in any of your pictures, when you stripped down to that lingerie."

"You're forgetting my bathing suit stuff."

"I haven't forgotten. The lingerie was more intimate."

"Made me look more available, you mean."

"I guess so."

"Don't guess." She pursed her lips. He could see secrets stacked up in her eyes, inscribed like petroglyphs in a language he could not fathom. "You wanted to make love to me, the way I was, then." She did not wait for an answer. "Stupid question, really. Would it pique your interest a bit more to know that Soliel is my daughter?"

Colin swallowed hard, trying to make room in his throat for a response. The lump there decided to stay. He felt his heart speed up. He paled.

"Yes, Colin. Soliel—your previous 'date.' The one you were so … preoccupied with, or should I say during? I'd think that given the opportunity you'd be more than eager to make love to my daughter. The results weren't so tabloid-worthy, were they?"

"I didn't know," he choked out.

"But it shouldn't make any difference, should it? I guess sex may really be all in the mind, like they say." Her gaze critiqued him, seeking flaws when before it sufficed with approbation. "Still … I'd think that would be your dream encounter, to have sex with the daughter of the woman you fantasize about while masturbating. And you really couldn't get it up that second time."

"It happens."

"It doesn't happen to me."

"It won't happen again." *Not as long as I can distance myself from that damned horse video,* Colin thought. "Sometimes under the best conditions, with the sexiest woman in the world, the rhythm just gets bollixed."

"We'll see, won't we?"

Valentina rewarded him with a low-slung, sturdy vixen with genuine breasts, the type whose strong, saucy walk was both an announcement and a warning to those who would aspire to get between her legs. Her name was JodyRae and carnality was her main ingredient. She shamed the anorexic bimbos of men's mags and provided a full-body workout for Colin. All the time he pounded her, he was thinking of how much better he would perform if he ever got another shot at Soliel. Valentina, naturally, had anticipated this. The time for Soliel had passed, and JodyRae was just a warm-up for what was to follow.

Colin had been told the new girl's name was Bettina, and he found her already undressed and waiting for him the moment he entered the chamber. She did not say much of anything and only seemed dimly aware of what he was doing. Her body was flabby instead of detailed, pale in an unhealthy way, and her movements against him were clumsy and ineffectual, as though she was doped, or not accustomed to getting laid well. She smelled bad, a combination of body odor and starchy diet, plus a diapery pall that put Colin in mind of nurseries and baby drool.

This one was a bedflop; no potential and no hope beyond a quick ram in the rack. What the hell was Valentina thinking?

Bettina grunted a few inarticulate words; Colin shellacked his expression and played strictly to the camera. Okay, she was obviously doped; it wasn't as if he'd never ridden that train himself.

He pushed off her and wiped down with the towel that was always there, waiting, on a small valet rack. Bettina was still making noise and when he actually paid attention he saw that she continued to murmur and thrust against air as though he was still inside her. Her arms looped around nothing above her; a ghost embrace.

That was when he finally realized: *She's mentally retarded.*

He could not get to the shower fast enough.

In his street duds, in the corridor, not twenty minutes later, he ran into Soliel. His brain was racing, trying to find some way to scour the previous hour out of every convolution.

"It's you," she said, looking at his crotch. They all did.

"Hey." Panic formed a fireball in Colin's head. He was trying to summon cheap charm and seductive small talk, to cultivate Valentina's daughter—for later—and all that would display was YOU FUCKED A SLOBBERING RETARD, UNH-UNH-UNH. His machine gun nest of pheromones was dozing on duty.

"I have to kind of explain. About my mom."

"You don't have to explain anything. I just—"

She overrode him. "No, stop. You don't understand, even if you think you do. It might all seem very strange. But she does it for love."

He stood absorbing her, sensing his snap judgment was off. He could see Valentina in her daughter now, around the eyes, in the shape of the mouth, in the general body carriage. The prevailing make-up fashions of the fifties would have made Soliel's brows thicker and she probably would have bangs over her considerable expanse of forehead. She smelled pleasantly of night-blooming jasmine. When she said *she does it for love* she had reached out and touched Colin's hand, in entreaty, then withdrawn it hastily, as though stung.

"What, even to the point of throwing her daughter into the mix, and watching her fuck?"

"That's not it. It's subject to my approval. I saw some of your movies and I said okay."

Colin abruptly remembered the capacity of Soliel's limousine-sized vagina. She had seen his dick in a few adult films and voted yea. She had volunteered to fuck him based on seeing his movies in the same way Colin was actualizing his vintage fantasies about

Valentina Sykes. It scuffed his ego. He had treated Soliel like a charity fuck while she'd been going to the races.

"And you did it for your mom." He tried his best to sound wounded.

She touched his face. "Hey. You were wonderful. Really. I gotta go."

Somehow it didn't surprise Colin that his next "date" was a man. His name was Larry, and Colin forgot it as soon as he heard it. He'd done boy-on-boy scenes before, so it was no big deal. By the end of the month he had also fucked a bilateral amputee and a toothless Skids sterno-drinker who cackled and stank of piss.

He got a bonus when he actually made the wino come.

Hence, when he had to fuck a cadaver, he appreciated its cleanliness.

"I hate it," said Soliel. "She's gone overboard. It's become like a tug-of-war between you and her."

"She's not going to win," Colin said, mopping his groin with a damp towel. "I can fuck anything she throws at me, but I want you to be honest and tell me something."

Soliel's nipples were tumid from her latest climax. She teased them idly and the reverberations tingled her toes. She hefted Colin's cock. "The truth, you have to work for."

"Does Valentina want me to fuck her?"

Soliel shot him a glance. "Does that mean what you really want is to fuck my mom?" She began pumping. "Does that get you hard?"

"I wanted to fuck your mother when she was an image, an ideal. I toyed with the idea of fucking her when I met her, as a challenge. Now, after jumping through hoops for her, the answer is no. It must have been kind of the same for you, I mean, growing up with a manipulator."

"Yeah ... what I'd expect to happen next is, now that you've rejected the notion of fucking her, she'd try to find a way to make you want to do it anyway, if that makes any sense."

"It makes too much sense."

Soliel had shown up on Colin's doorstep between his "dates" with Dayna, the amputee, and the cadaver (whose name Colin never did learn).

"I'm sorry I was rude the other day. Here." She'd handed Colin a little box of chocolates.

Colin was honestly moved, insofar as he could be. "Did your mom send you?"

"No. I need you to help ... um, fill a void in my life." Her gaze came up steely and wanton. "And if you laugh, I'll break your teeth out of your head with a wrench."

Colin had not laughed, and pulled her into his arms instead. He spent private time wondering whether she was a spy, just as she doubted any and all of his motives. In a bizarre way, they were a good couple—mutual interests kept their relationship completely indoors.

Soliel loved sex with Colin. She whipped him up like a berserk rider, telling him that her size, her capacity, caused him to swell even larger inside her. Their sex became a runaway engine with the governor dumped, terminating in high-speed collision and the popcorn stutter of machine-gun multiple orgasms. It was worse than a letter to *Penthouse*.

Colin loved sex with Soliel. But then, Colin loved sex with anyone. It was his reason for being; he did what he was good at, and it was more than fun—it was why Valentina had hired him. The more he fucked Soliel, the more the old Valentina, the movie-fantasy Valentina, seemed to emerge from her daughter. Colin would never admit that his relationship with Soliel had the power to ground and stabilize him in a healing way, so he just stuck with the fantasy.

And when Colin was working, he fucked whatever flavor Valentina could conjure up from her kettle of pleasures and nightmares, until the day she actually drew him aside for a warning.

By now, Colin was used to being shocked, so Valentina's attempt to cushion him came as a complete surprise.

"Normally, I'd let you navigate on your own," she told him. "But if there is one cultural constant that cuts across every ideal of what is sexually attractive around the world, it is the absence of disease. You've done dirty-filthy-nasty, and it's not the same. I'm talking about you having sex with someone who is diseased."

"We talking AIDS, here?"

"No. You are in no danger of contracting anything. I'm more concerned with the danger of you not being able to handle the idea of making love to a partner who is diseased, repellently so. I'm talking about sights you may not want to see, smells you definitely don't want to inhale, and textures that would make you sick to your stomach."

"I fucked a dead person for you, Valentina."

"That's clinical. Not the same."

"What about the chick with no limbs and the screaming wino lady?"

"This is different."

"No it isn't. Are you offering me the opportunity to refuse?"

"I'd rather you didn't. We've come a long way and I have big plans for you."

"Then what's my incentive? I got a bonus for getting the wino lady's rocks off."

"You'll get a bonus for this."

"I want something new. I want you to give up something valuable. The money is nothing to you."

"You want my daughter, by now, I suspect."

"I already have your daughter." The sense of power over Valentina at last was giving Colin a hard-on. "I want you."

"Young man, haven't you given up your wet dream of screwing a woman old enough to be your—" She stopped. She had spieled off this script already.

"Not this particular old woman."

"You'd be disappointed."

"More disappointed than I was when I fucked a dead body?"

"You're going to insist, aren't you?"

Colin held fast, not giving an inch … so to speak.

"It seems I've outsmarted myself." Her crooked little smile resurged. She appeared to run scenarios in her head. "And what would I be giving up, exactly, that seems so valuable to you?"

"Power. You're going to have to relax your grip on things, just once."

"Why, Colin, are you going to make me come?"

"Yes or no."

Valentina released a long, slow breath of consideration. "You do this, today, and you can have what you want."

"Plus the money."

Valentina laughed. "Goes without saying, greedy boy." She chuckled. "You'll have to promise to be gentle."

They regarded each other, both knowing the market value of promises.

The chamber was darker than it ever had been before.

Colin was aware of walking down the corridor and turning right in the usual way, but in some way flirtatiously beyond the reach of his senses, this room felt different from the room in which all his previous tests had been conducted. There was no light, so much as luminescence. It was a mushroom-damp nocturnal environment, like a cavern of bats. The air was hothouse-thick and Colin's estimate put the chamber itself at body temperature.

It was a different room. Somehow Valentina had slid the facets of her spider's web puzzle-box around and caused him to take a familiar, by-rote route to a new destination.

Here the bed was canopied. Directly above it a bank of powerful full-spectrum UV tubes glowed, and as Colin approached—slowly—he picked out the vague rush of humidifiers, misting the atmosphere. Vents engirded the room at waist height. As Colin passed beneath the crimson glow of a heat lamp in the ceiling, he could make out a row of TV monitors above the vents, across from the bed. All dark. He felt the heat seek to penetrate the top of his skull; he shaded his eyes.

"Come on." It was Soliel, using the sort of tone with which one might coax a puppy. She revealed herself to be nearby the bed when she stepped into a pool of chromatic light. She was clothed.

"Okay," Colin ventured in anticipation of some weird punchline. "You care to give me a clue?"

Soliel withdrew a drape and the eyes of bed's occupant rolled to register Colin. Its mass lolled, as though from internal tremors, and Colin could perceive its basic form as humanoid—head, limbs, genitalia. In no respect did it violate the law of bilateral symmetry, not exactly, but the shifting nature of its gelatinous form made it seem shapeless. That maw, a hole punched in putty, could be a mouth; the upper appendages could pass for arms since the longer one had several fingers. It suffered from bedsores. Bilirubin-colored smudges mottled its surface like the spoor of leukemia. From what Colin could see of its pubis, he guessed it to be female.

Soliel passed by Colin like a wraith, kissing him lightly on the cheek. "I'll just leave you two alone."

"That's no goddamned answer."

She spun on him. "It's what you wanted."

"The more you talk, the less sense you make." He was getting angry, working up a good mad.

"That's Valentina's daughter, you idiot. That's Soliel. I'm just a hired gun. Like you." She stalked off and was enveloped by the dim haze that masked the limits of the chamber.

"Valentina! "

The monitors snowed briefly blue, then resolved into Valentina's image; her face, replicated in a row of screens.

Colin spoke to the screens. "You just violated my bullshit ceiling and I'm outta here as of now."

"No, you're not." The sound system was refined enough to make her transmitted voice sound intimately close. "You're going to stay here, Colin, and do what you do better than anyone."

Colin heard the door thunk shut with airlock finality. He was pretty sure he was not actually imprisoned, and wanted to know what Valentina thought she had, to keep him here.

"I'm sorry about the disease story; it is partially true. Technically."

"What about Soliel?"

"The woman you thought was Soliel is named Adela. She's been receiving regular injections, and it was necessary for you to make love to her in order to become immunized, yourself. The rest of the participants were to help you overcome your own fears and prejudices, so you could be effective here, with the real Soliel."

Colin's arms folded tightly, defensively. He didn't know where to look for the cameras, so he addressed the screens and tried not to look at the fleshy plasmodium awaiting him in bed.

"No," he said. "I don't think so."

"Then you haven't thought enough. There's nothing here that you haven't dealt with already. You can't claim to be repulsed and expect me to believe you."

"What if I have a headache?"

"What if I tell you that the mentally impaired young lady you mounted so manfully kept on making those grunts and thrusting motions until she died? Now that must've been a *headache*. What if I tell you the coroner could only identify JodyRae's remains by her dental records and a crookedly-healed fibula she broke when she was nine, and—what do you know— you were the last person to see her before parts of her got, well, metabolized?"

"Excuse me?"

"You know—digested."

"Eaten?"

"Not exactly in the sense of chewed-up-and-swallowed, but essentially, they provided nourishment." She lowered her voice into a tone Colin recalled from the movies, whenever her character got dead honest. "I love my daughter, Colin. More than anything. You saw me only as a manipulative old crone, a puppet mistress. That's what I was in a lot of movies made a long time ago, and you reinforced your biases by watching those movies and passing judgment on me. I project a hard exterior, like armor, because I'm an actress, and on occasion I can act very well. But more than that, I really do love my daughter. That probably doesn't 'track' for you, real love, I mean."

"It doesn't mean I have to get intimate with the Blob, here, either."

"Oh, but it does. Remember Catherine Ankrum, the fold-out woman? She died. I have you on tape with her just before she died to feed my little girl. Sex with the dead is also still against the law in this state, and I believe you indulged in a bit of that, as well."

In that moment, Colin tracked. Valentina liked to watch, and she was probably pretty good at *recording*, too. Videotape, from multiple angles, of Colin with *all* his partners, these past weeks. All her victims; now all *his* victims. Not counting the corpse from the morgue, that was what? At least six murders whose names he could almost remember? He'd be painted as a sexually predatory serial killer, and nobody would be interested in the innocence of a porn actor.

Soliel waited. She had been waiting such a long time, for a man that was right for her ... which meant that she had spent even more time fantasizing and mentally preparing. She would expect not to be disappointed.

"You don't possess many true intimacies," said Valentina. "But the ones you have are sufficient to damn you a hundred-fold. Skin, hair, prints, blood, semen, DNA ..." She left unspoken the part about how the brand of wealth that underwrote Colin's services could also buy the best legal pit bulls available—to be fired at will toward Colin's credibility in a salvo of torpedoes with teeth.

He wanted, more than anything, to revert to the unreal version of Soliel, and the fantasy that they had formed a human bond. She had slipped his grasp and walked out of the room. That woman was really named Adela, and she hadn't been much to look at, but she'd left a pang in Colin's gut, and by now she was catching a train that would whisk her into the coal-mine blackness of a subway tunnel whose depths smelled metallic and alien, like the real Soliel. He had taken up Valentina's challenge to bypass the fate of adult film hopefuls all over the world—a world where young meat could erode to nothing in a handful of years. A world that included dippy dream relationships, like the one he had with the fake Soliel, only as a preamble to the usual fucking and sucking …

There was no flattery here, no seduction. His partner did not look like all the other chicks, and Colin began to fall out of love—with his image of himself, his staying power, his ability to take and have anyone.

He disrobed with Valentina's face surrounding him on a dozen screens. He had been servicing her all along, not that he minded. He fancied himself, above all, a pro.

Now he was a pro with obligations and entanglements. He needed to avoid being arrested, should his ego force him to walk out, or consumed, should his libido fail this new standard before him. He detested responsibilities, but could exploit them to kick-start his good old autopilot.

With a rising erection, Colin approached the bed and commenced his foreplay. It was no longer fun to do what he was good at.

On the Dangers of Simultaneity, Or, Ungh, Mmmm, Oh-Baby-Yeah, Aaah, Oooh ... UH-OH!
by Robert Devereaux

I've related elsewhere the catastrophe that befell when, one Christmas Eve in the late sixties, the archangel Michael, entrusted with the whole ball o' wax while God was vacationing, inadvertently allowed Santa Claus and the Tooth Fairy to cross paths.

By no means was that the archangel's only screw-up. Michael was renowned for screw-ups. But his other major gaffe, which the heavenly host oohed and aahed and tut-tutted over for eternities afterward (though God proved kinder), came when he unleashed, by mischance, the Orgasm Fairy upon the world.

Before the ninth of February 1964, no lovers had ever truly had a simultaneous orgasm, which is to say, one in which amorous jet-fuel propels them at precisely the same moment along precisely the same giddy arc of glee. Michael, you see, had been given the crucial task of assuring unaligned orgasms, since God knew what would happen if two human beings ever experienced such a conjunction. So, around the clock, God's spy into the world's bedrooms tracked copulators (and those who, either through cross-genital stroking, or through mutual masturbation and the visual stimulation it brings, likewise approached synchronous derailments) to ensure that, if only by a hair's breadth, the sexual surge came upon them asynchronously.

For centuries, Michael's sneeze built.

His nostrils tingled as he knocked out of phase the oral bespurtments of Burr and Hamilton weeks before the lovers' quarrel which history—swallowing Hamilton's spin with as much zeal as Burr his sperm—ever after passed off as political in nature.

Michael's right index finger hitched to his upper lip even as its tip flicked toward Toklas and Stein, putting a hair fracture in what would otherwise have been a perfect union. No matter. The pink roses of their twinned mouths and vulvas bloomed with sufficient ooze and pucker that, by any measure, there was plenty of there there.

But the archangel's sneeze peaked just as the Beatles laid their first chord atop the screams of young girls on The Ed Sullivan Show and, far more germane to this tale, at the exact moment that Hap and Meg Osborne, de-pajama'd in bed— Hap's pud cuntily beslubbered as it jaunted in and out of his wife—went ballistic. Michael blinked into the sneeze, losing his grip on the groaning pair. In that instant, there came a-borning between them the Orgasm Fairy.

Meg had known her impending climax would be grand. It skittered upward like a megalopolis of skyscrapers rising in time-lapse photography. And when those upswept edifices began jutting and thrusting into the heavens, her detonations pounded out with increasing force. Ka-boom! Ka-boom!! Oh-my-god-KA-BOOM!!!

No perverts they, Hap did his sexual pushups as Meg lay quiescent beneath him, and the bedroom lights they kept of course discreetly off. But an eel-like phosphorescence now coated the air between them. It writhed and wriggled to the bestial gruntings in their throats, to the slippery lock of their loins. The form it took was female. Suddenly Meg and her husband were making love to it as much as to one another.

Worse, Meg found it absolutely delightful!

"Honey," she gasped, "what's—?"

"I don't (umpfh!) know." His words strained up an octave, no longer his deep baritone nor the above-glasses quip-voice of his Sunday-morning funnypapers snap, but rather the scranneled woe-ache that piped from Hap's lips whenever his man-gloop blurted out inside her. "Jeepers, I can't stop myself from … you know!"

Nor could she.

The ghostly creature between them grew a new face and soul-kissed both of them, her moon-slick tongue setting Meg's mouth afire with steam and sizzle. Her wanton touch thrilled their bodies in every secret place. Then she vanished, slipping away like sun-glints passing across the hood of a Chevy. But unending orgasm billowed anew even as she vanished, threatening swift terminal overload.

But lo, effulgence unexpected flooded their bedroom with spun gold.

"Be not dismayed," said a distraught angel, for angel he surely had to be. His eyes flitted from Meg to Hap to the wall their ethereal lover had hurtled through. "Pray excuse the intrusion, pardon the liberties, no time, we'll talk on the way."

It was as if the angel embraced them, still coming, and zinged them smack into the bedroom wall. They broke no bones nor did they splat, but arrowed straight through, cradled in the arms of their protector, sweeping past neighborhood homes and out into the night.

Their thighs rocked deliciously. The agony of sensory overload had vanished when the angel enfolded them. In its place, pure pleasure sprang up. "I'm Michael," he said. "We've got to … ah, but there she … Damn!"

Moaning with love for Hap, Meg saw atrocity flash by: Another bedroom, bright and tacky. Upon the wall, a sequined matador on midnight velvet thrust an estoque into an enraged bull's back. But what hurt Meg's eyes was the pair of lovers that reached out of a muddle of melted flesh on the bed. The woman was bone-thin, olive-haired, saucer-eyed, her head atwitch on a stretched stalk. Her lover's mouth gaped, his shouts dopplering by as he struggled to free himself of their mingled putrescence.

"They're toast, alas. That's how you'd have been," Michael said, blithering on as they brushed treetops and sped through the night. "We've got to stop her before she mucks up the entire world." But what conceivable role, Meg wondered in among a continuing concatenation of body-explosions, could she and Hap play in stopping the Orgasm Fairy? For such was implied in the archangel's statement. He wasn't merely keeping them from turning into orgasmic pudding. She sensed too, even as they hurtled over forests and graveyards and light-scoured highways, that Michael maintained his task of unsynching lovers all over the globe. Though his face was as calm as wisdom itself, his mind appeared to boast more facets than the eyes of a swarm of fruit flies.

Said Hap in mid-hump, "Isn't that—?"

"It is." They swooped down into an extremely well-known theme park, eerily quiescent by night. Outlines of idled rides evoked TV memories as they slammed down into a brick walkway and passed along a brightly lit tunnel below.

Meg wasn't sure if her loss of breath came as part of her unending climax or because of what she saw next. Three huge-headed creatures, cartoonish above the waist, humanly naked below, were engaged in white-gloved prick-and-pussy stroking. At the tunnel's far end, an insane phosphorescence corkscrewed up into nothingness. Despite her orgasm, Meg giggled. Then she covered her mouth, at once aghast and aroused. Smoke rose from cotton fingers that caressed squirming thighs. Gloves caught fire. Yet Meg's childhood fantasy friends moaned with pleasure through neck-gauze beneath beak and snout, as below the belt they sizzled and flared.

Again the archangel swept Meg and Hap away, a swift smack upward past hums of fluorescent light, then a zoom into darkness. "We're gaining on her," insisted Michael as Hap gasped, "I love you." It was unclear whether he was addressing Meg, or the archangel, or both. Not that it mattered. It was all love. Every shred of life was love. Such was the message of this unending, unifying, edifying climax.

"We'll outfox her," declared Michael as they changed course, trebling their breakneck pace. Meg was blessed with a glimpse inside the archangel's mind. Like skate-scorings on ice, swift tangents etched along the hunted fairy's erratic track, sweeping beyond its obscure end into God-granted certainty.

The Pacific coast, California perhaps. A full somber moon silvered upon a sea of crushed grape. Upon a crag, there loomed a mansion. They burst through it into an opulent bedroom even as the creature they pursued did the same from the opposite wall.

On the bed, a zesty platinum blonde, nipples stopper-hard, rode the stickshift of a grimacing young stud, his hair as tossed and golden on the pillow as waves of wheat in sunlight. "Hang on," said Michael, sweeping her and Hap onto the mattress. Like streamwater sculpting boulders, they slid over the climaxing pair, melding with them, embracing them. The Orgasm Fairy, not yet halted in her mad career, slipped in among them. Meg and Hap kept coming, joining their gasps and groans with the couple on the bed. By God, the warmth and fragrance that rose from them! Meg's mouth tasted the ramping woman's left nipple as the man on whom she performed the buck-and-weave caressed Hap's unstoppable cock where it slipped in and out of Meg.

The archangel issued new directives to the Orgasm Fairy, which she at once obeyed. Meg didn't understand what he said, but the gist—an order to convert mayhem into benevolence—became one with the love the foursome shared.

It was absurd.

All Meg had learned about love in her thirty-three years told her that one needed time to know someone before sex meant anything at all. Not so now. Orgasm, precisely synched and blessed by an angelic presence, opened them up, brought out the best in them, made plain the divinity they shared, the unequivocal love that spilled out of them and into them. At last, their orgasm peaked for real this time, a tower of Everests high. They started an extremely long slow descent, wheeing and wowing like a quartet that Verdi had never quite managed to compose.

Michael gestured at the Orgasm Fairy, who at once vanished in a flurry of sparkles. Her loss devastated them all. "I'm sorry." The archangel was touched by their bereavement. "Sorry as well about—" but he didn't have to conclude the thought, for he had swept her and Hap up in his arms and was already on the move. The young man's pussy-prod slipped out of Meg's fist as her mate's own quim-pleaser de-vulva'd with a pop from the blonde's mouth, like an all-day sucker eased out to renew the joy of its insertion. Anguish warped the young couple's faces, an anguish mirrored, Meg knew, by hers and Hap's.

The archangel sped them backward along their route, soothing, cuddling, assuring them that all would be okay. And Meg felt the sorrow of parting from perfection, even as Hap and Michael embraced and consoled her. Their bedroom bloomed up about them. Aromas of arousal floated in the air, a delight and a torment: her arousal, and Hap's, and that of the unknown pair.

"Happy trails," said Michael.

"But how will we find them again?" Even as the words formed on her lips, he gestured above her nightstand where a paper wafted down like a feather, falling between her clock-radio and her crook-necked lamp. Names in gold script, a phone number writ large.

"Wait!" cried Meg.

The angel halted in his swirl.

"Please," she said. "What's heaven like?"

Michael smiled. Just before he vanished, he uttered a soft single word. Meg couldn't parse it but it went straight to her heart. "Oh, Hap," she sighed. "We are blessed indeed."

"Yes, Meg," agreed Hap. "We are."

"Are you thinking what I'm thinking?" In her eye, deviltry glowed.

"You betcha!"

Together they leaped for the phone, laughing as they fumble-punched its buttons. The phone at the other end, in a California mansion by the sea, rang once before it was picked up.

As for Michael, he was ready to fall abject at the feet of The Lord, particularly since even God's toejam gives off an irresistible ambrosial scent akin to that of aroused organs.

But there was no need to grovel.

The Head Cheese beamed. The Orgasm Fairy's hands were busy beneath His robes.

God nodded. "Good work, boy. You wasted no time correcting your mistake. Five deaths is too damn bad, I'll grant you. But hey, it's a small price to pay for the emergence of this delightful creature. That's very nice, little one. Your mouth, please."

She complied.

"Besides, Michael, look over yonder."

Upon a nearby cloud sat the puddled couple, still puddled but blissed out. They were making goo-goo eyes at one another and squirming in the most heavenly of ways. One flesh they had become, united as blissfully as the androgynous creatures Plato had painted in *The Symposium*.

Next cloud over, the trio of lovers from that extremely well-known theme park were whole again, flames undone, their huge cartoon heads alive and integral to them. The sight pleased him. I wish I could describe them for you. But the aforesaid theme park and the exceedingly famous characters these three had once depicted—which now, in some peculiar way, they had become—are the intellectual (yeah, right, make me laugh!) property of a highly litigious and soulless corporation. Still, I think you can guess who they are by the shapes of their ears, the fuzzy grays, the bright yellows, the tell-tale hat with its tell-tale hue and ribbon, the eyelashed eyes. I have unshakable faith in the imaginations of my readers.

"Henceforth," said God, "I entrust the Orgasm Fairy with the task of ensuring that simultaneous orgasms don't happen. As she is so very talented, however, she shall be allowed to bring lovers of her choosing extremely close to simultaneity, to join in if she likes, and to give them unforgettable joy. Only the good ones, of course. The nasty, naughty, Godforsaken baddies—by which I mean the bluenoses; the intolerant blithering screwballs on the extremes of an issue; busybody anti-choicers; the so-called Christian right who are misguided miscreants all; soldiers everywhere who allow themselves to be duped by the murderers who appear to be in charge of their lives, but really aren't; dolts, bullies, shortsheeters, tireslashers, blasted numbnuts tailgaters, and others of that nasty little ilk—shall go straight to hell. Ain't no way I'll give those little bastards and bitches any pleasures worth the having."

Michael tried to hide his concern.

"Hey, pardner," said God, chucking him under the chin without moving from His throne, indeed without so much as uncupping His hands from the Orgasm Fairy's sweet pair of luscious, prick-sproinging boobies. "Cheer up. You done good. But I have other plans for you. I'm considering, maybe in five years' time, a sort of vacation … "

And as God filled Michael in on what the archangel's duties would be in his absence and the Orgasm Fairy's head dipped like a feathered cuckoo-bird craning for water, a quartet of TV'd moptops, 'midst twists and shouts as hearty as sex itself, sounded their second chord.

Creeps
by Steve Rasnic Tem

It creeps up on you.

Her eyes cut above the edge of the silk sheet, watching me, waiting for my next suggestion, or order—am I doing orders this time?—I can't remember. I must have dozed off and now I can't remember if it was orders this time, or suggestions, or who was delivering, who was on the receiving end. The end. The ends are important, all that matters really. The ends of the body, the moment, the climax.

It creeps up on you.

"What, Jake? What creeps?" Did I say it out loud? I had no idea. "Oh, the sheets? Great, aren't they?"

I've lost her name. Or I've escaped her name. It embarrasses me, seems so tacky, this terrible cliché of the one night stand. Didn't even get her name. And now the anxiety generated by that lapse seems ill-proportioned to the cause.

It creeps up on you.

"Jake, please." Dark eyes above the sheet. I can't see her mouth, so I guess I can't say for sure it was she who said my name. Maybe the voice was in my head. But somebody, somebody knows my name. An insect tingle of nervousness felt mostly in my hands making them flutter. Like a butterfly's wings, I think as I wiggle my fingers and she gasps thinking the gesture is something especially for her. It creeps up on you.

As I pull the sheet away, pull at her pale body, hips spongy under my fingers as I pull her onto my slippery dick, it creeps, the way I feel her opening around me, and the gentle tickle of electricity at the end of the penis where it touches the juncture of soft walls, and is held, and moved. It creeps.

Later I'm standing in front of the door mirror in the bathroom wiping myself off. She's left, chuckling at my clumsy attempts to get at her name. It's funny to her.

She's having fun. Sex is a joyful thing in her world. I may have felt that way at one time, in my teens perhaps, but I can't really remember. At this time in my life sex is a serious thing, a joyless thing. It creeps up on you.

When I examine myself in the mirror I'm again surprised that women would want to have sex with me. My body is soft, soft as a woman's really, the skin pasty, as if it might slide with your touch. The torso is full, near to swollen, not really fat, but somehow fat would look healthier. And the blue shadows, what are they? Under my nipples and along the rib beneath the heart, darker on one side of the neck than the other, creeping farther across my body with each ragged breath. I seem winded for hours after sex. And late at night around my eyes: blue sometimes dark as makeup, blurring my vision until every view becomes a memory.

Like something behind you, and you can feel the weight of it in the pit of your stomach, or something at the corner of your eye, a shadow slipping or a stray shininess as if from a detached retina. Or a distant weather pattern first felt as an ache above the knee, until its imminent arrival announces itself with knives in your hip joint. It creeps up on you. Like

ELAINE

Whom I remember most vividly the way she smelled, a sharpness in my nostrils increasing with the intensity of our sex, until when I licked her pussy, a moment always delayed, held off to magnify anticipation. The taste was a bleach scald in my nose and throat, a rapid chemical wash that made me wonder if her pubes were dyed, or if the sensation might be the result of a Clorox douche.

So frequent was this experience that I learned to begin with her ass, something I had been shy about with other women, but since smell had become the defining sensation in our relationship it seemed only natural to begin at her anus with tastings and nibblings and full thrusts of the face between her cheeks to breathe in the last hint of all that might be left after the processes of her day.

The very last thing each evening, actually, was to kiss Elaine on her lips, and with my tongue to return what I had found to her. This always appeared to be the best moment for her, in fact, as she invariably came with such force I fell into a sudden shyness, and could not look her in the face. It immediately recalled my father's warnings about women who appeared to enjoy the act too much, and how to taste a woman in that way was to behave "the way animals do."

If he had outlived my reluctance to talk about such things I would have explained to him how these were simply bodies we were talking about, flesh on flesh. Some of us who get old enough grow beyond embarrassment because we know all too well we're going to die anyway. So shouldn't we discover as much as possible about these frail, wounded bodies we must, eventually, lose? It creeps up on you, Dad. It creeps.

But one night during Elaine's best moment I discovered something different about her breath, something subtly wrong in the taste of her which summed up the vague changes in the smell of pubes, vagina, anus, sweat, and faint fecal gas I had been noticing all evening.

I felt as I do now, seeing in the mirror the blue shadows creep beneath my skin.

"Are you sick, Elaine? Is something wrong?" I asked, and she cried and told me about test results and prognoses and treatment plans but I was hearing little of it, so intensely developed had become my sense of smell that hearing was fading away and the only thing I was aware of was the stench creeping out of every pore.

That was the last evening I ever spent with my Elaine.

Make no mistake, I'm ashamed that I refused to be there for her during the ordeal whose details I would not even allow to penetrate my aromatic fog. And I'm afraid it's become a pattern with me. Now that I'm in my fifties I'm willing to try virtually anything with the bodies of my partners, no hesitation or embarrassment, but I flee at even a hint of illness.

Perhaps that's why my next partner after Elaine was

ANGELA

Who is one of the finest physical specimens I've ever known, male or female, a few inches taller than me on her long, muscular legs and torso like a boxer's, buttcheeks built up and out into natural handholds but just enough fullness and drop in the breasts to assure anyone she was female. Her groin had exquisite definition, a tightness that made her labia even more pronounced. In fact those lips were not as fatty as I was used to, but more like flaps of skin or web that hung down slightly as if incomplete, waiting for my fingers and tongue to stretch and caress them, to complete them. She'd shaved her pubic hair well away from her slit to highlight and display herself in the manner of so many women pictured in pornography. The strange thing is I've never gotten much out of pornography, haven't even owned any since my twenties. For some reason the bodies in the photos and films have never seemed real to me. I've discovered I must smell a body before it is real to me.

Angela constantly challenged my physical abilities in ways that weren't always pleasurable (not that sex is ever completely pleasurable for me). More than a few groin pulls and leg cramps occurred when flesh was stretched too tightly or a joint was bent contrary to its design. I did enjoy seeing her move her ankles behind her head and spreading her thighs in such a way that the interior of her pussy opened to a degree that shocked me. She was going to turn herself inside out one of these days, I thought, and I finally decided that was what she intended to suggest by this particular maneuver. Inside out as the organs rip open on contact with the outside air.

"Fuck me," she'd say with a strain in her voice, and I'd oblige, sliding deeper into her than I'd thought possible, the sounds of my pleasure blending with her pained exhalations. Of all my lovers she sounded as if she were having the least fun, but love sounds, of course, are deceptive: the sounds of sex and birth and torture and murder sounding so very much the same. It can give you the creeps.

So it threw me to discover that

JANICE

Made no sounds of any kind during intercourse. She both enjoyed and suffered in silence, her face oblivious to all bodily experience. Now and then a tear would leak from one of her eyes during hard fucking and I'd worry about hurting her—I'm not into hurting despite my appetite for exploration—but she gave me no clues as to her pleasure or pain so I would continue to ram myself into her, without feeling much pleasure myself. The space inside her seemed much too large and there was never enough friction between us, no give and take, so each time it was as if I were only fucking emptiness and once down that road there's no end in sight.

But the odd thing was I returned night after night to my Janice, thrusting myself into the darkness with my only roadmap a pattern of anxieties. Creeps and creeps galore as I rooted myself into nothing, waiting in vain for any glimmer of acknowledgment from her too-beautiful face.

Strange how the worst thing about these evenings with Janice was that I had too much time to think, to wonder at the deadness in her and why that deadness did not keep me from fucking her. How her total submissiveness might be confused with a generous and nurturing spirit and perhaps that was what men looked for in women when they said they valued these qualities. I hoped not, but could have argued the issue either way.

Did she suffer in silence? Of course she did, as even the most loquacious among us haven't enough words to express the horrors of life inside our frail, leaking bodies. It was largely because of Janice that I ceased to trust the language exchanged during love-making, so that when

ANNIE

Proclaimed her love for me I groaned wordlessly and fucked her all the harder, striving for a passion that would not permit her speech. I didn't give a fuck what she had to say, no, not really, because when she talked during our fucking it gave me the creeps, so intent was I on exploring her frail, skinny body, hardly more than a girl's and in peril of dissolution at any moment. She did not have the solidity about her I expected in a living person: her pubic hair was so thin and wispy I thought at first she had no bush at all. So appalled in fact was I by her insubstantiality that when next I came it was with

ELIZABETH

Who had augmented her despair so completely with folds of fat so numerous I might imagine her equipped with dozens of cunts I might require weeks to explore. But with so many cunts obviously she couldn't keep them all clean so if I went far enough into her flesh I discovered stench worse by far than anything I'd ever experienced with

ELAINE

Creeping back into my life at what surely must be the end of it. Not that at any doctor has told me that I'm unwell—I don't give them the chance, I won't even see them—but you can tell, can't you?, the weight of it a constant companion fucking you unawares, your resistance too low to fight off its advances, a glimmer off the edge of the eye a blue shadow beneath the skin, a hard-to-recognize smell that's here one day and gone the next but back again when you've felt confident it's been eradicated lingering on in the memory creeping back on you creeping back.

Elaine is virtually a different person, a dying person—but then we're all dying as I must have explained—her face having lost tone, mouth sagged from crying and the effort to stop, shoulders narrowed and breasts pushed in, nipples almost pointed at each other, hips nearly fleshless, pubes rank and almost always wet with a creeping nervous sweat, legs unsteady, with too much bone.

"Ah, Elaine," I sigh into her, unaccountably overjoyed at her return, the first such revisitation of my life, not bothered by the smell, the wheezy rawness of her voice as she urges me on, it all seeming so natural that she should come back and that people should end this way, smelling as all bodies must eventually smell, failing as all bodies fail in such a predictable way it becomes like a dance.

But it creeps up on you, even when you've come to accept it—or so you think—the inevitable failure and fading away, the smell lingering even after you're gone, it creeps, and as I look into Elaine's eyes, her face spread and opened up by the fucking, I'm terrified to go there, into that most unsafe place, relentless in the truths it has on display, because my body is a poor thing, a weak thing, and cannot bear the horror of that journey.

Torpor
by Charlee Jacob

Sometimes he would just wake up in the middle of the night.

What had he dreamed? Floating in the sea of blood, face down, feeling it bubbling up his nostrils, tasting ponderous rustiness. He felt as if he'd just been born. The feeling was gloriously gory. Flesh floated past, segments identifiable as fingers, ears, funk with no specific names. The horizons on the sea pulled back tightly like the edges of a scar. He was less buoyant. An island rose from the depths directly beneath him. It brought him almost completely out of the ocean swill, still face down but embracing a solid mass as opposed to inhaling plasma.

The mass had a face.

Len would wake up, discovering more than perspiration in his sheets. It was the only time he got an erection at all.

The rest of the time he didn't feel anything. And when he got out of bed to clean up the mess, he realized he still felt nothing. For the dreaming self was a whole other entity. Its fears and desires were as separated from the conscious ego as life was from death.

He put it aside, assured that the walls of his apathy hadn't been breached.

. . .

The first act was billed as TING AND LING ESTRUS, SISTERS CONJOINED IN LUST!

There were snorts about the obvious nature of the names. Len shrugged, sat down with his friend Phil, and prepared to watch whatever weirdness this turned out to be. Not that it would have any effect on him. Nothing ever did.

I feel nothing.

The curtain went up. Two naked women were facing each other, wrapped in passionate embrace. There were the sucking noises of a tongue sliding across another tongue, slurping up mutual saliva, lips earnestly pressed together. The women parted slightly above the waists to rub breasts, berry nipples like kernels of red corn about to pop. Their faces were attractive enough, more than Len would've expected in a run-down sex show like this one. Nothing spectacular.

Pelvises ground together, the insides of thighs glistening. Identical apple-shaped asses clenched as hands roamed, fondling one another lasciviously. Sighing as jet-enameled fingernails scratched down a sleek back. Groaning as a thumb, lubed in the mouth, slid up a rectum. Gasping as the right hand of each insinuated between the tightly fused bellies, snaking down, stroking sweet pink conch shell meat. Somewhere offstage wind chimes were shaken. A large bell was struck with a muffled clapper. A drum was beaten.

The women stepped apart a few inches. Everyone except Len gasped.

Len saw where they were linked. A rose strip of wavy tissue vibrated in ecstasy between their groins.

"They share a clit!" Phil whispered shrilly, slapping his knee. "Wild, huh? Ain't that the tastiest looking meat you ever peeped?"

"I've seen better," Len mumbled, sensibilities sparked by no curiosity. He heard zippers going down behind him, the sliding wet slap of erections being jerked by their owners. There was no rise in his own jeans nor was there likely to be, no matter what he saw tonight.

He sighed, resigning himself to hours of his friend trying to kickstart his emotions. Attempting to get the frozen exterior to crack, showing Len was as human as anybody.

Most folks who knew Len assumed it was some macho stonefaced act he put on. Probably because he looked burned or something, arms rippled rubiate with scar tissue. They didn't know what had really made him this way. There always had to be something, didn't there?

. . .

Twenty years ago Len decided to put away emotions as relics of some unevolved being. It wasn't because of the hysterical screams of the other five people he'd been imprisoned in the cellar with; although, well yes, of course that was a part of how he'd come to his decision. But it was how the maniac totally lost it at the end that made Len's mind up.

The fact that this loon did what he did to begin with (kidnapping six students from area colleges, three women and three men, to perform some ludicrous experiment conceived in brain hell) would seem to be an indication that he'd "lost it" long before. But Peter Munford hadn't acted the part of slavering psychopath. He'd been calm, methodical about his processes, scientifically detached. He even looked like a nerd: hair short and run through with Brylcream, tissue stuck where he'd cut himself shaving, shirt pocket protector. No one would have picked him as a dangerous type.

Len still remembered the first unsettling sight of the basement. The kegs of salt, large peg boards, gallon jars of translucent lard, the block and tackle. He wasn't feeling anything then. He was terrified, as were the others, squatting down, chained to the damp brick wall.

Nobody wanted to look up. That initial eye-search of the cellar when each was dragged in—ether cloying in their nostrils-had revealed a ceiling covered in cat skins. Mummified heads still attached drooped mutely, tails dangled limply—the only whole parts of the carcasses.

Over two weeks, when Munford donned his slick plastic apron, Len's emotions soared to a fever pitch of visual shock (I didn't know the human body could look like that...), and anxiety (am I to be next?), and guilt (take one of the others!). The first to receive the monster's attentions had Len shrieking along, throat as raw as a third degree burn. The second had him staring, slack-jawed in the kind of sickened fascination that makes people slow down to gawk at highway accidents. The third went through it so badly that Len actually fainted. During the ordeal of the fourth Len underwent textbook hysterical blindness, nothing but a black hole around him.

Munford sped up, slowed down, made notes in blood, mumbled to himself.

"I never seem to get the eyelids right. Why do they have to be so thin?"

"The asshole is a real test of patience. Maybe if I just left about an inch's diameter? No, that's cheating. You never learn by taking the easy path."

"Nicked through the abdominal wall. A knot of intestine is coming through. Damn … suppose I should pause here and suture this."

He experimented with technique, apparently deaf to the decibels reverberating within the close underground walls. It was a wonder no one ever heard. But Munford's farmhouse was out in the country. And none was around to take notice when he loaded what was left into the back of his van to take them into the city.

"Hello?" he'd say into a telephone. "You need to send an ambulance to (whatever lonely park or deserted alley he'd dropped the wounded soul in) right away. Someone's badly injured."

When the beast strung the fifth up and carefully selected a blade, something intangible broke inside Len. Her name was Natalie, the only one of the victims he knew. She was in his psych class and he was always turning around to find her staring dreamily at him. Not an especially pretty girl, she had a way about her. A calmness of demeanor, total grace, Madonna eyes.

Not that Len was ever attracted to her. He'd never have asked her out. In point of fact, he didn't date at all, never having found anyone who appealed to him.

But once they were prisoners in Munford's basement, Natalie was all that kept Len from a complete slide from sanity.

"We'll get out of this," she kept promising. "I know that's difficult to believe. But we'll survive."

"And you get this from—what? Faith?" Len asked, ratcheting the words out in nervous laughter.

She'd smiled sweetly. "I just feel it."

Then Munford hoisted her up. Right away Len could tell the fiend wasn't his usual detached self. He studied Natalie a moment, suspended from that ceiling of flayed pets.

"Maybe I should take him first," Munford said, half-turning to Len.

Len ducked back so fast he struck his head against the brick. "Not me!" Chains jangled like unraveling bowels. Feeling craven, he tried to avoid looking at Natalie. But something about her eyes always drew his gaze, be it in class, on campus, or in this meat-littered cellar.

Her red hair hung across her pale, pinched face. She smiled at him. Actually *smiled*. As if to say, "It's okay. I understand."

Munford swung back and prepared to cut her hair and shave her head. Crimson tresses fell like strips of organs. Then he started on the flesh.

Len couldn't look away. His fingers dug into the dirt, nails snapping off at the quicks, sweat running down his arms to pool in the furrows, creating salty mud. Ripples of heat flashed across him, boiling in waves he was sure would roast him alive. He'd be nothing but umbra, like the shapes of Japanese in Hiroshima imprinted on buildings after the bomb burned the rest away. Yet he seemed frozen, unable to hurt as he gripped the floor so hard he broke four of his own fingers. Watching as Munford scraped and gently tugged, as he would on an orange rind, careful not to damage the fruit.

Len couldn't shut his eyes. Not as she was transformed before him. He was desperate to help her. He pulled violently against his chains, springing toward the spot where Munford worked but never reaching it, falling back like a pit bull on a short leash. Finally he stayed down, shuddering, helpless.

Natalie didn't scream. The tide of her blood hitting the

floor was louder. She just stared as Munford began to murmur, then rant.

"This isn't right … rosewater in her veins … Lord, I'm peeling back the scalp of the sky—!"

Finally Munford's eyes locked with hers, the knife trembling in red mist. Tears shone on Natalie's steak cheeks as she smiled.

Actually smiled at the monster.

Munford dropped his tools, put his face against her divested breast and screamed, louder than any of his victims. The bricks in the wall rumbled, pieces of fur drifted down from the carcass-lined ceiling. Len's chains thrummed like tuning forks.

This was when Len found the switch inside himself that severed the emotions. Stopped trembling, ceased sweating, no longer cared. Because he'd understood finally how feelings were nothing but the curse of the victim and the downfall of the butcher. They tore you apart, aged you toward early death, made the ending twice as hard. They were the passions of nightmare. He'd have no more. Perhaps there were none left but if there were, he wouldn't let them out again.

I feel nothing.

Munford took Natalie down, tenderly setting her upon a blanket. He phoned for help before he left. The police came, finding the four pelts in various stages of tanning, the fifth incomplete, drying on the table. An ambulance came, siren like some injured wolf baying at the moon.

Len thought as the ambulance careened down the winding country road to the highway, *Don't give in, Mr Wolf Moon's paralyzed and doesn't care. The suffering sails away, once you're in torpor.*

Len spent two years in a mental ward, immobile except for a constant mindless masturbation that never achieved anything. He never returned to college. Natalie, naturally, didn't either. She was sent to some clinic for those with catastrophic injuries.

Len didn't even wonder if he'd really left that shadowy cellar to come back into the light. Now, the dark and the light were pretty much the same to him. Numb.

. . .

"If somethin' here don't get you hot, bud, nothin' will," Phil said as they walked into another tent that exhorted its act as MR. MEAL.

A man on stilts thumped around the arena, absurdly long trousers making him look like a regular clown at any circus. He stopped next to a ladder as tall as he was. Nothing sensational about that.

Until he undid his fly buttons and his dick flopped out, hanging five feet to dangle where the stilts pretended his knees were.

A woman in a short spangled costume danced out, beaming, generous mouth splashed with scarlet lipstick. She climbed the stout ladder, pausing with her head level with the clown's exposed groin. Up this high, everyone could see she wore no underwear. Her tight little ass was tanned without bikini lines.

"Tissue?" a midget carrying a box of them offered.

Len shook his head but noticed Phil took a couple.

The woman began to haul up the length of flaccid dick, sliding the head to her lips. She began licking it, tongue sliding across the notch in the top, around the glans. The penis grew, veins throbbing, length hardening, growing in her hands. If she were to drop it, it would probably go all the way to the ground now. It animated like a rope some magician has spoken an incantation over. Len wondered if she was going to climb it to disappear at the end.

Like that could be real.

She sucked it into her mouth, cheeks blowing a bellows. Her throat worked, like an expert hooker or an anaconda. The clown's eyes closed, a grimace working his face. The length began to disappear into her mouth. Down. Going where? Why didn't she gag? She worked up to Mr. Meat's scrotum, saliva dribbling from the corners of her mouth, lipstick smearing obscenely.

Somebody shouted, "Look!" Fingers pointed. The ones that could shake free from their own throttled chickens, that is.

Under her sequined dress, between her legs, a knot appeared in her beaver. Then a bulge. Next Len could actually make out the head. It inched out through her pussy, rubbing her clit till her eyes fluttered in ecstasy. She licked and sucked harder. The erection slid through till it reached her painted toenails, like an impossibly long flesh-colored turd.

Daubed with scarlet lipstick.

An image infiltrated his mind through this potent vision of impossible fellatio. One of blood and the carnival of illusions. Of corium concupiscence and deep psychological disgrace. It was only a flicker, imprinting on the eyes, lingering in debased revelation. It drowned in sanguinated delight. It was the taste of biology's metals. It was an island rising, rising.

Len shook himself, focused on the real scene in front of him. The stiltclown's *Guinness Book* dick continued to go through the woman doing the sideshow blowjob, sliding down the ladder's steps.

Mr. Meat grabbed hold of the ladder as his hips shook. The head of the bizarre cock spat out a stream of come that would have filled a bucket. It splattered the dirt floor of the tent.

"Guess that means he doesn't expect her to swallow," Phil commented.

The woman began the slow regurgitation of the cock. It looked like she was being throttled by a sausage alien. As it vanished up through her cunt, she trembled so hard with orgasm that she nearly fell off the ladder. Len was walking away.

Phil tossed his own semen-clotted tissues in the trash barrel and caught up

"What d'ya think? Could they have rigged it?"

"Can we go home now?" Len asked in lieu of an answer to the secrets of bawdy prestidigitators.

Phil grinned and punched Len's arm. "No way. Gotta see what's next. Gonna get through to you yet. You can't dwell in rhinocerosity forever."

The next tent advertised its star as PHATIMA. Four strongmen in leopardskin tights wheeled her in on a dolly. The woman, who had to weigh five or six hundred pounds, was helped to stand. The billowing muu-muu she wore was removed. The men used their hands to spread apart the heaps of flesh from her armpits that all but concealed her breasts, prying apart the immense butt cheeks to reveal scalloped hemorrhoidal shadows in between. (Nothing up her sleeves or arse.)

Then they began grabbing meat. They dropped it where the audience could watch it quiver on the stage. She made faces like it hurt, but there was no blood. They used their fingers, scooping rolls of fat curd off, slowly scraping away pounds.

I feel nothing ... But can't take my eyes off it, ought to be blood, should be red, revealing as nothing else ...

Len bit his lip. His groin had been warm for an instant, but wasn't now. What triggered it? His palm hurt from making a fist so tight that his short nails cut him.

He focused back where the fat woman was now mostly thin (except there was no blood, no red). Only her belly protruded, a good two feet in front of her.

She was helped to lie down on her back, legs spread. One of the musclemen knelt between her now-enviable thighs. She moaned, hitching her hips as he stuck his fist up her cooze, knuckles grazing the labia. She bucked harder under the onslaught by the wrist, next the forearm, his elbow eventually grinding the notch of her clitoris.

When he pulled out a tumor big as a lopsided basketball, the audience cheered. Phatima reclined, accepting a cigarette from another muscleman, tears shining on her cheeks.

Len yawned, not really tired. But the jaws needed to stretch, like a man sitting before a boring array of television sitcoms has to walk before his knees petrify.

"Man, she's gorgeous now," Phil noted.

Len glanced at her.

"Is she?" he asked, distracted.

No, it was too little. Or not enough. Of what, he was afraid to know.

. . .

"Only one at a time," said the unkempt man at the last tent's entrance. The sign advertised MONA LISA.

Phil and Len watched a balding accountant type stagger out. The fellow began puking into the grass, strings of bile-pasta clinging to his chin.

"I gotta see whatever made that guy hurl. You remember him from the stilt act? He got so hot, he started humpin' his chair," Phil said eagerly.

"You go first then," Len offered. He didn't want to go in at all. He wanted to go to a bar and get drunk. Then go home and pass out. Not that he went wild when he drank. The only difference between that and his normal ossified state was the enhanced ability to sleep. Otherwise he had trouble. Too many nightmares of trying to leap out of those chains, of sleek maroon, of anatomical wonders which beggared description. Of mortification.

Mortification? Rot, decay, decomposition?

Not like the singular dream of the island gracefully rising.

Phil paid the man and followed him into the tent.

Len first met Phil while looking for Natalie. From sanatoriums to research hospitals. Phil worked in the last one, a place specializing in epidermal devastations. A doctor there, a genius named Dorfmun, had perfected a drug called Necrocillin. It proved efficacious in helping victims burned over ninety percent of their bodies. It also was an immense relief to patients suffering from flesh-eating bacteria. It maintained a condition free from infection—and the usual subsequent necrosis.

Even though Len thought Phil was a jerk, he'd worked where Natalie had last been. He'd known her.

Phil couldn't offer him hope. "She was in a real bad way, bud. She up and died. Even on the Necrocillin, some die 'cause they just can't go on like that. Who'd want to live that way?"

Len waited outside the tent, looking at his own arms, sticking out of the sleeveless T-shirt. At the wide excoriations where he'd used a razor blade, flaking off modest layers of skin at a time. At the strip-mine gouge scars where he'd prospected for virtue but never found forgiveness.

The facility shut down a couple years back. Len got Phil a job at the stockyards where he worked. A place where being cold-blooded was an asset.

Phil came back out, trembling from head to foot. His eyes were watering and he kept clutching his queasy gut.

"I take it this isn't the painting by Da Vinci?" Len asked quietly. Phil swallowed hard.

Len arched an obtuse eyebrow. "Thought you had a strong stomach, after working at the skin home."

Phil's hands shook. "Actually, I worked in the laundry there. I never saw anybody," he admitted.

Len glared at him. Phil had led him to believe he'd been an orderly. That he'd known Natalie.

Phil had no other friends. Had he lied just so Len would hang out with him?

Come to think of it, Len had no other friends either. He was too scarred and cold.

"You want in?" The bearded barker cocked his head slightly, eyeing Len.

Something about his stare made Len's flesh itch. He couldn't help thinking about the ceiling of dead cats, fur falling down in maggoty scraplets. That's what the guy's mangy hair and beard resembled.

"Don't," Phil whispered. "It's gross."

A switch for his usual earthy gusto. What could be so bad that Phil was spooked?

"You dragged me out here when I didn't want to come, and now you want me to turn back?" Len asked laconically. He would have laughed if he could.

Phil's response was a moderate nod, not able to meet Len's gaze.

Len pulled a few wrinkled dollars from his jean's pocket. "Let's go," he told the barker.

The tent's interior was surprisingly clean. There was a large vat in the center. Len peered at the viscous red liquid inside. He stepped closer, seeing bubbles.

Suddenly a body bobbed to the top and floated there. Len moved closer. At first glance it looked like an oversized newborn baby, still covered in blood and placenta. You had to look closer to see there was no skin.

Well, not much anyway.

That wasn't to say there was no flesh. There was plenty of that. Sleek, shimmering mounds of it, damp hollows between sparkling curves. Len abruptly understood the twist in some morticians who routinely got off on the dead. Groping burn victims for the last vestiges of true heat. Putting their sallow dicks between the torn lips of some face that had traveled at high speed through a windshield. Lying on top of what had lain a long time in the woods. It wasn't because the deceased couldn't protest, making them the most helpless victims anywhere. It was a whole other animal, perverse amid the lush landscape of the human form in its most compelling aspect.

Anyway, this chick wasn't dead. And she wasn't completely flayed. She still had the round white epidermis on her right breast, in the V of her groin, and on the soles of her feet.

Len gasped. "Natalie …"

Eyes opened in the meaty sockets. The gaze fixed on him tenderly, a smile bisecting the hamburger face.

Raw arms reached out.

Len's body grew hot everywhere. A trickle of sweat he mistook for tears popped down his cheek. Something growing in his jeans burned like a brand. He ran the next few steps to the vat, feet moving as if they belonged to somebody else.

At that moment he, would've torn through chains to reach her.

He'd done that before. Or, rather, he'd tried to.

In the maniac's basement, as Munford scraped Natalie's plain flesh, peeling off ordinariness. All the horrors Len had already witnessed in that cellar culminated in a synapse-singeing burst of his own madness. His desire to fuck this divested goddess. That she'd had a crush on him in college, Len had always known. But up to that moment he'd never really looked at her.

His passion had felt like sickness. In the cellar, this was the real reason he'd turned off his emotions. He'd been mortified at this obscenity in himself.

Mortification? Rot, decay, decomposition? No, only shame. He wasn't denying the victim's traumatic-born hysteria or the psychopath's brutal lunacy. Just his own abrupt derangement. He'd talked himself into believing that emotions were gateways to vulnerability and terrorisms of empathy. But the truth was that he'd disgusted himself. Because who could be so headfucked as to only feel desire for a woman after she'd lost her skin?

"Len?" the pared lips spoke. "It's all right. Please, make love to me."

He stared down into her eyes. Those he'd loved before, even if the rest of her had meant nothing then. They possessed some sort of power. Even Peter Munford had fallen under their spell enough to stop his rabid acts. Apparently they could even grant the return of Len's passions.

He heard the sound of ripping cloth. Len discovered he was tearing off his clothes. The barker did nothing but stand there, placidly observing.

"Won't I hurt you?" Len asked her, climbing carefully into the vat. Her body dipped down briefly, submerging her. Then she rose back up again, an island beneath him.

"There's no pain. Necrocillin is truly the drug of wonders," she replied.

The thick red solution was warm, shellacking them in scarlet. He marveled at the shimmering Martian moonscapes of Natalie's curves, the lost worlds of hollows. He ran his palms lightly across her breasts, left one skinned and sans nipple, right with papilla swelling into garnet stone. The pubic V was dusted with fine hairs like pollen, the labia a livid pink. Parts of her adopted a sheen under the tent lights, rainbows resplendent as in aged tenderloin beef: prisms of ruined color. What the human form might have been if God had rested on the sixth day instead of the seventh, his work left unfinished.

She undulated, hips coming up as he penetrated her. He moved in and out, slowly at first, but gradually gaining speed as arousal shook his senses. He imagined the inside of her womb as looking like the rest of her, a glossy convoluted cinnabar. He leaned down to kiss her mouth, sticky as flypaper, sweet and salty. She brought her hands to his head, fingers without nails running through his hair, gliding down his back, slipping between his buttocks. Her vaginal muscles worked like a well-greased fist, gripping his erection, kneading it, his balls moving in the vat's solution like tomatoes swimming in aspic.

He ran his tongue over her chin, across the flensed cheeks, gorging on copper musk. Up the nose's delicate bridge where the cartilage was barely concealed. Across gauzy eyelids that Peter Munford hadn't attempted to "do." Len lapped like a dog at her hairless, skinless scalp as it dripped with the pungent, fungal taste of Necrocillin. He moved back down the face, tracing the throat, drawing a circle in saliva around the peeled left breast. He let his mouth flow down the hideless belly to the reef of skin at the thigh's juncture, working his tongue around the folds of the clitoris, then dipping it into the vaginal well. And he thought, *everywhere on her body—it's like she's the color, texture, and flavor of pussy.*

He put his cock in her again, rolling like a hard wave. The scars on his torso tingled against her skinless perfection. The vat's turgid sauce made him think they were merging in a sea of red come. And with these thoughts, Len's body spasmed with orgasm, splashing the liquid drug over the sides of the tub. Contractions inside Natalie assured him she was having her own.

They smiled at each other. He knew he couldn't be parted from her again. If something mystical in her eyes could always have caught his attention, something primal in this total, surreal nakedness of her body would hold him. His torpor was gone.

This was why he'd never been with a woman. Even before the weeks in that cellar (hypnotized by the grotesques Munford created, not finding them repulsive), Len had felt absolutely no attraction to jiggly fleshpots—traditional fare for young men.

It might be unnatural, but Natalie—as she was now—was what he found beautiful.

He'd forgotten the barker. When he looked up, the man was holding a scalpel.

That was when Len recognized him. Even with the beard and the mane.

"Munford!"

Len leaped out of the vat, ready to wrestle the blade from the monster. Natalie's soft voice cried, "Len, wait! He's not the same anymore. None of us is the same—"

"We've waited for you a long time," Munford said, stroking the scalpel's edge carefully. "We thought you'd never find her."

It was because of Phil that held stopped looking.

Len swung around to stare at Natalie. "You mean you know it's him?"

"Of course," she replied, looking now like a confection comprised completely of peeled cherries. "We met again at the last facility I was in. He was calling himself Dr. Dorfmun. He invented Necrocillin. For me."

"I really am a doctor. Well, not legally anymore," Munford told him. He gestured to Natalie. "You can be like this, too."

Len's expression was incredulous. "Why would I want that?"

Munford pointed at the array of self-mutilated areas in evidence on every part of Len's body, the destruction never as far deep as the full epidermis but maimed and eroded just the same.

"Seems you've been attempting it for years, " Munford said. "But you couldn't muster up enough nerve to go the distance."

It was true. Len knew. His soul knew. Every emotion inside him did, too.

He'd even tried to escape the chains, there in the basement. To get to Natalie, overcome with a mania that had overthrown his sexual repressions. And to make Munford stop working on her and do him. Fast, before he could change his mind, going back to believing all that crap society fed you about beauty being only skin deep.

. . .

Some other town. Another state. The barker brought the next rube in.

The guy stared at the stainless steel and glass. And at the large vat.

"I paid you five bucks just to see a Jacuzzi full of strawberry jelly?" the visitor asked, put out.

But then bubbles appeared and two islands rose from the deep. Looking for all the world like two newborn babies.

Seeing Things
by J.R. Corcorrhan

The phone embedded in the seat in front of me spilled out of its socket and onto my lap, as the pilot fought against the turbulence. I'd never used an airphone before, but I wondered, as its convex mouthpiece wobbled precariously on my groin, how many people had talked dirty into it? How many people had dialed 1-900-BLO-JOBS on its buttons, secretly beating off beneath the plastic food tray? How many passengers had arranged sonic foreplay with their spouses, who were waiting for them in the phone booths of airports down below? How many businessmen had logged onto the Net through their modem's laptops, browsing porn as their cocks pressed up against their Toshibas? How many ears had gotten hot with blood against this receiver? How many tongues had licked this mouthpiece, now hard against my crotch?

I quickly put the plastic handset back in its cradle, wondering what Bluto had done to me. I had never had thoughts like this before I'd met her. But her curiosity was contagious. And now everything seemed like fodder for fetish.

But I shouldn't blame Bluto, really, since I was the one who approached her first. Virtually, anyway. I met her online, responding to her description on ICUCME. I had bought a digital camera for my home computer—a new little egg-shaped jobbie that promised to help my home business with its overhyped video conferencing features—but when I found out that it required that my customers own a camera just like it, I had no other use for it than play. So one night I explored the ICUCME software that came bundled with it, and found myself logged on to a directory of other Net surfers with video cameras and nothing better to do than look at each other's gonads through their computer monitors. The whole place seemed fun—somehow sterile, but entertainingly lewd. Everyone in the "live chat" directory had funky names like "Long Dong Silver" and "CyberCunt" and each name included descriptions of what they might do on camera if you clicked on them. A bit shy, I decided to take my first dive into this stuff with a soft-core description. Bluto's name was on the top of the list—with a description that simply read: "I'm a blonde and I like to watch ... DO YOU?"—so I clicked on her name and a frame instantly popped up enclosing her beautiful face.

Her hair was straight and long, the strands parted above her left temple. Her head leaned forward a bit as she apparently looked down at the camera, one bright blue eye scanning the frame and looking right at me. Her golden hair fell down over the right side of her face, almost covering the black patch I spotted over her right eye.

"Um, hello," she said, in a voice that sounded innocent, but playful. I realized then that that I had been gawking at her patch and she had been waiting for me to say something first.

Self-consciousness brought heat to my face as a picture of me-looking-at-her suddenly popped up beside her frame. I could see my cheeks tint red. "Hi, uh, Bluto," I muttered weakly.

"That's me," she said, reading the hesitation in my voice like a question.

We took some time sizing each other up. I was uncomfortable, but blown away by how *present* she seemed. I used Windows, but now my computer really felt like a window for the first time. It was unnerving but utterly fair and just—as if the neighborhood peeping Tom had caught me spying on the neighborhood peeping Tom. Or something weird like that. An honest meeting of the eyes in a place where the eyes never should have met to begin with.

"So," I continued, to break the silence that crackled out from my computer speakers. "What is it you like to watch?" I wondered how well she could see with one eye.

She cocked her head to one side, tossing the hair over the patch more fully. I couldn't tell if she was looking into the camera or watching her monitor or just teasing me. "It's not a question of what or whom. I just like to watch." She smiled. "You know. I like watching."

"I see." I didn't, really, but I didn't know what else to say. She was spectacular.

"Well, maybe that's the difference between you and me—" Her face changed angles—she was giving me her profile. She was probably getting bored, maybe reviewing the list of other ICUCME users for someone else to look at it. "You see. But I watch." I heard some clicking: keyboard keys.

Figuring she was going to hang up, I took a chance, trying to sound like an old pro at flirting on this tele-com stuff, mustering my best smile and saying: "I like watching you so far. But I wish I could see more …"

Her one eye turned to pin me down and her voice turned catty. "Let me guess. You like my patch."

I nodded.

"You wanna see it?"

"Yeah," I said. "Why hide it? It's sexy."

She smirked and turned a bit towards me, acting coy. Then a hand reached forward and blocked my view until she was just a black window on my screen and some noise on my speakers. I saw myself in the other frame, looking confused.

Her voice came out of my computer: "That's what it looks like. I'm blind in one eye and that's all I see. But when I watch—"

She lifted the hand. The frame flashed with bright flesh-tones and then focused. The camera was angled between her legs, casually parted so I could see her crotch. But it was blocked by a thin black panty—a triangle of black fabric that looked as if it were torn from the same cloth as her eye patch. Only it was blacker in the middle—stained with her wetness.

Bluto groaned under breath, "This is what it's like when I watch."

The hand that had blocked my view slid down to peel aside the cloth, teasing me with a quick peek at her thin pink lips before she inserted her long finger. I saw a gleam of light on her knuckle as she slowly pulled it out and then pressed it back in again. I couldn't really see anything that I hadn't seen in movies before, but the movement of her hand and novelty of having a masturbating woman live on screen before me was enough to turn me on. The hair that surrounded her fingers was thick and rich and blonde, matted dark with her juices. I could almost smell her, feel her wrapping herself around me.

I slid a hand down inside the elastic of my boxers, groping my groin, timing a necessary stroke with her quickening finger-work. In my peripheral vision, I could see the look on my face, watching me watching her on screen with my mouth slack and open. With my free hand, I reached up and tried to turn my camera away, angling it toward my cock—which I had finally pulled free of my pants and had begun pulling madly—so she could watch me, too. After all, she said she liked to watch and it was the least I could do.

"No," Bluto called, her voice disarmingly soft as it purred over my speakers. "Let me watch you. Don't change a thing."

I obeyed. But I didn't want to watch myself—it was a distraction and I could tell by the faintness of the pulsing in my hand that it was giving me stage fright. I found the "minimize" button on the window that contained my image. That helped me focus on her as she tugged her panties down her thighs. My dick "maximized," heavy in my grip. Her lips puckered bright pink and shiny; she made sure I could see inside them by spreading the vulva with two wet fingers, while her other hand fell down to tease her asshole with a pinky. Her ass was flexing hard and she began mashing her clitoris with an outstretched thumb, working her pelvis up and down in the leather chair. All I could hear now was heavy breathing—hers and mine, mingled and quickening at the same pace as if breathing with the same lungs, exhaling through the same throats, licking the same lips. The unity of our timing was perfect. There was no echo.

Before I knew I was coming, a ropelet of jizz flew up and hit my monitor right where her pussy was thrashing. A sudden bolt of heat shot up my spine as I continued to pump it out, my flailing grip seeming miles away from me, as if someone else's hands—I imagined they were Bluto's hands— were reaching out to jerk me off across cyberspace. The orgasm was electric, my legs and chest shuddering from the glorious sizzle of pulsing pleasure. The come coursed over the back of my palm and over my balls, my eyes glazing, blurring my stare at the screen. Bluto, I could see, was exploding, just a heartbeat behind me, her voice raspy and loud as she groaned and panted, the image blurry and choppy from the speed of her finger fucking.

Then her hand—wet and shiny with her juices—blocked my sight again before it occluded my vision, and I stared at the black frame, waiting, listening, wondering what I should say. The goo under my thighs was getting cold, creeping under my ass and tickling me. I turned and grabbed a rag to clean up a bit as I waited for her return.

Fleshtones again, then her beautiful face came back to my screen. She had pulled the hair back away from her temples. Her forehead was slick with sweat and the hair that surrounded it held a few beads of it, like oil on a string. I could finally see the patch that covered her eye, black and full and somehow perfect.

"I don't think I want to watch that," she said, and I suddenly remembered that she could still see me—and had been watching me the whole time. I was blushing again, but it didn't matter now. I stopped cleaning up. I waited for her to do something. I felt like quickly hanging up, running away from my embarrassment, but I couldn't get myself to do it. She was too wonderful. I couldn't delete her image so crudely, with just a click of a button.

"Not bad for your first time," she said, lighting a cigarette. The smoke clouded my view.

My jaw dropped. "You mean you knew I was a virgin to cybersex? What gave it away?"

"Seen it a million times. So why don't you tell me what it looked like."

That was a weird way of putting the old "Was it good for you?" question, but I tried my best in order to keep her online. It was all so new to me that it was hard to put in words. There was a distance about the act that made it both less intimate and more primal. It was odd not seeing her whole body in the frame at once—hell, I hadn't even seen her breasts—but it was intensely arousing as the rawness of it all made the passion so densely focused. The sound of my beating off had mentally cross-dubbed over the image of her masturbation, and that sound somehow unified us.

We talked for hours. I met her again online for eight nights in a row. She never showed me her face when we made virtual love, but she asked to watch me doing all sorts of different things: fucking my hands, fingering my ass, cupping my balls, rubbing my nipples. Things I never did to myself before. It didn't feel so hot, really, but knowing she was watching so intensely with her one blazing eye got me off all the same. She taught me how to use my camera in interesting ways—how to refocus quickly for sudden close-ups, generate perfectly sensual negative images, do trick shots with mirrors and cellophane, and save these things as movies, or what she called "video captures," on my computer. She once made me shoot my wad into an ornate brandy tumbler I had propped up precariously on top of the camera lens, just so she could see what it looked like when my gob hit the bottom of the glass. She meant it when she said she liked to watch. And though I soon deduced that she had been saving our escapades on her hard drive as often as I had, we both preferred to watch each other live. Hell, we even enjoyed just bullshitting with each other, talking about the weather. She liked to watch, but she also began to like me as much as I liked her. And the next thing I knew I was on a plane headed to Dallas so she could not only watch me in the flesh, but feel all I had for her to feel, too. And vice-versa.

It would be another thirty minutes until I landed. I picked up the airphone and dialed her, just to make it real.

. . .

When I rang her doorbell, I noticed that the last name on her mailbox beside it read Gunningham. I had assumed Bluto was short for Blutarski or something like that, but I was obviously wrong. That was good. Her handle would give me a topic for conversation if we found ourselves uncomfortably speechless once we were confronted with each other's presence.

I heard her footsteps approach on what sounded like a hardwood floor, then an odd silence. Wondering what was up, I noticed movement behind a peephole smack dab in front of my eyes. I should have known. After a surprising number of locks were turned, the door swung open.

Beneath a high ceiling with a bare bright bulb, Bluto leaned against the open jamb and smiled. She was large—much larger than a computer screen could ever communicate: a full head taller than me and strong boned. Her hips were full, straining the plaid boxer shorts she wore. Her breasts hung heavy, pulling down the thin shoulders of her tank top like giant pears on a tremulous vine. She had just a slight curve of what might otherwise be called a beer belly—it was cute, different. She was tan, sweating a little from the Texas heat. Her smile was gorgeous, with large teeth. Despite her size, she looked far younger and far less devilish than she had on-screen, her long hair held back behind her ears with a pink scrunchie.

I probably wouldn't have recognized her at all if it weren't for the patch, the familiar black mound over where her left eye should have been. But the patch she wore was a different than the one she wore online—this one was hard black leather.

The difference turned me on as she leaned forward and gave me a welcoming kiss. Her lips were heaven: syrupy smooth. "Thanks for coming, you look great," she said as she grabbed my hand and ushered me inside.

She sat me on her couch and offered to get me a beer. I accepted. While she was gone I unzipped my carry-on and pulled out a little gift I'd gotten her at a layover in Denver—one of those silly glass baubles with a diorama inside that snow when you shake it. She'd told me once that she hadn't seen much snow in Texas, so I thought she'd like to have one to look at on the warm days of winter.

I sat on the couch and waited for her, sizing up her living room. The averageness of it all was a surprise—for some reason I expected her to live in a plush love den with leather beanbags and an artful arrangement of dildos on the coffee table. Instead, a fistful of remote controls sat dress-right-dress on a birch wood table, beside a potted plant. And like most people these days, she had a big screen TV, the centerpiece of a huge entertainment center, which included what appeared to be three VCRs. She had numerous framed posters of TV programs. White sheer curtains absorbed the sunlight blaring into the room; she could see out but people on the street couldn't see in. I wondered how she could watch the TV with all the glare it threw on its large glass screen.

"Here's your beer," she whispered, handing me a cold bottle over one shoulder with a long tan arm and gently resting her head on my other one. It felt good to be held by her, but I couldn't stand having my back to her with a sofa between us. I tried twisting around to see her face to face, but she held me more tightly. I looked around the room, wondering if I should put down my beer so I could stroke her cheek or something. I found her looking at me in the big TV's reflection.

"You're so real," she said. I could hear saliva crinkle in the corners of her mouth as she smiled. "I think I like you better this way."

"I like you any way I can get you," I replied, nuzzling her cheek with my ear. I put the beer bottle between my legs and touched the forearm laying across my chest. "I got you a gift," I said, leaning forward and holding on to her arm, picking up the snow globe and slipping it into her hand before leaning back.

With her chin back on my shoulder, she held the glass sideways in her palm, shaking it languidly in front of my face. Stupid me: a placard at the base of the glass dome read "Apocalypse Now" and the snow was really nuclear fallout dropping down on a waylaid cityscape. I hadn't even looked at the damned thing when I bought it. I might as well have shown up on her doorstep sniffing a dozen plastic roses.

"I—"

"It's beautiful," she said, in a voice that was warm and honest and preciously free of online static. I stared at her hands—long and smooth, shaking the snowy glass with a slow, purposeful flick of the wrist. She shook it for long enough that I felt my crotch begin to pulse. I wondered how long it would be before we finally did what we both knew we were going to do.

She slid away, sensing the curiosity behind my silence, maybe even smelling my arousal. "Come here," she called as she stepped away from the couch. "I want to show you my system."

I set my beer on the coffee table and followed. Her computer was in her bedroom. I knew that, since I'd seen her lean back on her bed numerous times during our ICUCME sessions. But I had no idea how much equipment she really had to make it all work: two monitors, each at least twice as large as my own back home. Two huge computer cases, standing on their sides like the Twin Towers. Two cameras: one egg-shaped like mine, only much more sophisticated, beside a camcorder—the portable kind—fairly large and propped up on a tripod next to her desk, one red dot glowing menacingly above its lens. A wire trailed from it to behind her computer.

She sat on the bed and patted the terry cloth summer quilting beside her, showing me where I should sit. "What do you think?" she asked as I took my spot, face to face with her desk.

"It's enormous. How can you afford all this?"

Wrong question. She looked away, giving me that "you're boring me" turn of the head she had done on ICUCME that first night. Then she looked down at the snowball in her hand. She smiled and shook it furiously. "Disability insurance, if you must know."

Her eye. I should have guessed. I put an arm around her shoulder.

She looked over at me, her one eye wet and searching, her black patch solid and unmoving: "But I'm not disabled. I hate that word. I'm able to see just fine. Missing an eye isn't like missing a leg or something. I can see just as well as anyone else. Eyes are like kidneys—you don't really need two to see."

I nodded, watching her blue eye well up with enough tears for two before they spilled over the rim and ran down her cheek. I hated seeing her cry but wanted her to let it out. I brushed her cheek with the back of my palm.

"I used to be a damned good cameraman. Worked for Eyewitness News at KGAS. You ever watch it?"

I raised an eyebrow and shook my head, stroking the temple over her eye patch. Her forehead was hot.

"Oh, of course not." She chuckled, sucking in some of the snot in her nose like a little girl. It was cute; she was sensing the absurdity of her tears and my comfort. "Then you never saw my grand finale on the news. I guess no one remembers it anymore, anyway."

"What do you mean?"

She looked down and up at me again. Then away, as if watching a memory on her computer screens. She was done crying, but the tears clung to her chin, reflecting the light they threw off. "We were on location, shooting a massive tornado that was miles away from the city, but threatening to hit Dallas if the weather changed. Really dramatic moment for Dallas. We shot it from a safe distance on the interstate. But it turned and came after us. We threw our gear in the van and hauled ass out of there. Hauled ass. But I was smart enough to keep shooting that motherfucker through the back window as it chased after us." She looked down at the glass ball again, and shook it violently. "Some damned good footage. I even won an award." She pulled away from me, standing up and putting the bauble down beside her keyboard, like a trophy. Then she motioned at her patch with an upturned palm, as if that were an award, too. She knelt down in front me, crossing her arms on my knees, confronting me with the truth.

I figured the rest. "My God. The tornado wrecked the van. And you lost your eye."

"Like I said, award-winning footage. Don't get me wrong, it was well worth it. Very well worth it. Not only did I get an extreme close-up of an oncoming tornado, but I even kept rolling when the damned thing lifted our van twenty-five feet into the air—" She cocked her head to one side, looking up at me in intense concentration. "But the viewfinder." She tapped the patch. "Right here. And you know what? I still kept shooting the whole time."

Her gaze was profound, the pupil of her eye as deep and round as the black patch on the opposite side of her face. I instantly fell into it, as if joining her at the bottom of a pit where she wrestled with the pain. "Bluto ... I'm ... .I'm so sorry."

She shrugged and quickly began undoing my pants. "Don't be silly. It was the greatest thrill of my life." She leaned her head forward. "And just thinking about it turns me on."

The look in her eyes wasn't one of pain. It was desire. I wasn't ready for it at all, but her mouth was suddenly on my dick, her tongue hot and slick around the shaft. She began gently pulling up and down on it with a tight kiss, stiffening my limp flesh into hard lumber in seven heartbeats. I closed my eyes, trying to absorb every sensation, soaking up her warm pleasure, tightening the muscles in my legs. Just when I felt ready to burst, she pulled off with an audible pop and stroked me slowly with one hand, the other sliding up my shirt. I looked down and our eyes met. "God, I've wanted this for so long," she said, her lips gleaming around a beautiful smile.

So did I. Finally having her hot hands on my pulsing cock instead of my own, I knew I could come at any minute, but wanted it to last forever. I promised myself I would hold back as best I could, even though this was the one thing I had been waiting for during the whole flight to Dallas. "Don't stop," I said, quickly unbuttoning my shirt and then leaning awkwardly on one buttcheek to brush the side of her face. "Please don't stop."

She gently pushed my chest, suggesting that I lean back on the bed. I did so, closing my eyes. I could hear fabric being quickly pulled free from skin—hers and mine—as her hand continued to work on my groin in her smooth and wonderful palm. She switched hands, apparently to pull her shirt free. This second hand was surprisingly wet and cold—perhaps slickened with her own saliva or pussy juice, but it felt thicker than that, more like lubrication jelly. I moaned with pleasure, eager to be cooled down yet stroked more harshly. She did so, deliberately yanking my boner tightly and roughly in her fist, even though her tempo was much slower than before.

Then she stopped, holding it still, tight. I felt myself pulsing in her grip like an arm in a blood pressure sleeve. Curious, I looked down and saw her naked shoulders and breasts. She had taken off her pink scrunchie, and her hair had fallen down around long bulbous tits that hung from her shoulders like fleshy eggplants. Her nipples stood up purple and erect. I was dying to lean forward and suck them but her head dropped down on my lap with a snap of her neck. One arm lashed out to push me back again and her blonde hair spilled down over my belly, blocking her face. I closed my eyes and concentrated, holding the back of her head gently with my hands, prepared for the moment when her mouth would meet my penis again. Gently, she teased the head of my dick with the hard tip of her tongue. The hand that had pushed me back slithered down around my ass and then toggled my balls, rolling them softly between her fingers. I wanted to explode then, but I held my breath and forced myself to hold back. Then I felt thin lips nuzzle against me, holding me there right on the precipice of entry. I could even feel the very edges of those lips—so thin and tickly—as they swiped over my knob and teased the hole on end of my cock. She repeated the movement, sending waves of heat flashing across my chest. It tickled like hell and felt sort of cold, but the teasing brush of sex made my back arch and my legs stiffen. I could feel my dick straining on its own to penetrate inside. But she held back, only kissing me with those delightful lips.

"Oh, man," she uttered. "You look so good. So fucking good."

I felt fast breath on the balls she jiggled in her hand, a chill washing over my lower stomach. She was giving me head and talking at the same time. It felt amazing.

I craned my neck, watching her sultry head move around on my crotch, frustrated when her blonde hair blocked my vision.

"I wish I could see more," she said, with just a hint of bitterness. She moaned, pushing more air around my balls with her hot breath. The lips continued to kiss me, more eagerly now, swathing quickly around my dickhead as if puckering on a tart lollipop. "I wish I could see you, really see you," she continued, sending waves around my groin. I felt the same way, watching her head bob around on my lap.

I reached down and swiped her hair to one side, answering her call, knowing that it would turn her on if I watched what she was doing, just like we did it online. But when my hand moved her hair I noticed that her patch wasn't there.

Her eye met mine, wide open and hungry. My pecker stood up, purple and pulsing against the other side of her face, nestled in her wet and puckering eye socket. She kept her good eye glued to mine as she slowly moved her head in semicircles, occasionally flicking a tongue up and down along the base of my cock as the lips of the wound where her eye should have been pressed against me. She let go of my balls and lapped them up into her mouth as I pressed precariously deeper into her socket.

Horrified, I shuddered and watched as my cock erupted and spit creamy white semen into the pink hole on her face. It ran down her cheek as I quickly leaned forward, pulling my balls out of her mouth. I took her in my arms, sliding down on the floor with her.

I lay there holding her silently, feeling her full body against mine, listening to our heavy breathing as our ribcages and pelvises ground into each other, my head buried between her neck and her shoulder for what seemed like a very long time.

"Now it's my turn," she whispered into my ear, writhing beneath me and reaching around my ass to slide my flacid-but-rising cock inside of her. "I want to see you in close-up."

I wasn't sure I wanted this anymore, but she felt so warm and juicy inside. Reassuring and real. I closed my eyes and concentrated, giving up resistance and remembering how much I had enjoyed her. What she had done sickened me, but she had wanted it. Part of me must have wanted it, too. And now she wanted more. I lifted my torso and began slowly pushing myself in and out of her, eyes tightly closed. I was still relatively limp, but each pump of my pelvis felt better and better, and I felt my cock getting more and more full inside of her tightening cunt with each penetration. She moaned deeply as I slid my head down and took her left breast into my mouth, gripping the hard nub of her nipple between my lips.

As my dick pulsed back to life, I pushed deeper inside of her, fucking her with as much might as I could muster. She egged me on, grinding against me as I moved my mouth to her opposite tit, fondling the wet nipple I'd left behind with a free hand. I teased it before gripping her ass with it, squeezing as she flexed around me with her hard muscles. I was getting deep, fucking her hard, and our bodies were slapping together loudly. I could feel my cock smacking against her cervix, a hard wall inside her. I slowed down, thinking I was hurting her as she groaned and shuddered, but her ass worked madly and she said "You're almost there," as her body begged me to continue.

I let go of her tit with my mouth and faced her. She moaned. For the first time ever I saw what she looked like when she was getting off. She had closed her eye. The other one was open, gleaming in the shadows with the remains of my goo. But as I bucked into her I smiled: she looked happier than I had ever seen her before. And as she squirmed and writhed beneath me, I realized that this was the best sex we'd ever had.

My crotch burned with pleasure as my balls slapped against the soft tight flesh above her asshole. Her breathing was hot and heavy and I could tell she was ready to come. "Harder," she cried. "Fuck me hard."

I obeyed, pummeling her pussy, scoring deep with each thrust. It felt fantastic, even though it hurt when my dickhead slammed against her hardness within, smacking all the way up inside her where it seemed dry and brittle. I had staying power now—I was nowhere near orgasm. I could enjoy this moment forever.

I thrust into her violently and squeezed her ass more tightly, sliding a finger around to tickle her anus. It was sopping wet with her juice and her muscles were working furiously down there. Her head flailed and she shuddered: "Oh god—I'm coming, baby," she panted. "I'm—coming."

I slammed as deep as I could, and then held there, grinding myself as deep as I could, feeling her vulva press around my pubic bone. She fought me and I held on, her body exploding as her hips bucked against mine, her back arched and her breasts heaving and slapping against me.

Then I felt something crunch deep inside her. Something harder than me. Not something, but some things, like billiard balls being racked up on a lead table.

It pinched. As much as I hated to, I pulled out and leaned back on my haunches to watch her.

Bluto's head fell back and she lay on the floor, gently turning her head from side to side, panting as her breasts heaved and her orgasm continued. Her nipples had softened into large purple circles on her chest, thick with blood. I finally knew why she called herself Bluto: I saw that her big toes were painted blue. But above, between her legs and down her thighs, I saw more than I wanted to.

Something white squeezed its way out of her. A gooey eyeball with a bright blue iris. A little infrared light in its pupil.

Three more spilled out, each a different color, leaving a wet trail behind them. One rolled across the carpet and tapped lightly against my knee. It was hot as charcoal.

Breathing heavily, Bluto suddenly sat up, leaned forward and picked one up. She lifted it to her eye socket, looking as if she were simply scratching her eye with three fingers before she lowered her hand again. I knew it was made of glass. But it looked right at me, with a sick shining gleam. And it wanted to see more.

I was up and out of the front door with my pants around my ankles before she could get up.

. . .

It feels like everyone on the plane is looking at me. The plane shudders from turbulence and they all look away. It feels like we just flew over a twister.

The airphone is in front of me again, and it's staring at me, too. Daring me. I pick it up, slide my credit card through the magnetic strip and call. Bluto answers, softly. She knows it's me.

"Can you see?" I ask, knowing she understands, and finally understanding myself.

"I'm watching you now."

"And later?" I ask.

Silently, she hangs up the phone. She doesn't have to reply. I know she'll be there, on ICUCME, waiting for me. She needs me now. And I need her.

Holding the whining receiver on my lap, the plane buckles from the Texas turbulence. I hold my lurching stomach and peer out the airplane's square window, seeing blue, seeing her everywhere there is sky.

Before the White Asylum
by Rob Hardin

I was arranging a display in the corner when I felt her walk in. The door tinkled behind her and the blue streak of a woman's heels caught the afternoon sunlight. That was all I saw and all I wanted to see: I kept her bad news at the limit of my vision. I stayed calm by mumbling to myself, by ever-so-quietly shouting down the static. Jimmy, the owner, had left me in charge of the place. That wasn't the smartest idea I'd ever heard, but I thought it might be some kind of test. A guy like him, who'd run a hardware store in Portland for seventeen years, probably knew exactly how far to push it. Me, I'd only been released from the Palmer Center for seven months.

When she didn't say jack, I went on stacking a pyramid of roach-fogger spray cans, figuring that was best. Some guys would have gotten up to offer help, but I couldn't see the point. She wasn't the type who needed any help.

She walked over to me and her blue heels led to legs. When I looked up, I saw who wanted my attention: the charmed-life type, a brat so put together I figured she was headed for the showroom. She was all cheekbones and derision, pale as chalk, with lips that kept secrets and a nose that went slightly too narrow. Her eyes were cool gray and didn't seem to care what they saw. I tried to look bored but I had to take in the rest.

She had a spare, sculpted torso caressed by clothes that dove tail-first off some Italian runway. Hips from a lathe of second-generation wealth. Three diamond-shaped spaces, between her ankles, knees and thighs, that gleamed in the dusty light.

"Sorry to bother you," she said sarcastically. "We're building shelves and I think I need some braces."

My stare climbed her torso until I was looking at her mouth. "You-you think you need braces or you know it for a f-fact?"

She clicked her tongue. "This is a hardware store, isn't it? Maybe if you stop staring at my chest you'll be able to figure it out."

I smiled and exhaled—choking with anger, but trying to stay friendly nevertheless. It was a nasty summer afternoon, the kind where you're pissed off just because you're sweating and they won't let you walk around naked. Then suddenly came this snotty posturing empress—so flawless I could only savor her obliquely in shyness and shame—accusing me of something I'd never do.

"I wasn't looking at your chest," I told her, faking a yawn. "It was your mouth, I guess. I was watching you say the words."

I prayed to the jerk in the clouds to control my temper. Don't fuck up, I told myself. Don't fuck up or you're definitely out of here. A guy like me, with a record and a mental history? If I cracked up again, I'd have nowhere to go but the cage.

She stepped back, pushing out her décolletage. I couldn't tell whether she was feeling proud or just taunting me with her body. Whatever the reason, she managed to make me look. Her breasts were full, of course—a little too full for a woman that statuesque.

She caught me looking and snorted. "Just get the braces and quit acting like a creep."

If the owner had been around, I might have stopped myself from answering. He sure as hell should have been, for his own sake. "Look, Miss," I said, trying not to stutter. "I told you I wasn't—that I wasn't looking at you and that's the truth. I'm being real n-nice—I'm being nice if you think about it—so try to show some respect."

But she didn't care what I said. "Yeah, right," she said. "You're doing me a favor by staring. Just. Get. The. Stuff."

She shouldn't have said that. I was being very polite.

"I don't think you should be accusing me of stuff. And you shouldn't be giving me orders."

She laughed with outrage—outrage that was hypocritical, like everything else about her. "Excuse me? Didn't I just walk into a store and ask to buy something? Didn't you just respond by checking out my body? This is bullshit, okay? Just find my braces and let me get out of here."

I was losing it. I was smacking my fist into my palm to emphasize the words. "What do you think-t-think you got that would make me? You think I'm some machine—Some fucking stupid guy who'll do anything—and you can just order him around—and you can just stick out your-your—talk shit because I looked, lie because I looked, only I didn't fucking look—"

A pair of garden shears hung just behind her. The orange grips glowed in the sun. With one snip, I could cut away two pairs of straps and she'd be standing there, naked and ashamed in the brutal sunlight. I reached behind her—

"I know the owner," she said, smiling calmly. "Joe or whatever. I could get you in trouble."

Of course I froze.

She'll pay for that, I thought. And I knew how to make her pay. I felt it go through me, what I called the cold emotion. It helped me stay calm whenever I stopped being polite.

I could have thrown her on the floor and fucked her right there. Believe me, I wanted to. But I knew what would happen if I did. Sure she'd respond—but no one else would accept that obvious fact. A minute of screaming and it wouldn't matter how damp her panties looked. They'd all turn on me, the people outside. They'd come through the door and pin me down. I could see the outcome: I'd be back in some institution, shot full of Haldol and gibbering for a goddamned year.

I hated them all. I wanted to smash in their faces. And knowing what she wanted made me hate her, too. That's when I calmed down and stopped panting. My eyes refocused.

"This is boring," I said flatly. I walked over to the front door and locked it. If she noticed at all, she did a good job of pretending she didn't.

"You started it," she said.

"Doesn't matter," I told her as I grabbed a flashlight. "I'm going into the back to look for your braces." And I left her standing there. I felt like taking my time.

As I passed through the curtain, a string of bells jingled. The bells were supposed to tell me when thieves decided to go exploring. That alarm went off, all right, but no one was listening—least of all, me.

The back room was cool and relatively dark. It felt damp, like a basement. On sweltering days, I liked dipping my head in there. One small window above my head gave the place just enough light. Right now, I was more interested in seeing faces than part numbers or the shapes of screwdriver heads. I crammed the flashlight into my pocket and let my eyes adjust until I could make out the piles of overstock. The braces were in one of three mounted wire baskets, I couldn't remember which. Then the bells jingled again. I heard breathing behind me—so close I could almost feel it against my cock.

She had followed me in, of course—like I knew she would. I counted three beats in cut-time, and then she was there saying, "What's taking you so long?"

"Hey, get back to the front of the store," I told her. She didn't budge. "I told you I'd have them in a minute." For a second, the tips of her breasts just touched my back.

I turned around slowly. "You gonna go back out there?" I asked.

"You gonna find what I told you to find?" she shot back, mocking my voice.

Brick wall. Fine. I tried a different tack.

"Look, I don't mean to be disrespectful," I told her. "But I like this job and I'd sort of like to keep it." Obviously, I don't wanna keep my job that bad, I thought.

I heard her snort. She didn't move. She just kept staring at me.

I hate being watched.

My whole stupid life, I've hated being watched. I can still feel every set of nasty blurred eyes in my past—eyes I never looked at directly unless I was punching them shut. I can still feel my father staring at me, as he made me stand in the corner with a mouthful of shaving cream; older kids in the neighborhood looking down at me and cracking up. They said they'd be my friends if I licked their piss off the gravel. No matter what I did, there was always somebody watching and laughing and tearing the hairs out of my arms. I'd wake up yelling whenever I dreamed of eyes.

Feeling her eyes on my back made it that much harder to find her piece of shit braces. Some of the shelves were numbered on a grid. I couldn't read the code yet and she wasn't waiting for me to learn. I didn't hear her tap her heels—she didn't have to. The sound was in my mind whether it was outside or not.

I moved down the row of shelves. I could feel her heel behind me: Tap, tap, tap. The sound made me picture her legs. I kept seeing them spread apart, the curve of her calves straining as she stretched herself wide open for some terminal loser. I could feel her impatient breathing. I knew that the tips of her breasts were still level with the small of my back. All I had to do was to arch backward to feel them against me.

Don't say anything, I thought-screamed to her in the dark.

"I'm waiting," she said anyway. "What's taking you so long?"

And then she clicked her tongue.

I wheeled around and slammed her ass down on the table. For a second, she fought me. Then she just went limp and leaned against the wall. Tools were jangling above us. It felt like something was about to fall on me. Believe me, I wouldn't have cared. "What do you want from me?" I heard myself shout. I grabbed her shoulders and shook her hard.

And then she began to cry.

Suddenly I was back home with my mother, trying not to hear her shriek through my bedroom wall. Shrieking at her empty room, at the hole in her life, at the black-hole bruises on her arms. I was squirming again, pounding the bed with my fist, shrinking into myself and saying it over and over: "I'll never treat a woman like that. I'll never treat a woman the way he treated her."

And then I was hitting the wall behind her, and holding her head against my chest, and telling her. "It's OK, baby, it's OK.

Daddy's here, he's right here and he'll never leave you. Daddy's here and nobody's gonna hurt you no more." She put her thumb in her mouth. And then I noticed her neck. She bore a faint greenish-brown bruise in that spot, which traced the hollows of her neck down to her clavicle, a place where she'd hurt herself as I did, like so many others I'd known. If she hadn't been so pale I might not have noticed.

"They hurt you, didn't they?" I asked her and she nodded like a little girl. "They hurt you and you hated it. But you like it now." She nodded and said uh-huh: a baby-toy voice.

I slid my fingers around her wrist and tugged, almost pulling her thumb out of her mouth. "You shouldn't be doing this," I said. "It's bad for you." She wasn't looking me in the eyes anymore. She was ashamed and I was glad. "I w-wanna," she said, pouting. And I yanked her thumb out of her mouth completely and held her wrist against the wall. "I told you it was bad for you," I said. She was struggling half-heartedly and whining a little. I loved to hear her whine.

She kept pouting and making baby noises with her mouth. It all seemed fake. She knew what was going to happen. I knew too, but I felt so corny it made me sick.

I grabbed a fistful of hair, slammed her against the wall, and kissed her softly. My cock was pulsating and I looked at her as if I were already inside her. In a way, I was. I pushed my cock against her leg, savoring the bend of her thigh. I was already fucking her. The rest was technical.

I slid her other wrist down between her legs, jostling her slightly, adjusting her as if she were a marionette. But her legs opened wide all by themselves. She was used to putting on a little show. I brought her hand up to her breast and moved it back and forth. Her fingers were slack, her entire body was passive. I rubbed the back of her hand on my cock. It felt as if the fabric wasn't even there. Her legs scissored as she rocked and moaned. "I saw that," I told her, catching one of her knees. I let go, then softly slapped her face. She looked at me carefully. Slowly, her free hand slithered down, lifted her dress slightly, and kept slithering until her fingertips reached her panties.

I looked down. They were blue and slightly damp.

I lifted her chin until the back of her head touched the wall. "Did I tell you that you could lift your dress?" I asked. Her eyes unclouded: It was like she really saw me.

Her hand moved in circles over the fabric of her panties and I began to slide her body down the wall. I held her there in the corner. She looked up with narrowed eyes. "There's nothing else under my dress," she said. "You could lay me down on the floor and just ram it in."

I stopped to look at her. Silence. I heard the front door open, tinkling, held there for a moment, then swiftly shut. Keys locked the door. She didn't tense up and I didn't give a shit. I was busy trying to memorize her face. The gray eyes with shadows underneath, shadows I'd only just found. Grotesquely sexual lips, cartoon-full with a heart-crease just below her nose.

I hoisted her up. She tried to pull me back down to her, but that didn't work. After I stood her up, she leaned, her back against the wall. Wasting no time, she raised one leg and pressed her knee against my cock. "Dry-humping works better if you lie on the floor," she said.

I pounded the wall behind her and slapped her cheek. I slid my lips across hers, our noses touching, looking into what I now knew was her self-punishing gaze. I hated her for making me pass that ticket into her hand, the ticket that admitted her image into all my dreams, where I couldn't edit her out. For people who grow up in state hospitals, emotions run too close to the surface. She must have known I couldn't control what I saw.

I grabbed her by the arm and threw her onto the sofa on the back room. I could feel them watching me, the faces, though part of me knew they weren't really there. It felt like eyes crawling along my neck. I forced her beneath me and rubbed my cock on her neck, petting her, slapping her, twisting her until she had her back to me. I pushed the back of her head down until her ass pressed against me and her spine had that perfect curve. Her ass was too full in places, more obscene than perfect. Every flaw I found couldn't save me, made my cock even harder, let her beauty control me again. I eased my cock into her and kneaded her ass with my hands. I reached over and pulled her hair: back and forth, back and forth, until I was ramming it into her. She couldn't see me. She mustn't see my face.

Then I turned her around and buried her face in my lap. "I can't look at you," I told her. "It hurts me to see you." I pictured myself in a pit dense with rotting brown and black leaves where I drowned her and ground her against their dry skeletal powder and they couldn't see us, though they kept trying to see, and we had our place underneath where I inched inside her, and my body performed acts while I analyzed the sensations, and I pulled her up by the arms and showed them her eyes, and I showed them her body, and I thought they might come on themselves in their secret places, straining to see her, and I wanted to hold her against a window and expose her ass like an X-ray of my dreams. It's OK now, I told her, don't cry, they won't hurt you anymore, it's OK now, I'll keep you here for as long as it takes, I'll keep you and never leave you, I'll hold you just like this, hold you and open you, and wet my sex with your tears, and make you lick away your own tears, make you understand that no matter what they did to you, no matter what they took, you still matter, and I'll make you feel cared for, poor little thing, I'll tuck you in at night, my own little girl, and I'll be the last to love you, the last one, always—

. . .

When it was over, I stared at the spot directly in front of me until I could actually see what I was looking at: the braces. Everything I'd wanted—everything—was there all the time.

I grabbed them and shoved them into a plastic trash bag. But she wasn't budging.

"What's your name?" she asked. Like she was ever going to see me again.

"Corey," I told her. "Corey Wiley. And your name is—?"

"Rachael," she said. I'd heard the name before. She kept looking down, still ashamed of something she wasn't talking about, and the shame in her averted gaze played me, finally, and I let myself look at her more than I should have, until I wanted to lock her in a room and own her always. I heard myself ask: "Where do you live?"

She shook her head and smiled. "Around the corner, obviously. Wanna help me carry the braces home?" I hit the light button on my watch: three-fifteen p.m.? No way.

A breeze passed. I studied her face. "You live around here? I thought you were from a better neighborhood."

She snorted. "I'm not even from here. I'm from hell. Get used to that."

I didn't say anything. I just took the braces out to the front of the store and came back for her. I carried her out into the harsh afternoon light and set her down. "I can't deliver anything right now," I told her. "I'm the only guy working at the store. Gimme your address, write your information on this. I'll bring it all tonight, around eight, after dark."

A slow half-smile tilted in my direction. "See ya."

With one finger, I hooked her chin. "Hold up. You still gotta pay me." Her smile changed.

"No, I don't," she said in a sing-song. "I'm Jimmy's wife."

I shrugged good-bye, not bothering to look up at her face. I knew what I'd find there, the power it had over me. Those blue-heeled legs retreated; the door jingled as if nothing had happened. That was how I wanted it—no grief for Jimmy, no Rachael, no hex on me. But that's not how it looked to me. Not anymore.

I counted to five-hundred as slowly as I could. And then I locked up the store like the day was already over. I walked out the door toward the river, hands buried in wool pockets too thick for July, not caring which road led to the river or how long it took to get there or, most of all, if I got lost and they found me like that, mumbling to myself. I could feel their laughter—bastards—as they watched me howl by the roadside. The hard light was dying and I just didn't care where I was.

Blue Boy
by M. Christian

"Sure you won't?" Mr. Oleander said, fondling the fine, supple neck of a sweet young thing. As a boss, Oleander was a lethargic mountain—slow but unstoppable in his decisions. Luckily for the firm of Oleander, Destar and West—designers of fine imitation antiques—his mountain was formed by tried and true decisions. Luckily for Prosper, Oleander considered gestures just that—and not a personal affront if refused.

So Prosper could, and did, shake his head: a slow tired movement of boredom.

Oleander continued to trace the contours of the young girl's lovely neck and shoulders. Even Prosper, who had seen his share of lovely necks and who rarely would have looked this one's way, had to watch—hypnotized by the subtle geometries of her throat and beginning slope of chest.

The girl was in a perfect lithograph dress. She was an ideal Alice, a snapshot Dorothy, or an identical Wendy. She was crinoline, lace, and tiny cream-colored shoes. Her dress was a slightly bluer blue than her skin. Her sunset glowing hair was highlighted by a pink silk bow.

"I know she's not exactly your type—but are you positive?" Oleander said again. The girl was balanced perfectly on his fat knee. Together, the girl and Oleander were another picture—he a rolling surge of dark, strong meat, pressed into a fine Osaka suit. The picture wouldn't have been pretty, if the girl hadn't been—

—she was such a lovely shade of blue.

Prosper had enjoyed his share in his young life. Maybe not Dorothies, Wendies, or Alices but many Hucks, Rudolphs, Troys, and Rocks. A great many. A great many—far above the national average. Still, this one, this one girl, was such a lovely shade. Despite the lack of interest in her sex, Prosper still had to watch her if just for her magnificent shade: early dawn, shallow ocean, a lovely bird's wing.

Lovely, lovely blue.

With refinement and dexterity, as if cautious not to disturb the girl, Oleander reached out a fat, walnut-colored hand. Prosper knew from twenty years of Hucks and Rocks and the rest that she wouldn't bat an eyebrow. Letting a lemonade and peppermint smile play around her porcelain features, she absently kicked her little legs—balancing on his massive knee—as Oleander moved. She didn't hesitate, or even pause, as Oleander picked up the finely crafted wooden box from his desk.

Simple in its beauty. Teak. Oleander skillfully opened it with one hand, a gesture rehearsed by endless repetition. In another age, it would have been lighting a cigarette, producing identification, or checking a pocket watch.

Oleander took the young girl's head and tilted it back. Animated with a girlish glow, she complied. Then he kissed her fine throat, just a grazing of his thick lips along the cerulean column of her neck.

"Don't know what you're missing."

Again, Prosper shook his head. He knew exactly what he was missing. Exactly; he knew what had been in the box and what was now in his boss's hand, knew the antique straight-razor's weight, its contours, and even its oily smell—if not precisely then its very close kin. Prosper knew the way it fell into the skin, the way the steaming blood poured out and onto the hand. He knew the feel of rope, the greasy mass of a pistol, the heft of a candlestick, and much, much more.

He knew the smell, after: copper and salt. Knew it all very well. Twenty years well.

Mr. Oleander slit the girl's fine blue throat. The razor slid back into her skin, two inches at least. A very fine knife. A good razor. The kind of quality that one would correctly assume for the leading partner of Oleander, Destar, and West. For a beat of his heart, Prosper was caught by the act of Oleander slitting the girl's throat—but it was a catch of reminiscence rather than attraction.

Seen one, seen a thousand.

The girl's blood poured out of her, running down the razor and over Oleander's hand. The leading partner had an expert's, a connoisseur's, touch—as the blood ran, he tipped his razor just-so and pale blue blood, even paler blue than the girl's skin, flowed and splattered onto the same-colored carpeting.

A gourmet's touch: none of the new sky, Robin's egg blood fell on his lovely suit. Instead, it soaked her dress, all but making it vanish with the flow—fainter blue against fainter blue.

As the girl died, Oleander put his lips to her cheek, kissing her softly as she drained of fluid, potential, future, and re-sale value.

Oleander tipped the dead girl from his lap with a practiced movement: gripping her neck from behind and pushing her slight body away from him—till she dangled like a cold puppet at the end of his huge arm. Being careful to avoid the quickly evaporating pool of azure blood at his feet, Oleander took the small corpse to a carefully unfurnished corner of his vast office and dropped her with a tumble of slack limbs.

Dabbling at his immaculate hands with a lovely lace handkerchief, Oleander sat down again and smiled a contented play of dazzling eyes and widely grinning lips: "Much better—does wonders for the blood pressure, you know. Doctor's orders."

Prosper nodded, smiling back but feeling nothing. Nothing at all.

"Now—" Oleander said, knitting his large fingers together over his belly and fixing Prosper with calm eyes "—about the redesign of those Jivaro skinning knives…."

. . .

Somewhere, he was unsure of where, exactly—some program or other (television background), paper article (laying around the office), or just common knowledge ("You know—")—Prosper had heard that certain occupations were manufactured en masse. Street cleaners, simple clerks, clowns, prostitutes, ticket collectors, repair people, etc., stream out of one of the huge upstate factories.

The newspaper vendor in the lobby was different from when he entered that morning. He remembered his slightly lopsided head, his minor facial twitch. Abnormalities both subtle and gross were a common design theme: what better to exorcise the hate and fear of the unusual than on disposable, and easily replaceable Blues?

For some reason he remembered his irritating (another commonalty) voice and his scowering eyes. Someone must have blown out his brains, stabbed him, slit his throat, crushed his skull or any one of a thousand other outlets early in the day. His stall was clean, immaculate—without even the tell-tale of another Blue mopping up his blood.

Prosper bought his evening paper without even a thought for the old proprietor—after all, he'd only been there since last night. Someone had stuck a sawed-off shotgun into the belly of his predecessor the afternoon before. Prosper remembered it clearly, mainly because he'd had to walk through a pool of his quickly evaporating blood to buy a nicotine stick.

Outside, Prosper let the city wash over him; the usual sights and sounds of his way home blurring into a endlessly repeating kaleidoscope of store-fronts, smiling commuters, flickering advertisements ("20% Discount on All Custom Blues!", "Blue Quick Learn—Don't Waste Valuable Training Time!"), and diligently working street cleaners, simple clerks, clowns, prostitutes, ticket collectors, repair people—who were replaced as soon as someone killed them—from that huge manufacturing pool.

The frustration was a wire in Prosper. As he usually did, had done, for almost three months now, he thought about killing. He thought about it as he entered the subway, looking at the pleasant-faced girl in the ticket-booth, at her sparkling smile and firework eyes. He thought about taking her head in his hands and banging it, again and again, against the pink-tiled wall of the subway platform. He knew exactly how it would feel: the echoing vibration of each *smack!* of her against the wall. The way her head would shake in his hands, how the feel of it, the solidity of it, would change as her skull cracked, changed shape with each fevered impact. He knew exactly how the sound would change as the back of her head flattened then seeped blood—blue, quickly evaporating blood.

He knew, after a point, as he slammed her harder and harder against the tiles, that her blood would seep and then splatter. He knew there was a special, magical moment when her skull would simply collapse from his passionate, diligent pounding and in one instant he'd go from holding an intact head in his hands to holding a globe of broken plates, mushy tissue and brains, and seeping squirting blood.

Done one, done a thousand. Prosper passed her his ticket and she let him onto the platform.

He knew he should still be thinking about work, mulling over the nuances of Mr. Oleander's timbre and choice of words—but all he could seem to summon up was a overwhelming sadness and a deep, all but hidden whip-cord of painful frustration.

Again, he debated killing. There were several Blues on the platform: an old-looking couple scowling at all the young and energetic, an arrogant buck in a leather jacket, a tiny boy in a (naturally) blue sailor suit who cried hysterically and annoyingly, a very pleasant-looking young man in an white shirt and tight jeans.

Looking at the latter, he ran a quick fantasy though his mind—with the perfect detail that came from many, many (too many) real experiences. The platform wasn't all that crowded: there was more than enough room for a quick one. The details rolled through his mind in perfect clarity (*Done one*—): walk up to his perfect, bountiful Blue form; a quick slap to knock him off balance; a tear at his shirt to view the perfect geometry of his chest; a shove to bring him to his knees; jam his too-hard cock in his mouth; feel him swallow and gulp it down through his artificial moans and false complaints; maybe he'd fuck him, turn him 'round, yank down those jeans and home his cock in his warm and also expertly designed asshole, or maybe he'd just crush his throat around his cock as he sucked at him till he was gripping his own pulsing cock in a steaming bath of blue blood (—*done a thousand*).

Done a thousand, why do one more?

The train pulled into the station, sliding in with no noise save for the screams and wet sounds of the little boy's body. Prosper blinked, joining the queue to enter, suddenly realizing he had missed whomever had tossed him onto the tracks. Distracted....

In the train, he took his usual seat. Across from him, a pair of Blue workmen in stained and dirty coveralls were bagging the corpse of a old lady and cleaning the wall and seat where she had been sitting. The map of the brilliantly-colored routes was all but obscured by her rapidly vanishing blood. With the absentness of trying to remember the next line of a popular song, or what he'd had for breakfast the day before, Prosper tried to determine what the murder weapon would be. He had all but decided on a katana, because of the very clean way her head had been separated from her body, the way her blood (disappearing quickly into the subway car's rarefied air) had fanned onto the route map, but then noticed the tall, thin black man sitting two seats back—and the Maori ceremonial knife in his lap (still a faint blue). One of their own products. A very successful line.

Again, Prosper remembered his therapist. He'd selected Gordon more or less on a whim, after visiting three or four of his profession. Gordon had an easy voice, a sleepy style that went completely against the hysteria that Prosper seemed to feel day after day. It made it easier to talk to the man, to have a still pool to drop his sharp, rattling angers and frustrations into for an hour.

"Set a goal, Josh. Make it simple. No big plans, no immediate reward. The strangle-job is a good one but you still think about it too much. Just do it. Set yourself a time limit—say tomorrow at lunch or the first thing in the morning. Carry a knife if it'll make you feel better. Be spontaneous rather than plotting. When you feel like it, just do it. You take the subway, right? Just push one onto the tracks. The more you wait, the more frustrated you'll be. You'll be surprised at how much better you'll feel—"

The others hadn't worked out and Prosper wasn't sure if it was because their analyses were too accurate, disturbing ("I want to prescribe you something—"), ("I think you should consider more extensive therapy—"), or simply because he didn't find them at all attractive.

But Gordon he did. He liked, more than anything, to just stare into the man's pool eyes and think about kissing his cheeks and stroking what must be his finely shaped chest and back. He never really thought much about his suggestions, if at all—just his eyes, and how he might move and smile stripped of his professional demeanor, as well as his usual cotton draw-strings and leather sandals.

Westerberg. The neighborhood smelled of dusk, the slow-moving Mongusti river, and bad Chinese food. Once again, walking home, Prosper thought about killing. Even though the Gung Ho had been closed since someone had machine-gunned down the Blue staff one night and the owner hadn't gotten around to replacing them or reopening the place, the neighborhood, by law, had its proportion. A boy in plus-fours and suspenders bounced a ball on one corner, a panhandler (drug palsy, missing teeth, aggressive palm) moved through the commuting crowd, a Playmate of the Moment lounged against one of the Gung Ho's boarded up windows, Spandex skirt hiked high to show off a lack of panties as she scowled her disdain at them all. The only one who caught Prosper's direct attention was a cop icon, who watched them leave the station with mirrored-sun-glasses and an abusive "Fucking homo queer" to Prosper.

He thought about killing him: automatic and fully detailed. The cop would be slow, since he was an icon: easy to push him over his bike, simple to fumble his revolver out of his holster (against his surprisingly feeble protests), click the hammer back and fire three or four rounds into his helmeted head. He guessed that he would scream and plead as he clicked the hammer back. He supposed that the cop would soil his immaculate uniform with blue piss as he cried like a tortured baby. He knew, fucking knew, that his head would explode with the first round, his face blooming forward against the shock wave of the bullet passing through his head, confined by the helmet.

Prosper shook his head sadly and entered his building. He was surprised, pleasantly, to find the lobby and elevator free of the evidence of murder. It lifted his spirits somewhat to have a clean slate for once, a unique situation, and he felt his muscles relax against their gripping tightness of frustration. Yeah, maybe, he thought. Maybe tonight. A fresh start—something unique. He started to think about his kitchen, his sample case of half-a-dozen finely crafted weapons. Hadn't done a circular saw in a while, hadn't done a spear since two years ago (at the Mass Murder Street Fair), shotguns were fun and he had the one, unused, that his father had given him for his birthday two years ago.

But the feeling vanished, evaporating as everything seemed to, in just a few moments as he put his key in his door and went in.

"The first developments in Blue technology—" boomed the announcer from the blaring television "—were, of course, in the field of nanomolecular engineering, leading to the first prototype fetus in 2015—"

The channel flipped as he hung his coat. "Cerulean Industries today announced a new line of Blues dedicated to less-represented ethnic types. As part of the Stereotype Series, Cerulean plans a modification of the current Gook, Kike, and Nig—" The announcer was, as always, new: Prosper caught sight of her as he walked in, noting the standard saccharine smile and glittering eyes. He doubted, again, if he'd turn in to watch the audience poll of how to kill her at the end of the broadcast.

"Oh," said Troy from the couch, taking his eyes off the flickering set for just a moment to nail Prosper with arrogant boredom, "You're home." The television flipped, again and again, till it finally settled on a flashy commercial for a new line of Sex/Death Blues called Come Hither. Strobed with whites and royals, the commercials painted Troy's normally dark blue skin almost purple.

Prosper went into the kitchen and poured himself two fingers of scotch, kicking back the flames and closing his eyes. From the living room, Troy said, "So, shithead, are you gonna kill me tonight or what?"

Prosper smiled till his cheeks hurt and knocked back another drink.

. . .

"So how was work, 'dear'?"

The liquor burned, a flaming trail from the back of his throat to the unknown depths of his stomach. The sensation felt good—feeling anything felt good.

Prosper shrugged, breathing heavy over the sink. He didn't see, didn't care, if Troy saw the gesture.

"Had a very exciting day, myself. Saw a *Life Without Hope* I hadn't seen before."

"Happy for you," Prosper said, panting into the sink, fighting the liquor that was struggling back up. Troy had been an indulgence. Oleander, Destar, and West paid well enough that he could easily afford someone every few days or so. He'd had Troy for three months. An eternity for a Blue.

"Almost enough to get out of fucking bed for."

His breath was acid, it burned his sinuses. The pain was real and sharp. Enjoying the sensation, he panted till the room started to tilt. Troy had originally been part of something elaborate. But like things had been recently, it had never materialized. Troy became almost like furniture. Almost—but not as comfortable.

"You would have loved it. Tristan—you know, the illegitimate son of Vera-De and Despar Cosmo, heir to the Cosmo fortune—has this problem. An intimate, manly problem. And he was having all kinds of trouble keeping people from finding out. That is till this one person, and, you know, I can't recall completely if he was Blue or not, just happened to speak to the wrong person." Troy tsk-tsked, still fixated, on the flickering screen. "Poor Tristan—"

The knife's handle was cold, and that surprised Prosper. Maybe it came from keeping it in a dark kitchen drawer or maybe it was just that his blood was so hot, hammering with heat.

He took it out of the drawer (cool, cool in his hand) and walked the four steps from his kitchen to the living room. Troy started to turn his head, as if on finely-machined bearings. A movement beyond anyone save his make, model. Pulse jumping his vision, Prosper still managed to ponder, as he walked and raised the knife, that he didn't really understand their mechanics, the details of them. You didn't need to know exactly how a bus worked to ride on one, or how a screen worked to watch it—or even turn it off.

Tension thrummed in his arm as Prosper stabbed down. The leather of the couch drank the blade till it hit something more solid than its stuffing. The impact jerked up his arm.

Troy looked at the vibrating knife, then turned back to the screen. A sound, something like a sarcastic sigh bereft of true feeling, slipped from his azure lips.

Prosper swung hard, slamming his knotted fist into the side of Troy's head. The sound of his skull cracking was as sharp as a voltage spark in the room. Troy's whole body jerked to one side with the blow, and a deep-toned groan grumbled from his chest.

In one practiced move, Prosper grasped the knife again with one strong hand, knotting Troy's silk shirt with the other. Hauling the Blue up, he expertly flipped the knife around and brought it with a blurring fury to his throat.

Troy breathed, deeply and slowly, eyes straining up toward Prosper. Prosper looked down at the tip of Troy's nose, just visible beyond his perfect hair.

Prosper's cock was stone, iron. He ground his pelvis against the thick resistance of the back of the couch, relishing in the feeling, the humming frustration coming from the Blue.

After time had passed, glacial and tense, Troy pushed forward, sliding his neck along the knife blade. Prosper saw him move, felt the knife glide across his alluring neck and smelled Troy's blood mixing with the stale room air, salt and copper adding to dust and stale sunlight.

Prosper pulled back on the knife, moving it away from Troy's straining neck. When he had gone so far that his muscles were straining in his right arm, Prosper crumpled his fingers into a shaking fist and slammed it into the back of Troy's head, at the same time snaking the knife out of the way as he fell.

"Motherfucker—" panted Troy from the narrow valley between the screen and the couch, panting and rubbing the side of his head. Even from where he stood, Prosper could see that his neck was softly bleeding.

Leaving him there, Prosper went back to the kitchen and put the knife away. Troy wouldn't touch it. Blues couldn't. The thought of killing Troy churned Prosper's stomach, knotting his guts with frustrated boredom. Troy would just have to wait. Living to die, Troy was aching to be killed. Killing him might be deadly dull, but keeping him breathing was, at least, not.

Crossing the living room with heavy steps, Prosper claimed his coat and opened the door. "If you kill anyone else I don't want to fucking hear about it," Troy said, glaring up at him with brilliant blue eyes.

Without looking back, Prosper stepped outside and slammed the door behind him.

. . .

The stairwell was old and echoing, carrying a heavy drum-beat tune from the machines in the basement. It was a place Prosper liked to go. He kept it in reserve against the heavy boredom—intentionally going there only when things Got Very Bad. He'd been there maybe five times since his problem first started. He wondered, feeling the depression and anger rise in his chest like warm lead, how many times he'd visit it again. Hundreds? Thousands? And isn't one trip pretty much like them all?

Labor was cheap, since life was. A dirty and all-but-abandoned stairwell was rare, a priceless gift. Hanging on the cool metal of the railing, Prosper kicked at some of the crumbling stonework that had fallen on the landing from high above. One. Two. Three. The impact bounced up to him, a wet and harsh sound. With it he caught a vision of thin standing water over tile, rust inching up the banister, mildew like slow red ripples crawling up the walls.

Go out, he told himself. Just do it. Go out. Walk someplace, anyplace. Get a gun and do it. Don't worry about freshness, uniqueness—just break out of it. You know that's the way, you can feel it.

Anything. Remember that young one two years ago, the one outside the museum, how you slid the knife in under his ribs and watched his pale blood trickle out? Got soaked all the way through, holding him in your lap and letting his blood leak. Remember how you held him, and rocked him as he bled early morning sky onto the sidewalk?

Or the one you surprised last fall. Remember him? Body-builder icon, all full of himself and his royal muscles. God, what a monster—all bluff and steam. Remember how you dragged him out of that bar, smashed him to the street with a barstool, then stood there, on his head, as he screamed and tried to reach up and knock you off? Remember your little improv dance number that lasted until his skull gave up and you fell through spongy turquoise brain, landing with a jar on the concrete? Laugh riot that one—

Remember the boy? Looking maybe, just barely, eighteen? Such a delightful present to yourself. A special treat, a glorious gift. All night he lasted. So skillful you were with the scalpel, the cuts. From sex to sapphire blood, from the wetness of his mouth, his ass, to the wetness of his wounds, his holes. He was so good, remember, that you snapped his neck with the dawn—applause for a night in purest heaven?

How many glorious others, Prosper? One? Two? Three?

The splash broke him from his self-examination. Looking up from his internal gaze, Prosper's knees prickled from crouching too long at the railing. The sound bounced around him, finally landing on his ears and then his thoughts. Standing against the pins and needles, he looked down the stairs.

"Hello." Black leather pants, a thin coating over a finely honed body. White T-shirt over a perfect ribbed chest—nipples showing through as he moved. Streaks of blond eyebrows drawing perfect attention to pale blue eyes. A finely shaped face, a pleasant fall between full and thin. Good bones. Lips like a perfect stroke of a brush. They looked as if they might taste, and feel, like silk.

"Fine night for it," he said, smiling at Prosper, bathing him in light, despite the fading sun.

"For what?" Prosper managed to get out, still trying to climb back into the real world from his thoughts and ennui.

"Navel gazing," he said, smiling a flash of white teeth.

"'Fraid I've been doing way too much of that, of late. Hard to climb back out sometimes."

"Problem?"

"Nothing that won't get better, I guess."

He was standing close. Prosper could feel the burning between them. His eyes hummed from going from his delicious shape to his ideal face. Blue eyes. Nice teeth. Tight body.

"If there's anything I can do—" he went to the railing and stared out at nothing—maybe hypnotized by the dust dancing in the fading sunlight. Maybe just standing there, waiting for Prosper.

Even though it wasn't exactly his style, Prosper ran a finger up his spine, tracing the bumps of his bones with a gentle touch. He made a soft sound and smiled back at Prosper, grinning lights.

Prosper stepped up and in, bathing his chilled, nervous self in his warmth. His cock was metal—iron or steel—and ached with a good kind of muscle ache.

He brought his hands around his chest, feeling his tits—flat and hard—with his palms, the tips of his fingers. Prosper hadn't felt anything like him for … he hadn't felt anything like him. Ever. He was dazzling, alive with sparkling. Prosper found it hard to look at any one single thing about him—his blond hair, the lovely slope of the back of his neck. He kissed the back of his neck, feeling his nipples with his gently stroking fingers as his own grazed his strong, tight back.

He moaned, high and sweet, pushing back against his straining cock.

Hands falling to his waist, he pulled his T-shirt out of the tight pants. Giving permission, he lifted his hands above his head. The shirt came off.

Turning 'round, he smiled. Chest, firm and cool. He had a silken belly, a gentle patch that played so well with the strength of his muscles: something gentle mixed with the strength.

Prosper kissed him, feeling a faint lingering of wine, a memory of ... garlic? ... from dinner. Their tongues touched and danced, a ballet, warm and wet, firm and coarse. Prosper felt them burn, ignite. Distantly, he knew he was rubbing his cock through his pants, knew he was tugging at his own waistband, pulling down Prosper's zipper.

The stairwell was cool, touching cold, but his cock was still hot as his hands explored him. Like a fever, Prosper felt his desire blast through him. He started working at his own pants. "Take 'em off," he managed to say between their kisses.

He helped, doing magic with his own zipper and buttons. They were tight, so he backed up against the railing for leverage before managing to work them down over his strong hips, corded thighs.

Kissing him again, as penetrating as a fuck, as aggressive, he turned and bent him over the railing.

He was like an oven inside. A wet, tight, oven. Prosper fucked him, feeling almost afraid that the heat of his asshole was going to burn his cock, was going to light him like a fuse and blow him away.

So good, Prosper managed to think; so hot, so new.

Then he let go, his orgasm mixing with a high point in his own moans. Relief and the little death surged through Prosper as he managed (barely) to step back and shove his still-hard cock into his pants.

So hot, so hot—he thought. *So nice and refreshing. Only one thing to make it better—perfect—*

Quick and hard, he knocked him off-balance by kicking the back of his knee. Dropping hard, hand skipping across the rusted metal railing, he collapsed. Feet perfectly aligned with his head, Prosper then kicked in his face. The impact was hard and meaty, traveling up Prosper's leg like electrical current—straight to his cock and his smile.

The man moaned and whimpered, clutching his mouth. He looked up at Prosper with shocked and scared blue eyes—

Prosper kicked him again, aiming for his jaw. He connected again, and the stairwell echoed with the wet gong of skull bones on the railing.

Kneeling down, Prosper took his wheezing, gasping face in his hands. "So new," he said, as he slammed him back, again and again, against the metal. It became a fevered blur, a motion like walking, like pedaling a bicycle (after all, you never forget how)—impact after impact, gong of metal after gong. One flowing perfectly, hotly, into another. One. Two. Three. Four. On and on, a background rhythm.

Then there wasn't enough of his head to pound. Prosper was kneeling in a slowly growing pool, holding thick fragments of bone and sticky blood.

"Very nice," he said, in an absent kind of voice, standing up.

Brushing his hands on his pants, he was startled by how sticky they were. Looking down, he saw the mess his pants had become.

The roar came up from his gut, his stomach, his balls. It tore through his lungs and up his throat. It escaped as nausea, and he felt the liquor boiling up.

Then the impact. From behind. A flash of an azure hand and he fell, down to his knees, onto the sticky floor, the red blood.

Red.

. . .

Pain woke him. Pain and the strangeness behind his eyes. He remembered being given something, and having something taken. What was gone wasn't obvious, glaring, but he felt it. It was as if something had been moved beyond his reach, pushed back so he could see it—maybe even understand it, distantly—but couldn't do it. That part of him was gone. The humming frustration, the ability, was gone—exorcised from him. He couldn't, ever, kill—or even fight back.

Something given: He brushed a brilliant blue hand across his brilliant blue brow, feeling the sweat the hot sun brought to his forehead.

Looking up and down the alley he saw people moving to and fro at either end. Some looked his way but most didn't even notice him. It was early, most were too busy going and coming to walk down, to indulge in anything Blue—in killing him.

Slowly, dancing back into the shadows, Prosper thought: *Unique. Smiling: Yes, unique—*

Her Master's Hand
by Dominick Cancilla

Even though she had expected it, Sasha jumped when her husband's fingers brushed the ridge of her collarbone. The cold fingertips sent goosebumps rippling across her skin, a pleasant disturbance in the still waters of her flesh. The warmth of her lover lying beside her made Sasha forget the cold envelope of night surrounding their bed, and the soft touch became a focus for her need.

She lay still as the single point of contact moved down her chest, meandering maddeningly to the most sensitive place on her breast and then circling it slowly. Arousal rose within her, bringing with it the sour aftertaste of too many years spent not knowing how wonderful sex could be.

From their first joining so long ago on a second date, sex with Josh had been rushed and seemingly only for his benefit. Until recently, Sasha had never understood what all the fuss was about. She was surprised by how quickly things had changed, and by the fact that it had taken another woman to change them.

Josh's hand was moving again, down her breast, coming to rest on her stomach where it would stay an unfulfilled promise until she had built up a healthy store of anticipative frustration.

Sasha tried to fill the agonizing stillness with thoughts of Melissa.

Josh had been with her when they met their new neighbor, and Sasha was irritated by the way his gaze kept dropping to the deep neckline of Melissa's blouse where the wings of a tattooed butterfly peeked from beneath black lace. The younger woman's easy sensuality and perfect body made Sasha fear for her position as the sole object of Josh's desire. Her fear had boiled into resentment and hatred over the following weeks as Josh became so preoccupied with trying to make their new neighbor feel welcome that her name began to creep into the frantic words of his lovemaking.

His obsession grew until Sasha could no longer bear it. She waited until Josh was away and then went to confront the woman who was stealing the attentions of her only love.

Melissa had been better than kind, better than understanding. She'd shown Sasha a windowless room where the bare wood floors were carved with symbols that seemed to writhe in the light of the black candles which lined the walls. There, Melissa had explained that her state of attunement to the plane of separation would only be weakened by the intimate attentions of a man, and shown Sasha a chest in which she kept arcane items that helped soothe her passions when they threatened to overwhelm her.

At first, Sasha had been shocked by the contents of the trunk, so far did they stray from the likes of the pleasure devices she'd seen advertised in the magazines that Josh thought he kept hidden from her.

When they parted, Melissa had reassured Sasha that she had no designs on Josh, and as a sign of trust offered to make Sasha an intimate token of her own. Her description of the toy to be was both abhorrent and enticing, but nowhere near as fascinating as her description of the process by which it would come to be.

Two days later, Josh had sullied their bed with the name of a woman Sasha didn't know and spoken in his sleep of a sexual encounter in which his wife had no part. Steeled by anger and humiliation, she'd called Melissa from work the next day and accepted her offer.

Sasha came home early from work that same day, unable to get anything done with a pounding head and throat full of bile, only to be surprised by Josh's cries and Melissa's deep moans emanating from the bedroom. There was no feeling of surprise when she eased open the door to find Josh lying on their bed, Melissa straddling him. Her only reaction was a moment of clarity in which she found herself relieved that what she had deeply, secretly desired was finally coming to pass.

The bittersweet memory was interrupted as Josh's hand slid lower. Sasha parted her legs just a little more and closed her eyes. She cried out when the roving fingers reached the center of her desire. For a moment, Sasha saw blood, Melissa's grin, and a crescent-moon blade in her mind's eye before the intensity of her body's sensation overwhelmed her.

It lasted just long enough to leave Sasha needing more. She moaned in disappointment when the touch of Josh's hand left her.

"Don't worry, I'm not done yet," her lover whispered, rolling onto and intertwining with her.

They moved toward the next level of lovemaking, pausing only momentarily while Melissa placed Josh's hand on the headboard shelf with the rest of the toys. It's too bad, Sasha thought, that her husband couldn't know what the rest of him was missing.

Madly, Deeply
by Connie Wilkins

No pleasure is so intense that Devlin can't imagine a scenario even more extreme—or pain, for that matter. At least you don't get bored with someone like that. Scared, sometimes, and frustrated that he can find his ultimate release only on film—but, no, not bored.

He has come so close to going too far—I might even allow him to go as far as he wished, if I could do it and live. But I'd be doing it for him, not for his damned art.

What he'll do for his art goes beyond sanity. I realized that the day he injected dye into his balls so he could X-ray the path his own sperm traveled. My mouth gaped open with shock as he drove the hypodermic into his testicle; his own mouth distorted as a ragged gust of air screamed through it—and then he fumbled for the second needle and thrust it toward me. "Lenne ... the other side ... help ... I can't—" I grabbed the hypo from his shaking hand. My hand shook too. "Do it Lenne, quick, please, hurry—do it!" Begging turns me on. But this ... the lines on his angular face deepened and he grabbed my hand and yanked it toward his crotch. "Do it! Now, damn it!"

The pain of his grip enraged me enough to go through with it—I've never been submissive. "Hold still then, damn you!" I none too gently probed his right testicle with my fingers until I found its firm core. His cock began to jerk erect at my touch. I drove the needle in hard, pressed the plunger, yanked it out, and his cock leapt and spattered drops of come on my arm.

Then he threw up.

. . .

Devlin is obsessed with the deep insides of things. His video equipment is state-of-the-art, like the tiny fiber-optic endoscope that rides atop his thrusting cock and lets a camera record his jets of semen and my swollen cervix dipping hungrily into the flow. To feel him inside, and see on the wall screen the spasming of my own depths: you don't get easily bored with someone who shows you that.

There are limits, though. The endoscope can go farther, all the way into the womb, but I wouldn't let Devlin try it himself. We found a gynecologist to thread it into my uterus—that was bad enough, but trying to explain *why* we wanted the videotape was even more difficult. Surely she must have recognized the tangled knot of art and obsession—and since she agreed without comment to perform the procedure, perhaps she understood something of it.

. . .

Devlin has taught me more than any film school ever could. He dismisses my digitally altered images as pop art, too Monty Python, and maybe he's right, but they help pay the rent. Sometimes he'll co-operate, sometimes not. It's his own monumental cock (state-of-the-art equipment!) in the film where my tiny naked figure twines around it and rubs against it and climbs onto it, writhing on its broad tip before crawling into its narrow slit, only to be expelled in a geyser of semen. But the figure tumbling in the waves inside my cunt and being sucked up by my greedy cervix is someone else. Devlin refused to ride the water slide necessary for the shots I needed.

He disdains such artificial manipulation, he tells me, even though he views that wave sequence over and over and the look in his eyes comes from someplace deeper than disdain. He wants, I know, to be that tiny figure, drawn deep, deep into the soft depths, back to the primal instant, the dark flash of life's beginning.

For his own work he claims a purity of vision, truth captured and revealed through editing and sequencing and pacing, not clever computer graphics. The sperm dyed by that injection took three weeks to reach the launching stage: twenty-one days of X-raying himself and combining the images and overlaying them onto two minutes of his naked body's progression from relaxation to erection. Computer simulation would have been so much easier—especially the transition to internal shots of blue-tinted come flooding my vagina, but it wouldn't have met his standards of truth.

"You can't capture everything literally," I tell him. "You can use visual metaphors, and record how people react—the groans, the contortions, what they shout in extremity—but you can't capture sensation itself any more than you can film the patterns and colors you see when you rub your eyes. That, at least, I can approximate with computer images."

Devlin frowns, and rubs his eyes. "There has to be a way to record from the inside! To channel images from the retina…."

I wince at the thought of fiber-optic cable inserted behind my eyeball, but I'm not really afraid. It's just speculation. This isn't his true, profound obsession. "That technology is bound to come," I agree. Then I try a distraction.

"I have an idea for a new sequence for the Web site. It's time to update—the paid hits are holding level or tapering off. What do you think of this?" I show him some rough sketches of my concept. "Should I get Henri with his pierced cock, or Luke for the contrast with Bianca's pale skin? Assuming Bianca has healed enough." Infected piercing attempts, she'd said when I asked about the bandages on her belly. I had made it more than clear that any piercings without my permission and she'd be out of a job, but even so I was surprised at how she'd cowered before my anger.

"I'll do this one myself."

"Not with Bianca, you won't!" Art or no art, I've told him that if he fucks anybody but me, I'm gone.

"No, of course not. This isn't Web site junk. I have some ideas for modifications—it'll be just us, taking it as far as it will go."

Just us … and the cameras. And, ultimately, that well-paying specialty market that appreciates art tinged with obsession.

One beauty of film is its plasticity. Cameras surround us discreetly, covering all angles; remote controls in Devlin's sleek glove dictate focus and virtual distance. We can try one thing, then another, "take it as far as it will go," and from all this footage he will shape a work of art with as much genius as a sculptor transforming a mass of clay into a Venus to stir men's blood.

Blood. I scan the satin sheets for stains. The last time we used this set was for the bondage scenario where I ripped the studs and rings out of Devlin's many piercings. They were becoming clichéd, and it seemed like a waste to simply unfasten them. He's almost healed now, but the ragged edges of his foreskin are still red under stress; an interesting effect on film.

The sheets are clean. The laundry did a good job. After today, though, I expect them to be stained beyond all hope.

We begin still as statues, back to back. In the final cut our bodies will be drained of color, pale as marble. Devlin's gloved hand tenses fractionally, directing zoom lenses to focus on my body. He watches on the wall screen, and I feel the stroke of his mind across my flesh as the multiple images sweep from downcast eyes over the curve of my cheek, the hollow of my throat (a subtle pulse there belying the semblance of stone,) the valley between my breasts and their full round curves. I see the screen through lowered lashes, see my nipples tauten. Bianca's silicon-pumped orbs might as well be water balloons when it comes to responsiveness, but my all-natural flesh swells with the need to be touched—stroked—tongued gently, and not so gently—sucked hard and harder, bitten. None of which is in this scenario.

I want to pull Devlin around and force his head to my breasts, his mouth to my swollen nipples, but I resist. The cameras have caught my desire; that's all that matters.

I do not resist a long, lingering stroke of my hands around my breasts and down over my belly to my mound. He can cut it later if he wants to. If I were editing the film I would make the shift to full color now, flesh tones flowing with my hands along the marble pallor of my body. Would I show the pale red crescent scars below my navel? Probably not. They have faded almost to nothing, but a film record remains of another time when we were "taking it as far as it will go." That time I stopped him in time. I can always stop him.

My skin aches with a tension that screams for more. I turn, press against Devlin's back, slide slowly down it, heated by the pressure of his firm body against mine.

I kneel behind him and reach my arms around his hips. He is already hard, but I make a show of working to arouse him, stroking, slipping a hand between his thighs to cup his full balls, licking and nuzzling his muscular buttocks. I am tempted to bite down hard, as he did when he left the tooth marks on my belly. Devlin has such a beautiful posterior; my clit throbs some-times with the urge to swell into a cock, to fuck his ass through and through. But that's a fantasy for another time.

Biting, though—I have a sudden vision of my teeth tearing his skin, peeling it away from those firm curves, like the dog tugging on the little girl's panties in the old sunscreen ad. I could blend images, show the clean lines of revealed muscula-ture with scarcely any blood, more as they'd appear in an anatomy book, or a Renaissance sketch.

That, too, is for another time. Now Devlin begins to turn, as though in response to my pleading touch. This is where he intends to gradually restore the flesh tones; it is his own arousal that warrants illumination by color.

There's something to be said for a man who can hold an erection indefinitely, at will, no matter what the stimulation, but there's a down side, too. Devlin never seems totally focused on me, or even on his own body. He can come on cue, of course, but his true orgasmic peak is reached only when he creates the perfect fuck on film. More than celluloid hits his cutting-room floor.

But this scenario calls for rapid response. Still kneeling, I stroke his engorged cock, take it gently into my mouth, then work it deeply and less and less gently in response to the urgent arching of his hips.

When he comes, the film will show only his face. Devlin does ecstasy (or agony) so well. I swallow, and scoop up the props concealed where the satin sheets brush the floor.

My arms are around his hips again, my body pressed against his thighs. A mass of multi-colored globes fills the valley between my breasts like jewel-toned grapes and rises about his withdrawn cock as though that had been their source. Gleaming, translucent, violet and blue and gold and blood-red, they are, in fact, capsules of dye.

Gradually I rise, working the thin-skinned globules upward between us. So fragile, so nearly bursting, like the yolks of exotic eggs. A few do burst, and thin streams of color trickle slowly between my breasts.

Devlin turns me, leans me backward onto the bed, and the smooth spheres spill across my body, their touch so sensuous, so fleeting that I shiver. A few are mounded in my navel; he plucks out two, wine-red, rolls them tantalizingly around my engorged nipples, then squeezes hard. Scarlet rivulets pour over my breasts like bright sauce on ice cream sundaes.

His cock is hardening again, his breathing becoming genuinely uneven. What comes next could so easily go … too far.

He has spread my thighs, and now he slips the cool, smooth globes inside me, one by one at first, then in multiples. I cannot keep my cunt from clenching around them, desperate to be filled with more than their elusive pressure provides. Finally, long past the point when I am sure I can stand no more, he thrusts his cock into me as though to drive the dye deeper. I want to arch, to buck against his hardness until release slams through me, but I know what comes next.

He withdraws in spite of my thighs' pleading grip, bends forward until his face presses hard into my belly. He is altering the script—I realize this change may be for the better—but his teeth dig so deeply into my soft flesh that the pain ignites my fury, and in that red haze I see what I had hidden from myself. Bianca's wounds were placed just so, positioned like my own faded scars, like these new ones.

I lied when I told him that if he fucks anybody but me, I'm gone. This time he's gone.

"No!" I scream. My nails at his eyeballs mean business. He draws back. "No, Dev, the knife! Remember? Cleaner, more elegant ... the knife."

He is shuddering now, obsession grappling with art. I slip the knife from beneath the pillow and press it into his hand, against his fingers, just long enough to impress his fingerprints upon it, then I snatch it back.

"Like this, remember?" He stares, dazed, as I draw the blade across my belly, barely breaking the skin. In one spot I press it in a quarter inch; a half inch. The pain means nothing. I wonder briefly if the original scenario can be salvaged, with its illusion of the knife plunged deep and the jewel-toned fountain springing forth; the extra, larger capsules still wait in the folds of satin sheets. I even let a vision of Devlin going all the way drift through my mind— but he would never find what he longs for, any more than those who split the fabled goose found golden eggs within its feathered belly.

No. I'm going to be the one to edit this film.

"It's all right," I whisper. "You can come in. All the way." The knife turns in my hand as he leans forward, intent in his madness. Then his face twists, contorts as though wracked by orgasm, and for one brief moment he is completely focused on me, then he shifts attention to his own pain. I force the knife sideways to be sure of an artery.

There can be no doubt that it is self-defense. Bianca will testify how close to madness he has come before. And the film is mine to edit.

I will still give Devlin what he wanted—even though it existed only in his fantasy. His body lies heavily across mine as my mind races with visions of how I will do it, how with my computer I will morph our images, shrink him, sink him at last so deeply into me that my dark mystery enfolds him and he is bound forever at that junction between life and not-life.

But first I'm going to throw up.

First Love
by Jay Russell

A death-goddess blonde dances on the metal platform above the bar. Pancake breasts hang from her body like dying flowers, the flaccid, bloody nipples big as Victorian roses. Her eyes are closed as she jerks to the music's dull throb like a wind-up toy running out of action. Purple Kaposi blotches on her arms and thighs glow like neon tattoos in the harsh spotlight. She has all the dignity of a bum who shits in the street and wipes his ass with his drinking hand.

I want her, I think, growing hard.

Quintano is suddenly there beside me. His crinkled silver jumpsuit glitters like a cracked fabric mirror. The bar's amber and ocher lighting melts into the material, swirling with every smooth movement of his lithe form. He reaches between my legs and roughly strokes me with his skeletal fingers. His hand lingers on my crotch as he nods ever so slightly toward the dancing girl, his multi-hued eyes whirling like sparkling, rainbow pinwheels. He smiles through filed gold teeth, flicks a reptilian tongue across his painted lips.

"Hors d'oeuvre?" he asks. I've never been able to make his peculiar accent. Somewhere west of affectation, perhaps.

Quintano must have somehow signaled to the dancer, for as I look up she stands directly above me, squatting on the mesh walkway.

A primal, excitingly rancid odor wafts from the shaved region between her legs as she tenses the muscles in her upper thighs. Through the music I hear her grunt with exertion as her distended, shaved labia redden and stir. They begin to flap, waving gently, slowly like sea anemones in an easy current. Her clitoris extends and swells, pulsing like a swollen vein as it escapes from between her blood-engorged lips. An anorexic tongue, it pokes in and out. The ultimate French kiss.

I watch the graceful pirouette of her sex and I sigh. Glorious, yes, but this is not what I have come for. I glance back at Quintano and shake my head. He shrugs, idly admires his manicured fiberglass nails, and walks toward the lift. I glance up, but the dancer has already wandered off. There are plenty of other customers. I join Quintano in the elevator.

I feel our ascension in my gut, though there are no indicator lights to mark the passage. I suddenly feel less tense and know that the lift has been programmed with subliminals.

Quintano, gods bless him, leaves nothing to chance.

I glance at my host, but Quintano's manufactured, multi-ethnic face is as unreadable as ever. The door swishes opens and I follow him down a long, brightly lit hallway that reeks of industrial disinfectant. Heavy ebony doors line either side of the corridor. I walk behind Quintano, the click of my heels against the slick tile echoing down the corridor like .22 caliber gunfire. Quintano moves without a sound, floating like a flower petal in the breeze.

A door opens to my right. A yellow man with flipper stumps and a mottled skull slithers out and flops across the hall. He propels himself by arching his scarred back like an inch-worm, gaining slight purchase with his jutting, bloodied chin. A hermaphrodite walks out behind him. S/he is naked, enormous penis and bulbous breasts flopping and jiggling with every step. S/he grabs the little man about the waist and drags him back inside the darkened chamber. The man barks and squeals as his flippers wave like clipped wings; he leaves a sticky, white trail on the tile. I stare at the door that slams shut behind them. I hear an ugly wet sound, like motor oil poured through a spinning fan, followed by a giggle and a high-pitched shriek.

I move on.

Quintano waits by a door at the end of the hall. As I approach he bares his pointed teeth and holds out his hand. I give him the envelope and he slips it in his pocket. He doesn't even look inside: Quintano has class. He takes my head between his long fingers and kisses me gently on the lips. He straightens his neon tie and disappears through an unnoticed doorway, leaving me with only the rosewater taste of his coarse tongue. And my fevered desire.

I open the door and step into a small anteroom. There is a wooden bench and a tall, antique wardrobe with full-length mirror. I feel the vibrations of unfamiliar chamber music projected through invisible speakers. A second, ornate door leads to … my deepest desire. I press a hand to the wood and my pulse begins to race.

I strip off my clothes and neatly hang them up. I stuff my socks in my shoes and lightly close the wardrobe door. I examine myself in the mirror. All the hair has been shaved from my body, leaving only a slight shock of thin curls about the pate. My almost-bald head looks unnaturally large, my silver-blue eyes slightly glazed—Quintano's magic elixir, I know—and my nipples jut out like ripe zits. I stare at my hairless crotch, run a hand over the stubble which is already desperate to grow back and try to imagine myself as I must once have been. A shimmering globule of pleasure dribbles from the head of my penis. I wipe it away with a finger and touch it to my lips, savoring the briny thickness.

I open the second door.

I can practically suck the warmth into my lungs as I cross the threshold. Electricity sizzles up and down my spine like arcs on a Jacob's ladder. The lighting is dim and I have removed my contact lenses, but I walk in the direction of the pale, fleshy glow.

She lies on a huge black mattress—a water bed I happily discover—naked and asleep. I gasp at the splendor of the reproduction, the perfection of Quintano's realization. I touch the back of my hand to her face and her brown eyes open, a loving smile breaking across her visage like surf on a virgin beach. The skin is warm and downy, the slight fuzz on her chin exactly as I remember.

I bend down and nuzzle my cheek against hers, find myself purring, kittenlike, without volition. She extends an ivory hand

and tenderly strokes my face. I crawl on top of her, maximizing the surface contact of flesh against flesh. I close my eyes and run my head down her neck, resting it briefly on her chest. I listen to her heart, the whispering rush of her blood. Our blood.

Her breasts are larger than I remember, but I ignore the discrepancy, for Quintano is nothing if not precise. More so, no doubt, than my own distant memories. I run my mouth over a supple, fleshy sphere, my tongue lathing the ripe plum of her nipple. I bite it lightly and it blossoms, engorging in my mouth. As I suckle, I press my hands together at my chest and slightly curl my back, tucking my knees. After a moment a flow of sweet, thick liquid begins and I grow hard—harder—as the savory fluid warms my throat and fills my belly.

Sated, I am tempted to doze at her breast, but there is so much more to know. I crawl down her body, maintaining the contact between my cheek and her pliant skin. I run my hands along her waist, feel her nurturing heat with my fingertips, the immaculately architectured musculature of her torso. I slide my face down her taut stomach, rolling slightly to one side where the dark thatch of wiry hair begins. As my chin grazes her thigh, she parts her legs and a trace of ocean tickles my nose. I open my eyes for just a moment and gasp at the wonder of folded pink softness that beckons me.

The origin of the world.

I try, at first—out of habit—to enter with my mouth, but my mistake is soon clear. Relaxing, I bow my head and force the crown between her welcoming, wet lips. I slip in easily and feel her moist warmth envelop my shorn scalp. There is some slight resistance as I lift my chin, but elasticity returns as my forehead plunges through the expanding slit. I become slightly panicked as my nose passes out of the open air and into her darkness, but somehow I am still able to breathe in the blind wetness. As my mouth passes through I poke out my tongue and revel in the sweet taste of primal salt and memory.

I experience a second brief panic as my shoulders become wedged against her pelvic bone and I get stuck, but a quick twist to the left solves the problem. I trail my arms at my side as

I squeeze my torso into the narrow gap, then bring them under my chin as I inch my midsection through the slit.

With my elbows available for leverage I pull my pelvis through quite easily. My erect penis poses a brief dilemma—an unusual, even comic puzzle in penetration. But another half turn enables me to draw the organ comfortably inside as her wondrous cunt expands almost knowingly for the glans which, unfamiliarly, enters last. I feel a brief twinge as my swollen balls resist admission, but with a tug and a wet slap they pop inside.

It is difficult to hear over my own strained grunts and mewls, but the beat of her heart provides a distantly familiar and comforting soundtrack. Only my ankles and feet remain outside now, and with a last flex of tendon I draw them in and the entrance snaps shut behind me.

It is utterly black, now, and my eyes are useless. Every nerve ending crackles with sensation. I hear not only with my ears, but through my bones and organs. I sense my heartbeat changing, slowing to match the booming, pervasive pattern of her own.

I squirm around as I try to find a comfortable position. I push off the soft walls of her uterus until I find my place, then curl my legs up beneath me and clasp my hands beside my cheek. Warm liquid begins to fill the womb, rising about my thighs as I hunch my back.

I wedge my thumb into my mouth and begin to suck, the lingering memory of her rich milk still warming my belly. As the amniotic fluid laps at my crotch I ejaculate into it with astonishing intensity, the orgasm filling my every sense. My penis softens and shrivels and my testicles contract into my body cavity.

The liquid is chest deep, thick and soothing like a honey hot spring. I am floating in an ancient sea now. Floating without cold, without pain, joined in a primordial and eternal bond.

The liquid laps over my chin.

"Mama," I coo and it fills my mouth, my throat. I kick. I sense a perfect, loving hand rubbing swollen abdomen as splendid darkness descends.

Small Bubbles
by Samuel Cross

Michael fought to catch his breath. His heart pounded, his hands tingled, he was in a cold sweat. Either he'd eaten some bad meat—or he was about to get laid.

Michael got hold of himself. Now wasn't the time to come unraveled. Not again. He breathed deep, but then a small noise rose from his throat. Lorenzo took him by the hips and pulled him close.

"I know you've been watching," Lorenzo said.

. . .

Michael was out of element. He rarely went out evenings and hadn't dated in years. But Lorenzo had shown interest. That was something new, and he was *hot*. His brown eyes could nail a guy right down with a glance. Over six feet tall, his muscular body was as good as those men in magazines. He smelled subtly of sweat and spice. Full lips in an intelligent face. Dark skin. Hairy arms and—

Well, he'd shown interest.

Michael never set foot inside Lorenzo's apartment until that evening, but he'd seen it many times. He watched Lorenzo painting his pictures. He wore a robe when he painted. Sometimes, the robe came open.

Some weekends—those wonderful, wonderful weekends— he watched Lorenzo entertain other men, doing the sort of thing he was doing now.

. . .

"You know?"

"Yeah," Lorenzo said. "I know." He held Michael very close. His breath was hot. Michael tried to think of something to say, some excuse for his secret indulgence. Lorenzo didn't look like he cared. His mouth was hungry. His eyes were on the top button of Michael's shirt, and the shadow of a smile brushed over his lips as he unfastened it.

"Oh," Michael said, more a gasp than a word. His chest muscles twitched at Lorenzo's touch. Like a virgin. Two buttons more, and Lorenzo buried his hand beneath the loosened shirt. He pulled at the tuft of hair under Michael's arm. He fondled Michael's nipples, pinching them between his thick thumb and index finger. Michael's cock reacted, stretching his slacks and poking at Lorenzo through his jeans. Mouth open, Michael closed his eyes.

"Oh...."

. . .

Lorenzo had paintings on the walls. Michael had seen them before with his eye pressed to the lens of his department store brand telescope, manhood spilling from his open fly and into his sweaty hands. So many paintings. So many people. A man drank wine from his lover's mouth. A woman knelt before a faceless queen in red boots laced high. An old-timer tied his mouth into knots and ejaculated upon his image in a mirror. More paintings, and still more. But Michael had only seen those facing his apartment window. Now he was surrounded by them. He hadn't even seen them all yet, but he felt their presence. They were watching him.

Lorenzo had painted all of those people. He worked very hard and very late.

. . .

Dizziness set in. Maybe it was the smell of oil and paint thinner seeping from everything. More likely it was Lorenzo's lips. Michael wondered if he'd forgotten how to kiss a man. People could be so judgmental about those things, and he wanted to do it right. Ah, but the motion came easily, and he knew just what to do when Lorenzo's tongue entered his mouth. Fear fell away like his shirt now cast upon the color-splattered floor. Michael took the bigger man in his arms. He squeezed and held on as tightly as he could.

A cool breeze drifted through the window, past the open blinds. By God, Lorenzo's back felt as though it was made of brick!

. . .

"Come over tonight," Lorenzo had said, just that morning.

Downtown traffic was at a standstill in the narrow street outside Michael's apartment building. Horns honked. Pedestrians rushed past to catch the bus. It was sunny and time for work, but Lorenzo had probably been up all night. He held a cup of coffee from the local deli in one hand, his keys in the other.

"That's my bus," Michael said. He looked at his shoes, then at the street. Lorenzo laughed. A controlled, masculine laugh.

"Don't be afraid," he said. "No one is watching. Fuck them if they are. I'm in the building across the street, apartment 510."

Michael nodded, unable to say no. They'd just met moments ago, literally bumping into each other on the sidewalk. Apologies led to conversation, and the conversation turned quickly to sex. The attraction was mutual, but Michael worried what people would think. Someone was always watching, judging. His landlady thought he was strange. What if she passed? What if she saw the sexual energy, so visible between them?

Michael caught the bus. At work, he fantasized of a romantic trip to the tropics as he rubbed himself under his desk.

. . .

Michael unfastened Lorenzo's pants and opened the zipper. Lorenzo helped him. Then, Michael got on his knees and parted the silk boxers with his hands and his nose. He took Lorenzo's flaccid cock and made it hard with his tongue. His mouth watered and Lorenzo's cock glistened as he moved his hips.

Cocksucker, Michael thought. The idea aroused him. Maybe he'd get into the swing of things after all.

Michael closed his eyes and imagined he was watching from a distance.

. . .

But another image intruded upon the fantasy. A glimpse, one that he hadn't fully taken in at the time, just a moment ago. Michael wondered—

Lorenzo's cock entered his face. Michael sucked, exploring the slit, the crown, savoring the ribbed muscle and the gentle bulge of blue veins. While he ate, the image became clearer. He stopped, and his blood turned cold.

. . .

"You are a quiet one," Lorenzo said. He pulled Michael to him, face to face with his wet cock dripping in front of him. He tore Michael's belt off with a snap. He discarded the belt, and pushed his hand down the front of Michael's pants.

"What do you want me to say?" Michael replied. He was shaking. Looking at that painting again, trying not to look.

"Don't say anything. Don't say a fucking word." Lorenzo said. He pulled aggressively at Michael's manhood, kissed him again. "You like that, Michael?"

"Yes."

"You want your pants off? Do you, Michael?"

"Yes." His eyes burned. He felt small and frail. Lorenzo lifted him right up, pushed him against a wall. The moment of weightlessness was incredible.

"Open your fucking eyes!" Lorenzo demanded. He pulled Michael's pants down to his knees, and now his hand worked with greater precision. "That's right," he said. "Look at me!"

Eyes open, so close, Michael saw and smelled the man he'd wanted. He felt him, his breath so near, his sweat so strong, and he wiped a tear away and groaned. It had been a long time. Too long, maybe. He lost sensation in his legs, and his anus tightened. By Christ, he already was going to come!

And facing a wall he couldn't have seen from his own apartment, he saw a painting of a man at a window, lips drawn, pants open, his small hard penis in his hand.

"That's me," Michael said. He said it twice, and then: "My God. That's *my apartment!*"

. . .

"It's not you."

Michael came. A gentle spill turned into a full orgasm. He tried to stop. He was afraid, but it was too late. Lorenzo tore open his own shirt and exposed his chest and belly. Come sprayed his skin, glistening and beautiful. Lorenzo rubbed the cream in, making little bubbles and oiling himself with the lather. He pulled Michael into him, and his flesh was warm.

"It's not you," Lorenzo repeated. He held on too tight with his chin on Michael's shoulder. His tongue curled around Michael's earlobe, and he whispered, "Don't be afraid. It's not you."

But Michael knew damn well that it was him. His cropped, blond hair. His thin lips, his smile. The red splotches smeared across his face a moment before orgasm. *Is that what I look like to him?* Michael's heart pounded, tears burning his cheeks. He was helpless, naked in Lorenzo's arms.

. . .

The longer Lorenzo held him, the more afraid he became. He wanted to push the man away and go home, but he hoped for a more subtle exit. He just needed to get dressed and say he had to go somewhere.

The more he looked at the painting, the more certain he became that it was painted from *inside* his apartment.

"That's my coffee table," Michael said. "That's my bookshelf."

Lorenzo shook his head. "It's not even you," he said one more time. "It's just that man. That silly, impotent bastard spying on us." He held Michael away and gestured toward the window. "Look. There he is now."

Past the open blinds and across the street was Michael's place. The lights were on. In the window was a telescope. Behind it, the silhouette of a man, hunched over, gazing through the eyepiece.

For the briefest moment, Michael felt as though he were in three places at once: in the window, in Lorenzo's room, and staring out from the painting. Three Michaels, all looking at each other, feeling for an instant almost nothing.

. . .

Michael broke from Lorenzo. He stumbled, pulling up his pants as he ran for the door.

"Come back!" Lorenzo said. "What are you doing?" But Michael didn't listen. Without his shirt or belt, he ran for the elevator, couldn't wait and hurried down the stairs. He fell into the street, rushed across and fled up to his room. He stopped at the door, realized he should have called the police. He couldn't go in there. Not with an intruder lurking. Catching his breath, he tried to think. He tried to think of the smart thing to do.

Gently at first, Michael knocked at his own door.

. . .

He knocked louder. And then, he got out his keys and turned the knob. He opened the door a crack and listened.

He went inside.

The lights were off, so he turned them on. The place was empty. He looked around. Yes, empty.

Across the way, Lorenzo was painting. He didn't look up, just kept painting, and Michael searched his apartment one more time before falling onto his couch.

It was quiet. It was very quiet, and he was alone, cold without his shirt. How long should he wait before he decided he'd imagined the intruder? An hour? Two? Already, he'd sort of settled into the notion. And, by God, it was quiet.

Payback's A Bitch
by Thomas S. Roche

NIGHTMARE CLUB, HOLLYWOOD: MIDNIGHT. A packed house filled with everything from smack-wasted deathrockers who haven't listened to a Cure album in ten years to black-and-turquoise Spandex metalgirls high on crystal meth and succulent distortion. The DeathKittens—the nastiest all-girl speed-thrash industrial-grindcore group ever to shatter eardrums and make the pathetic testicles of so-called "male" musicians shrink up and crawl into their body cavities whimpering and begging for mercy—are back and screaming for blood. Out of the scene for three fucking years since Miranda went up on drug charges, the Kittens are ready to blister the paint from the walls with their skull-cracking wall of sound guaranteed to melt your brains into putrescent green goo.

. . .

Jane Convulsion takes her old place at the keyboards, ripping out sounds out that haven't been heard this side of Mai Lai. Anya Claw and Tara Switchblade trade eviscerating riffs on matching metallic-gold Gibson SGs with feedback screaming like the gods at Ragnarok. Kara Fleshpound and Valerie Viscera respectively hold down the bass and drums with a congealed rumble that pounds your brain to bloody effluence. Above it all—wailing her trademark death-dirge—rises Miranda Icepick, fresh from prison with scars and jailhouse tattoos; her voice all fire and agony, her eyes haunted like something out of a cracked-out masochist's speedmetal Emily Dickinson pastiche.

Standing at the front of the seething mass is the legendary Erica Scream. Erica feels the surging bodies of rabid Catgirls (as the DK's affectionately call their fans) pressing herself hard against the front of the stage, pleasantly smashing and torturing her tits. Erica Scream: world-famous porn star, veteran of over a hundred triple-X features before her twenty-first birthday. And about three times that many amateur beyond-hardcore SM videos and Polaroids she shot herself, in private, over the years—first in her basement bedroom at Aunt Roonie's house, then in her run-down roach-infested tenth-floor walkup in the East Village, then in the luxury penthouses of various porno producers while she fought and crawled her way up the ladder toward stardom, and finally in the private playroom in her thirty-four-room mansion off Mulholland overlooking the smog-blanketed City of Angels. These videos and photographs document Erica Scream's enthusiasm for complicated masochistic scenes and passionate submission to her dream mistress. But Erica has never experienced her longed-for torture at the hands of another. She has saved herself for the ultimate bitch-goddess.

Since her early years, Erica has guessed, then suspected, and finally known beyond doubt that the goddess in question is destined to be Miranda Icepick.

Erica has spent countless nights of exquisite masochistic suffering wrapped in the cruel Miranda's auditory arms. She's watched every Kittens video a hundred times, her soul enveloped in longing as she drove her body to higher states of agony and pleasure. Erica masturbated nightly to Miranda's suicidal chanteuse since she was sixteen—first with her hand, then with a jumbo-size Hitomi ShakeDown she shoplifted from the local KwikDrug, and eventually with a pack of unfiltered Black Lungs, a bottle of Jack Daniels, her grandfather's pre-1900 ivory-handled straight-razor, a box of clothespins, a curling iron, a package of hypodermic needles, jugs of bacon grease from Camp Pendleton, and a nine-inch-by-three-inch Mister Dong donated to her collection by the Sleaze Emporium on Sunset Boulevard. The numerous Polaroids Erica sent to Miranda at the Dante Women's Prison were confiscated by prison officials who had a hell of a good time with them. Word finally got back to Miranda Icepick of what was being sent her way, and the descriptions of said Polaroids were, just maybe, even more outrageous and enticing than the photos themselves.

. . .

It didn't start with masochism. It rarely does. Erica Scream's first letters to Miranda in prison were innocent fan letters, with only the faintest hint of the intense sexual desire Erica felt for Miranda. Miranda was used to that—more than one porn star had already begged and pleaded her way into Miranda's bed. But soon, the caliber of Erica's gifts to Miranda began to change. With a little of Erica's money greasing the proper palms, she was able to slip some of her commercial-release hardcore tapes behind the walls of Dante. With the help of her inter-prison connections, Miranda arranged to watch the tapes late at night in Warden Richardson's office.

It was love at first sight.

The tapes were strictly C-quality fuck-and-suck stuff, but sleazy enough for the tastes of Miranda, who'd never been too proud to slum from time to time. And even in her most commercial incarnation, Erica did go in for the extreme stuff. She was commonly shown doing it with six men simultaneously. Another favorite scenario featured the voracious Erica's encounter with a sadistic prison warden and her six female guards.

Miranda fucked herself with the neck of an empty Smirnoff bottle to that gangbang scene, sprawled nude across the warden's desk with her prison blues in a rumpled heap on the desk chair. Warden Richardson, a Kittens fan from years back, had already gone down on her knees for Miranda while Miranda spread out on this very desk, so it only seemed appropriate that the rock star pleasure herself with the issue of the Warden's liquor cabinet—after polishing off the Smirnoff, of course.

Miranda came six times on that Smirnoff bottle, imagining what it would feel like to slide the well-greased glass appendage into Erica's cunt. Would she like that as much as she obviously liked the strap-ons of the guards in the video? Miranda felt quite sure that she would.

Miranda stepped up her pressure on Warden Richardson, and soon made arrangements to use the office every Friday night. She eagerly devoured Erica's gifts, ranging from the now-classic *I Was the Pope's Fuck-and-Suck Whore* to *Invading Lesbian Slime-Queen of Satanador Twelve*—Erica's one attempt at "legitimate" cinema, in which a hagged-out Bambi Bunz played the title role, limply holding a ray gun and hissing in a fake accent equal parts Rio de Janeiro, Nazi Germany and Alpha Centauri: "Take me to your leader!"

But Miranda's favorite scene was when Bambi gloated over the unfortunate captive, Ms. Scream, describing her plan for world domination as the ray gun quivered in her hand. "Yes, I will defile and degrade your slutty El Presidente! I vill force zat bitch to submit to my succulent und brutal caresses. She will become one with the SlimeGoddess and soon ze entire planet will belong to the Slime-Queen of Satanador Twelve!! But first, you, my dear, you will become a human specimen, an offering to my cruel taskmistresses the SlimeGoddess!! Bend over, bitch!"

Miranda climaxed with a moan when Bambi delivered that last ridiculous line—not so much because of Bambi's acting skills, which, let's face it, left a little to be desired even in her hardcore days—but because while the line was delivered the camera was focused on the look of sheer terror on co-star Erica Scream's face. And it was such deliciously convincing terror.

Miranda liked to see terror on Erica's face.

. . .

But despite the great pleasure the admittedly perverse Miranda took in her girlfriend's fetching squirmings in said cinema classics, there was something missing. Erica's videos, all triple-X but firmly within the bounds of commercial porn's legal guidelines, hinted at her intensely submissive and masochistic nature, but never spelled it out. Miranda was teased on an almost daily basis by the cruel guards at Dante, who took great delight in describing to Miranda all the things her demented girlfriend had done in the Polaroids—Polaroids that Miranda would never see, they were quick to remind her. Miranda heard rumors of the late-night fuck-parties in the back rooms of Dante cop bars, most notably Blue Belles (known for its wide-screen TV, which perpetually showed porno videos involving women in uniform) and Natasha's CopHouse (where every female cop or prison guard gets a free beer and a free Puerto Rican stogie). The prison guards and local cops from Dante, along with a liberal sprinkling of their friends from the LAPD, would get high as all fuck on prime weed and choice crack—and sure, sometimes even a little FuckDust—lifted from evidence rooms. They would polish off whole cases of Pabst Blue Ribbon. They would smoke putrid cigars and frig themselves fervently on the pool tables while passing around the Polaroids Erica had taken for Miranda and only for Miranda. Polaroids of her ultimate rituals of submission and suffering, offered to Miranda as the symbol of her desire.

Those photos had been stolen from Miranda. They had been passed from sweaty palm to sweaty palm until they were stained with the issue of the various guards' carnal pleasures. Even Warden Richardson, who had proven so willing to use her sloppy tongue—and sloppy the damn thing was—refused to return the photos to Miranda.

In fact, Miranda heard from certain loose-tongued guards— and they were all pretty loose-tongued, Miranda knew from repeated experience—that Warden Richardson didn't just turn a blind eye. The Warden had been in attendance at numerous of those late-night circle-jills—frigging herself at the sight of Erica's sufferings as eagerly as the horniest first-year rookie. The Warden, for all her eagerness to see to her star prisoner's simplistic carnal needs, was playing both sides of the fence.

And so, the images of the Polaroids grew in Miranda's mind, as she pictured all the complicated sufferings Erica had put herself through in the hopes of capturing Miranda's heart. And capture it she had, even more so because Miranda had never witnessed those sufferings, on film or anywhere else.

Miranda would have been happy to let bygones be bygones. If only the guards of Dante Women's Prison had furnished Miranda with her "valuables" upon her release from Dante,

Miranda would have forgiven. She would have washed her hands of the whole thing, and allowed the guards and the Warden their pleasures. She would have devoured the Polaroids, all her hungers finally satisfied. She would have gone back to her mansion in Beverly Hills, accepted the eternal submission and suffering of Erica Scream, forgotten the wrongs committed against her by the prison guards and the Warden.

But it had come back to Miranda, through a guard who kept her ears open and longed for Miranda's famous cruelty— she owned every Kittens album—that it wasn't just the Warden who attended those all-night fuck-fests in the cop bars.

No, it wasn't just Warden Richardson with her active, if unskilled, tongue. Another face had been seen bisected by a stogie while its owner frigged herself to Erica's Polaroids. District Attorney Courtney Petrusca, who had, with Governor Antonia Kwan, (so this guard said) engineered Miranda's routine traffic stop on the Santa Monica Freeway that had resulted in her arrest when three grams of FuckDust and an unregistered .45 automatic were discovered under the front seat, and a subsequent blood test had shown that Miranda had enough FuckDust in her bloodstream to kill most women her size.

In those days Miranda had done FuckDust almost as a matter of course before she ever mounted the L.A. freeways—shit, how else was she supposed to get up the balls to drive in L.A.? Besides, half the people on the freeways were high. According to Miranda's source, Governor Kwan had conspired with District Attorney Petrusca to have Miranda seized on that very night. Precisely because LAPD surveillance of Erica Scream—to which Governor Kwan had access because her spies in the LAPD Racketeering Intelligence Division spent a lot more time in surveillance of female porn stars than tailing gangsters—had shown that she was planning to send extensive documentation, photo and video, of her self-inflicted agonies to Miranda Icepick. And Miranda's incarceration at Dante would ensure that said documentation would fall into the right hands. Governor Kwan, Miranda's sources discovered, had *unusually* close ties to Warden Richardson.

So, from Miranda's intelligence, it appeared that more than just prison guards and wardens were achieving their climaxes with the contraband Polaroids of Erica Scream's complex erotic sufferings in their hands. A governor, and possibly a few judges, and what the hell, probably a senator or two, were enjoying these photographs as well. Who knew how high the conspiracy climbed?

The System had cheated Miranda out of her photos of Erica's submission to her. But one day, Miranda promised herself, she would see those sufferings performed live. She would make them happen, to Erica's repeated delight. One day, when Miranda had secured her release from Dante and the whole fucking penal system, she would see those sufferings repeated endlessly in the dressing room of some sleazy club in Hollywood—and then, with Erica's help, Miranda would wreak her bloody revenge. Then, it would be time for a little payback, Icepick-style.

And make no mistake. Payback's a bitch.

· · ·

Miranda had kicked the FuckDust in the joint. With the help of her many organized-crime connections and the large number of guards who were also DeathKittens fans, Miranda could have gotten all the FuckDust she wanted even if she'd ended up in Maximum Lockdown. She could have kept herself high for her whole three years of hard time. But she didn't. She went through the shakes, the screams, the pukes, the laughing fits, the weight loss, the Boris Karloffs (a type of seizure so named because of the forced rigidity of the arm muscles), even the phase of FuckDust withdrawal where your hair turns phosphorescent blue. She kind of liked that last part.

She did it because only a stone-cold sober bitch-queen could punch the number on those who did her wrong—and enjoy herself doing it. Those fuckers would pay, and Miranda would chuckle cruelly as she fucked them over.

They would pay, and Miranda would savor their unconditional surrender.

. . .

The limousine speeds smoothly down the Santa Monica Freeway. The driver keeps it right at the speed limit. Miranda coolly pours another glass of Dom Pérignon for herself and lifts the bottle, offering it to Erica.

Erica licks her lips nervously, indicating with a glance toward her martini glass that she prefers an ice-cold Smirnoff. She gets that herself, though, from the freezer above the seat, and the action has the intense air of servitude about it. Erica follows this up by lighting Miranda's Virginia Slim with her elegant ultraslim Death's-Head Zippo.

Erica sits obediently across the seat from Miranda, regarding her with wide-eyed admiration—you might even say "worship."

Erica is wearing a skintight latex corset which reveals the deep valley between her surgically-constructed 36DD breasts and her snow-white belly (nothing but long hours at the PendaSpring there, but even so a fetching little bulge jutting out beneath the flesh-hugging corset) with its intricate blue-black modern-primitive tattoos and the stainless-steel ring with its patented phosphorescent red GlowRuby pierced through her belly-button. Her matching leather miniskirt, decent by perhaps a quarter-inch, is so tight it looks sprayed on. Miranda can see that Erica isn't wearing any panties, only so-called "thigh-high stay-ups" from Maurice Soavi—fishnets which, in fact, come to just above Miranda's knees, therefore not living up to either hyphenate very well. Four hundred dollars a pair on Rodeo Drive, with their unique rips and tears added manually by the designer himself with a switchblade bought on the streets of Rome, accounting for seven-eighths of the price.

Erica's outfit, in fact, caused no small distraction at the DeathKittens concert earlier, leading the twenty-two-year-old correspondent from *RockTawk* to faint dead on the floor when he saw it.

"As I told you in my letters," Miranda says in her trademarked DeathKitten meow, "The videotapes you sent affected me ... profoundly. There's no question in my mind that you are destined to taste the ultimate pleasures of submission and torment at my hand. I will own you as if you have never existed except to service my most deplorable, depraved, nauseating, shocking, and overwhelmingly repulsive desires."

"Ooooh, baby," pants Erica, a shudder going through her body as she squirms on her seat and almost spills her Smirnoff. "I love it when you talk dirty."

Miranda tips her Dom Pérignon to Erica and utters a faint chuckle.

"And the Polaroids?" Erica continues in a desperate gasp, her voice a breathy whimper, threatening to become a moan of tangible sexual need. "What did you think of the Polaroids?"

Erica suddenly tosses the martini glass out the window. It shatters on the Santa Monica, sending ice-cold Smirnoff spraying through the night. Erica drops to her knees and crawls fetchingly across the floor of the limo, lifting her face to look up at Miranda, her eyes bright and wide with eager need.

"I'm going to do every single one of those things for you," pants Erica. "You're going to watch me suffer every filthy degradation I documented on those Polaroids—I've got them filed away in my filthy brain in alphabetical order, my oh-so-merciless and brutal mistress. What do you want to see first? Asphyxia? Or Zoophilia? Maybe I should just sort of mix them up, like start with "Queef" or "Quack" or something? What did you think of those Polaroids, my cruel and nasty bitch-goddess? I'm just dying to know."

"Uh, kind of a funny story, there," sighs Miranda thoughtfully.

"Yes?" whispers Erica, and her bright-eyed enthusiasm is enough to tug at the heartstrings even of the legendary Miranda Icepick.

Miranda mumbles incoherently for a few seconds; then, finally, she says: "I didn't actually get to see the Polaroids."

"Ooooh," whimpers Erica Scream, in the eternal and trademarked sound of her raw sexual desire that has engorged erectile tissue of all gender affiliations in cities and towns from South Pasadena to Ulaanbataar, Rejavik to Capetown. "That's so filthy of you. You're saving them, you brute, to enjoy them now that you've got my receptive and enthusiastically willing body all to yourself. You're such a dirty bird, my unforgiving and relentless Lady of Spain. I adore you."

"Yes, right. Well, then. Perhaps I should explain." Miranda knows she should really portion this exquisite humiliation out over the course of numerous manacled fuck-sessions, but then again, it's a little hard to predict how even an extreme masochist like Erica Scream is going to take this one. "In fact, I'm afraid those Polaroids which you so dutifully sent me have in fact been masturbated to by every prison guard at Dante, as well as Warden Richardson and, in fact—" Miranda Icepick giggles nervously, an uncharacteristically juvenile sound—"Several State Superior Court judges and probably the Governor, as well."

"Unnhh! Oh! Uh!" gasps Erica, her whole body shuddering in climax. "I can't believe you thought up that entire story just to humiliate and degrade me. You're such a filthy-minded pervert, I know you and I will make a perfect couple—"

Miranda Icepick clears her throat. Her ivory face reddens appreciably. "Well. Uh, look, Erica. I wish I'd thought it up. But, in fact, it's true."

Erica blanches. "What?"

Miranda coughs. "Hey, baby, look at it this way—*could* I make this shit up? Could anyone?"

There is a long moment of silence, broken only by the sound of gunfire ricocheting off the limo's bulletproof windows as the driver changes lanes.

Erica clears her throat.

"The fucking warden's been jilling off to my Polaroids?"

"You got it," sighs Miranda, finishing off her glass of Dom Pérignon. She savors the knowledge that there's still another bottle in the refrigerator.

Erica just stares at her lover for long, horrified minutes.

"But you were kidding about the governor," she finally says.

Miranda shakes her head. "Nope. The governor's definitely in on it, and I'm ninety-percent sure she had the Polaroids in mind the whole time. The bitch set me up so she could see you torment your malleable flesh with a curling iron. Sorry, babe."

Miranda would swear she can see Erica's dyed-black hair curling.

"The Governor."

"Right. Governor Kwan."

"That bitch who wants the death penalty for FuckDust trafficking."

Miranda takes out an emery board and starts buffing her nails disinterestedly.

"You're sure about this," Erica says.

Miranda shrugs. "You'll see in a few minutes."

"What?"

"Tonight, my sweet, revenge shall be ours."

"You fucking better believe it," growls Erica Scream, standing up so she bonks her head on the roof of the limo—and barely notices. She shrieks: "I'm going to toast some diseased goddamn gubernatorial pussy if you know what I fucking well mean!! There's going to be one mofo of a Superior-Court judicial clit-fry as soon as I get some fucking names!!! Gimme badge numbers! We'll see how those fucking guards like being Mirandized with a hatchet!!!!" Gasping, sputtering in anger, Erica falls to her knees, the wind suddenly going out of her sails. Her submissive nature once again dominating her moral (or perhaps, rather, immoral) outrage, she licks her deep-red lips and, panting softly, stares up at Miranda with eyes wide open in supplication, looking suspiciously for a moment like the Velveteen Rabbit.

Miranda laughs, the cruelty of that sound sending a shiver through Erica's body. Her arousal begins, once again, to mount.

"We shall take our revenge," whispers Miranda, toasting Erica with her now-empty glass. "Be patient, my sweet slave. Shit is going to go down."

"Yes, Mistress," pants Erica, and lowers her face to Miranda's knee.

. . .

The back room of the cop bar is packed to capacity and beyond. Every guard who's ever worked a shift at the Dante Women's Prison is crammed into a melange of seething copflesh. The word has spread like wildfire throughout the state. Were there merely fresh Polaroids to be had of Erica Scream's complex masochistic rituals, every guard throughout the network would rush to Natasha's CopHouse in Dante, California, to partake in the peace-officer ritual of the Erica Scream porn-fest circle-jill. From her contraband Polaroids, Erica has more fans among female cops than she had any reason to suspect.

But this night is special. It's not just a new set of well-used Polaroids that is to be passed around. Rather, it's Erica Scream herself.

The story is that Erica got wind of this So-Cal cop-bar ritual, and does not feel the least bit violated—or, rather, feels exactly as violated as she likes to be. Erica Scream, it is said, has been tormented by the lifelong fantasy of extreme submission to a roomful of female cops and prison guards.

And so (the story goes) Erica Scream threw her postal lover Miranda Icepick to the wind in favor of fleshly law-enforcement Nirvana. And she's coming to Natasha's CopHouse this very night to satisfy her lifelong craving—a brutal schtupping at the hands of a bar full of uniformed female peace officers.

And so Natasha's CopHouse is filled with every Southern Cal prison guard who ever climaxed while jilling herself to images of Erica Scream torturing herself for the love of Miranda Icepick. But it doesn't end there.

No. For Miranda, with the help of her compatriots, who so dearly loved to use their tongues on her behalf, has seen that these stories reached the highest levels of judicial government.

And so Natasha's CopHouse is graced on this foul night with those members of the judiciary who prize the sight of Erica Scream's tortured and suffering flesh above all else.

· · ·

Keep your panties on. It's ugly. It's real ugly. Law enforcement corruption is always ugly. Didn't you see *Serpico*?

. . .

This particular night, to accompany the submission of Erica Scream, the bar has received delivery of a fifty-five-gallon oil drum filled with FuckDust. A particularly attentive police captain saw that the barrel of FuckDust, confiscated in a bust, "disappeared" from an LAPD evidence room. The FuckDust is handed out in big glass tankards that say "Hefeweisen" on the side in cheesy Germanic letters. Cops and prison guards eat it with cheap steel spoons and sprinkle it on their pizza. Meanwhile Natasha herself, a drag queen and ex-LAPD cop—one of the pigs, in fact, who beat the shit out of Frank Cordell that fateful night when six separate VHS cameras immortalized the brutality of the LAPD—is toking a fat joint the size of a Havana King and humming loudly along with the silly techno soundtrack to the Erica Scream videos on the wide-screen TV she's purchased specially for tonight's event.

The door to Natasha's CopHouse swings open. Erica stands in the doorway, lit from behind by lights from the parking lot. Her flesh is outlined in the smoke from the bar. All eyes are on her. Silence. Silence. Silence. Then a low moan goes through the bar. Somebody tosses a baggie of FuckDust her way, and Erica empties it over her head, smearing the succulent intoxicant over her breasts as she tugs down the latex corset. She is careful not to get any into her mouth.

The LAPD cops and Dante prison guards, meanwhile, are heaving big spoonfuls of FuckDust into their gaping mouths and washing them down with bottles of Pabst.

In a moment, Erica has shed the latex corset and is hiking up her skirt. She wears nothing underneath, not even the faintest shred of a G-string. Erica has "FUCK ME FUCK ME FUCK ME YOU BRUTE" in elaborate Gothic lettering tattooed low on her abdomen where her pubic hair would have started—as any jerk-off who can rent porno down at the Quick-Vid knows.

She climbs onto the bar and drops to all fours and an approving cheer goes up from the crowd of law-enforcement officers. Spreading her legs and turning her hindquarters toward the crowd, Erica reaches back and delicately parts her swollen pussy-lips with her fingers. She begins to tease her erect, swollen, and pierced clitoris with her thumb. Erica moans loud enough to drown out the sounds of her recorded moans from the video screen—and then, she lets out her namesake: The Erica Scream.

Wailing as if in climax, Erica shudders and pounds herself up and down against the bar. Pabst Blue Ribbons and ashtrays full of FuckDust go scattering everywhere, until the floor is slick with a fetid slime composed of flat beer mixed with FuckDust.

A cheer goes up as Erica finishes her orgasm. The crowd of cops and guards begins to applaud.

Then, suddenly, a hush goes over the crowd.

From the swirling mass of blue and flesh-color, a figure emerges. Naked except for the blue cap of an LAPD captain (whom she has just finished orally servicing)—her hair freshly dyed phosphorescent green in the ladies' room on the spur of the moment—her eyes wide and glazed with FuckDust euphoria—Governor Kwan takes in her hand the thick shaft of the fourteen-inch strap-on fastened by a complicated array of black leather straps to her slim, muscled body.

"Scream, Erica," growls the Governor, drawling around her stogie, as she mercilessly drives her throbbing strap-on into the writhing body of Erica.

Erica throws her head back and screams as she has never screamed before, penetrated by twelve inches of hard-rubber gubernatorial cock, filled with the shaft of an elected official. Erica climaxes repeatedly as Governor Kwan drives her strap-on dildo home again and again amid the flashing images from the video screen.

The crowd shrieks its delirious approval of this new foul degradation to be added to Erica's already-impressive list.

Governor Kwan cackles her pleasure as she drives her cock into the kneeling woman, hearing every last moan and shudder of Erica's submission. The roomful of cops and prison guards falls upon itself, frantically fucking, licking, sucking, pounding, seething and exploding with gasps and moans of drug-induced ecstasy. Within the waves of FuckDust-inspired delirium, Governor Kwan lets out a belly-laugh of criminal pleasure—even as the first cop's screams turn from pleasure to agony. Even as the cop's eyes swell and then, amid the deafening strains of a DeathKittens song mingling with Erica's screams from the enormous speakers flanking the video screen, as the cop's eyes burst and spurt forth in a bloody swill of putrefaction, squirting and streaming across the naked bodies of the writhing and groaning peace officers covering the beer-slimy floor of the bar. Even as Erica utters yet another scream of ecstasy and climaxes in spasms on the Governor's thrusting strap-on. Even as the unfortunate LAPD officer, naked from the waist down but wearing the open shirt and the pointy cap of LA's finest, her shaved snatch and prodigious jet-black leather strap-on slick with lubricant and the juices of her fellow law enforcement officers, drops to her knees, screaming madly as her eyes spurt blood over her own breasts and then over the naked bodies of her frantically-porking compadres. Even as her head begins to swell. Even as vomit cascades from her parted lips and coats her jiggling breasts with their firm nipples. Even, it's true, as the cop's head explodes, spattering blood and brains over the squirming mass of naked cop-bodies that has also begun to swell and turn a putrescent red like rotting meat boiled after twelve days in the sun.

The governor laughs and drives her strap-on into the receptive and shuddering body of Erica Scream. Even as the naked and half-naked cops, around the room, packing and not packing, begin to scream and clutch their eyes. Even as their mouths spout phosphorescent-green vomit that spatters across the squirming bodies of their fellow blue knights. Even as all around the room, a dozen, two dozen, three dozen eyes explode in gouts of blood and spray uncontrollably amid the wails of agony from those whose heads have not yet exploded.

Even as Natasha, who never touches the FuckDust, realizes what's going on, opens her mouth desperately to scream, finds her mouth dry and, unable to utter her scream of terror, feels two jetting eyeballs shot from the blossoming face of that K-9 officer from Orange County—who decided she wanted one last beer—ram their way down her throat. Natasha drops to her knees, gasping for air, choking on eyeballs. She slumps face-up, death-spasms seizing her as the headless corpse of the K-9 officer gropes at her, spewing vomit, and then dissolves into a mass of fluorescent goo.

Only the K-9 officer's German Shepherd, Binky, stands unaffected, disinterestedly watching the dissolution of human flesh. The Shepherd issues a small yawn, whines and lies down on the floor, wishing she could get her belly scratched.

And still the orgy continues.

Even as the governor herself, looking around in sudden horror, begins to feel the sharp pains in her own eyes.

Her hips do not stop thrusting until after her head has burst, issuing torrents of bubbling green slime over a naked and writhing Erica Scream, who continues to climax, repeatedly, long after death-spasms of the Governor's jellifying body have ceased.

· · ·

Miranda Icepick, wearing her knee-high rubber boots with the stars on them ($399.95 at CyberSluts on Haight), walks amid the mass of still-warm and still-jiggling organic wreckage, the roomful of quivering remains that might, just possibly, have been human at some point in the distant past. Through some cruel twist of fate, the Erica Scream tape has reached its end, and is rewinding while a late-night rerun of *T.J. Hooker* plays on the wide-screen TV.

The Governor's headless corpse still twitches, the strap-on slick with gubernatorial blood and slime. Every now and then an obscene sound, like some sort of satanic belch, issues from the remains of the Governor's destroyed head and neck.

Miranda feels a lapping at her hand, and leans down to pat the friendly German Shepherd nuzzling her. She looks at the tag on the dog's collar. "Officer Binky. All right, come on, Binky," Miranda says softly. "You're one of us, now." None-too-subtly, Miranda leans over, edges Binky's wagging tail out of the way.

"Oooooh, lucky us," coos Miranda. "She's a bitch."

Face-up in the enormous, seething pool of disintegrating human remains, lies the panting, heaving, naked body of Erica Scream, her body slick with vomit, blood, ocular fluid, Pabst Blue Ribbon and liquefied human bodies.

The Governor's bones form a rather postmodern frame around Erica's naked body. Erica looks up at Miranda, her eyes wide, her lips parted and shimmering with unnamable organic substances. "Bitch," she spits, and Miranda chuckles, savoring the caress of that so oft-spoken, rarely-meant word.

Miranda's pretty sure Erica means it this time.

"Thank you," Miranda chuckles, and reaches out for Erica.

. . .

Watching the sun rise over Mulholland as the limo travels up into the hills, Miranda lights an unfiltered Black Lung and takes a sip of Dom Pérignon. "Dexandor Pentotharanide," she sighs, breathing smoke. "Or you can just call it *the bad stuff*. Mixed with pure enough FuckDust, it's totally undetectable outside of a laboratory. But you get that shit in your veins—and it's worse than Ebola Zaire in super-fast-forward. It was developed by the LAPD, you know." She flashes Erica a cool smile. "For urban pacification. You could call it that."

Officer Binky gives an affirmative whimper and nuzzles Miranda's hand.

Erica shudders on the seat, twitching and squirming as the memories of her night-long ordeal filter through her damaged brain. She's wrapped in Miranda's full-length black leather coat ($1,499.95 at Vetrano of Genoa on Rodeo Drive), but underneath the coat, Erica's naked and quivering body is still slick with gore and the faintly-glowing internal fluids of the Governor and about a dozen cops and prison guards. Erica has an eyeball stuck in her chestnut-brown hair, jiggling like it's still alive. Miranda could swear that's a fucking kidney plastered to Erica's left breast.

Coolly, Miranda plucks the suspected kidney off of Erica's tit, the eyeball out of her hair. She touches a button and the window of the limousine lowers soundlessly. Miranda tosses the kidney out onto the Santa Monica Freeway. She holds the eye-ball up, peering into it. "What're you looking at?" she growls with a twisted smile, and throws the eyeball out to join the kidney on the Santa Monica.

"Fuck you," whispers Erica. And then, "I love you," she says, like she means it, like the two statements are neither contradictory, nor even vaguely dissimilar.

"I know you do," says Miranda, as she bends forward and kisses Erica's vomit-slick lips. "Now."

On the floor, officer Binky rolls over and goes to sleep.

The sun is blazing in the sky as the thick slime of smog becomes visible in the valley. It's gonna be a scorcher.

Director of Dolls
by Anne Tourney

When does a woman become too old to play with dolls? So many textures of flesh to savor—taut rubber, silken bisque, pliant rag. Angela loves her collection of human lookalikes sitting like mute sentinels around her bedroom. Maybe, she thinks wryly, menopause brought on this obsession. Under soft-colored stage lights, with artfully applied makeup and hair tinted Botticelli gold, she can still pass for under forty. But each month brings another unwanted change; a dryness between her legs or a reminder of gravity found in the slackness of her breasts. She wipes off her make-up in the dark so she won't have to see the leathery hide under the pancake mask. She prods her skin for ominous crusts, swollen nodes—so far she has found only pockets of goose fat. The dolls seem to hold back the witch who keeps a vigil in Angela's bathroom mirror.

Because Angela hasn't had a lover for a long time, there is no one to see what she does with the manikins, to witness how she strips off their trousers or frilly underpants. Only Angela watches the friction of their sexless pubic mounds as she rubs their bodies together in simulated lust. Angela tries to overlook her own knobby fingers manipulating the dolls' perfectly molded limbs.

Her current favorites are a Victorian ice-skater—a collector's item she ordered from a home shopping channel during a weekend of gnawing solitude—and a grubby Barbie knock-off she found abandoned, its arms and legs bent in four directions like a swastika, in the hallway outside her apartment. She has christened the skater Eric; she calls the slut Goldie. Eric's painted black pompadour remains undisturbed as he slaves between Goldie's thighs, his invisible tongue struggling to find a cleft.

But Goldie comes out of their sexual bouts looking more slatternly than ever, her neck dislocated, her blonde hair whipped into a synthetic rat's nest. *Suck him*, Angela hisses, banging Goldie's skull against Eric's groin. *Suck him harder. Now, Eric, tell Goldie that you love her, in spite of what she is.* And Eric, anxious to please his director, gasps his devotion.

Goldie, grab his cock. What's the matter, can't you find it? Goldie claws helplessly at Eric's crotch. He groans in frustration through his sealed lips. The director relents, allowing her actors to couple the way they want to, genitals grinding against each other in a fury of squeaking surfaces. The girl-doll climaxes first. The violent rocking of her jointed torso nearly wrenches her head off its socket, and she screams like a mosquito as she comes. A gentleman to the end, Eric allows Goldie to finish her orgasm before he indulges in a couple of dignified grunts. But as the pair separates, Eric can't hold back his contempt. He kicks Goldie's face with the steel blade of his ice skate, leaving a vicious scratch across her mouth, nose, and eye. The skates are an extension of Eric's feet; the director has no choice but to let him wear them while he performs.

Angela lets the dolls fall to the floor. She opens her dressing gown and slips her hand under the waistband of her panties. Wet—she can still get so wet. She finds her clit under its fold of skin, like the hood of a priestess. Her fingers become the tip of a lover's tongue as she remembers one of the worshippers from her early days in the theater. They used to court her then, men and women alike, willing to wait months to taste her fruits. They brought her offerings of pleasure in so many forms. The imaginary tongue glides in languid figure-eights through the hollows of Angela's cunt. Her body used to hold a wealth of promise. As she lifts her hips in climax, a memory of that promise wells through her tingling pussy, radiates upward to her painfully sharp nipples, then withdraws.

. . .

The odor of nervous sweat stings Angela's nostrils as she steps into the theater. A dozen would-be actors are waiting for her, trying to look unconcerned about tonight's final audition. To Angela their attempted cool is pathetic and arousing at the same time. She imagines ordering them to stand in front of her—men on one side of the room, women on the other—and telling them to strip down to their gleaming skins. Their nipples would tighten and rise as they shivered in front of her, awaiting her direction. *You,* she would say, summoning the bitter blonde stripper whose name is Goldie, *come over here and kneel in front of Eric. Isn't he handsome? Bow your head and tell him how unworthy you are—no, no, keep your eyes on the floor. Now lift your head. Gently circle the head of his cock with your tongue. See him harden! Isn't he magnificent?*

Angela loves theater, has loved it since she was younger than the green colts who stand before her tonight. None of them is as beautiful as Angela was thirty years ago, or as tempting as the leading men she remembers. Eric is a possible exception. He is the son of a prominent San Francisco family, the sum of impeccably calculated breeding. You can see it in his careless black hair, the scuffmarks on his leather shoes. And, Angela supposes, you could see it in the parabola of his cock, which is probably as strong and well-made as the arc of a bridge. He is beaming at Angela now, a smile slick with flattery and need. Last night he confessed to her that if he didn't win the lead role, his parents would force him to give up acting.

"What would you do instead?" Angela asked.

"Stanford law school," Eric sighed. "They don't think I'll make it as an actor. Their goal is for me to be *comfortable.*"

Angela nodded in sympathy, though she secretly agrees with Eric's parents. Aside from his looks he is hateful on stage, pompous and strident. Goldie, whose hard little breasts and flaxen hair are well known in Tenderloin strip clubs, is frantic to play his leading lady. Her whine will clash with Eric's bray; they will hate each other long before the dress rehearsal. But in the deepest closet of her heart, Angela has decided to give Eric and Goldie the leading roles. She knows the play will fail. It will be the last of a string of arty productions that Angela has been allowed to direct, at a financial loss, because of who she was many years ago.

Why is she doing this?

Anxiety shocks Angela out of sleep every night, her night-gown slick and hot. Menopause again. Maybe even AIDS, she thinks in her wildest moments; when she was young, she could never get her fill of flesh. A Polish director whose work Angela once admired claimed that the purpose of experimental theater is to cross boundaries, surpass limits. Theater is about filling emptiness, he said. She holds that statement in her memory like a touchstone.

I still have the emptiness, Angela cries soundlessly. The dolls perched on her vanity table tilt their heads in a simulation of attention.

. . .

The doll museum: a treat for a nervous little girl who was happier playing with dolls than with other children. Among the aristocratic porcelain beauties slumped the kidskin bodies of worn-out hex figures and the contorted wax tools of voodoo. *They're antiques, dear*, Angela's mother reminded her, but that status only heightened their horrible power. Angela wasn't ready for the crushed rubber and shattered porcelain, the scabrous cheeks and blank eye sockets. The Pennsylvania-German hex doll had two heads—one human, one pig—attached to either end of a single torso. A Japanese geisha with black teeth slouched among her ratty wigs, which had failed to hide the frightfulness of her cracked skull. A terra cotta mother goddess from India boasted a monstrous vaginal cleft and a pair of funnels for breasts, each larger than her head. These were not toys, but ritual objects. Their faded surfaces hid a core of evil potential.

In her bedroom that night Angela's dolls turned into preda-tors. Angela was not powerful like the dolls, whose mocking gaze kept her from sleeping. They knew that she was afraid of almost everything, and that she often touched the tender flesh between her legs to soothe herself in bed. Their shrieks of laugh-ter drove Angela to unknown peaks of terror, where no caress could calm her.

The next day Angela poked out the dolls' eyes with a pencil, one by one, then twisted their heads backwards. Her mother was furious. She screwed each doll's head into its original position and locked the door of the cabinet where they lived. In the darkness the dolls beamed blind malevolence at the child who cowered in her bed. If she blinked, even breathed, the dolls would burst through the glass door and leap on her. They would claw the sheets, which were drenched with her urine, and tear her delicate human skin to bloody strips. Her eyes were parched from the effort of holding them open, in case she should miss a flash of movement from the totems that decorated her room.

. . .

Angela grew into a jittery teenager, her body at odds with her will. It wasn't until she took the stage at the age of seventeen that she felt at home in her own skin. In the theater her flesh became new flesh, the substance of whatever character she was playing. That flesh might weep, scream, or laugh hysterically, but it never lost its self-possession. On stage she was illuminated, vibrantly sexual. She lost her virginity to a sixty-year-old director, a vicious genius named Max Yelf, the director of a troupe called Dollsbody.

Yelf's mission was to drag theater off the stage and into the streets, into alleys and public toilets. Drama would be played out for audiences who would unwittingly become actors. "Let the observers shame themselves," he cried, "Reveal the true faces of their sexuality in public!" The trademarks of his productions were his nude, life-sized papier mâché dolls, each of which represented an obscene effigy of one of the actors. In Yelf's notorious play *The Doll's Crucifixion*, Angela played Mary Magdalene, witnessing the death of the doll that resembled her. It dangled from a makeshift cross, its head lolling, legs grotesquely spread to reveal a snatch of black yarn—Yelf's mockery of Angela's dyed blonde hair. The crowd moved in on Mary Magdalene, sniffing at her like animals, tugging at her costume. "Why stop there? Don't stop!" Yelf shouted. And the crowd went on. They tore off Angela's cloak, baring her, the men easing her to the ground while the women attended to her lips and breasts with feathery hands. As Angela's nipples stiffened, as her pussy swelled, Yelf beckoned frantically for the audience to help his lead actress to her orgasm. They descended on her in a flock of hands and mouths that sucked and licked and stroked her into a frenzy. In the middle of the dirty street, an entire crowd took Angela.

Everyone took Angela in those days, but there was no doubt that she belonged, at soul level, to Yelf. It was said among the actors that Yelf manipulated his papier mâché creations at night, directing them like an orgiastic army, and that these ceremonies helped him exert his will on the cast. Angela believed it. The man could make her do anything, no matter how humiliating or vile; her soul was a tiny mechanism tucked in his pocket. She imagined that he pulled it out at night to play with when she was sleeping in her bed, which smelled of urine because she had never fully broken that embarrassing childhood habit. She was a bed-wetting Coppelia, a doll brought imperfectly to life.

When Yelf abandoned her for a younger, more pliable actress, Angela was afraid to take a new lover. How would a lover respond to the dark cavity where her soul used to be? She collected an exotic array of sex toys, prosthetic penises and vaginas and breasts, with which she entertained herself alone. Sometimes she climaxed so hard in her sea of rubber flesh that she lost consciousness. She woke from those blackouts the way she did as a child, in a tangle of soaked sheets.

One night, in a spasm of drunken anger, Max Yelf toppled off a fire escape in an alley he was using as a stage and broke his neck. Angela saw her soul fly out of his pocket and land in the gutter below him. Somehow it seemed too late to retrieve it. In a ceremony that was part memorial, part exorcism, the remaining members of Dollsbody burned the creatures that had represented them. As Angela watched the dolls' faces, limbs, and genitals writhe in the flames, she realized that acting had never given her the role she really craved. When the sacrifice was over and the last paper shreds of the dolls were drifting over the city, Angela announced to the troupe that she would take Yelf's place.

. . .

Angela earned an underground fame for the plays she directed, some of them on stage, others in motel rooms, strip clubs, or even her own bedroom. During a performance of *Thirteen Disciples*, in which an audience watched a small crowd of men make love to her, Angela lost control for the first time in her directing career. The men were actors she had known for years, but as they stared down at her, all burning eyes and twitching, turgid cocks, they turned alien. Their sweat mingling in a miasma of desire, they moved in on their prey. Although the play was her own creation, Angela was suddenly weak with fear. With this fear came the much older dread of pissing herself—Angela's memory filled with the stench of ammonia. Alarm bells of shame clanged in her mind as her body betrayed her.

The men descended. Angela clenched her teeth and dug her heels into the mattress, willing herself to remain tense. If her muscles were tight, she wouldn't feel any pleasure, not even by accident. But when the chorus of male panting grew harsh, Angela's body rose to meet the ocean of skin and sweat. One cock entered her only to be pushed aside by another; for the weaker men, there was no choice but to spray Angela's breasts and belly. She began to enjoy the way her limbs were stroked and prodded through the silky bath of jism. Her body, slick and malleable, felt more like rubber than flesh. Her mouth and cunt were two empty O's, ready to be filled and filled again. The numbness in her breasts and thighs—did it come from the weight of the male bodies on top of her, or from this strange new experience of being played with like a toy? Teeth bit lightly at her nipples; muscular fingers squeezed her buttocks as a cock glided in and out of her soaked pussy. When the climax rolled over her and her body arched in a blinding spasm, all of her power as a director was lost. Normally Angela made a lot of noise when she came—this time only a wispy sigh drifted past her lips.

It would never happen again, Angela vowed. The actors had taken over, manipulating their director as if she were a cheaply made mannequin. She had experienced more shame in that passivity than she had felt in any other sex act. But she climaxed again later, with the help of a large rubber phallus, to the memory of her performance.

. . .

Angela has learned to protect her professional dignity, although lately it doesn't seem worth the trouble. She misses the orgies she used to conduct in the days before everyone was afraid of violence and disease and addiction. She misses the sexual dares that she and her fellow actors used to issue to each other: *You will sit beside me in the first row of the balcony at the opera. Wear nothing but a garter belt and stockings under a flimsy skirt. Slowly spread your legs, stretch your thighs into a rude sprawl. I will slide my hand between them, find your buttery hole, fit three fingers inside you, make you squirm on my hand until you cry out, coming.* That precise, erotic direction of the flesh—what had she found to match it? Plays seemed artificial by comparison, the stakes hollow. What did it mean to lose money or prestige if you lost the keen edge of pleasure, the risk of humiliation?

Alone in her apartment after the audition, Angela pours vodka into a highball glass. The first dose of comfort is harsh, but the next is smooth. The actors were dumbfounded when she announced her choice for the leading roles. As young as they are, they recognize Eric and Goldie as untalented strivers. Angela is already losing credibility. She pours another drink and sits down to play with the Eric and Goldie dolls, who are still nude from their earlier performance. So safe, their manufactured flesh! It won't shrivel or sicken; the only thing these lovers will communicate to each other is their mimicked passion. "I love you, I love you," Angela mutters. The female doll dances with simulated joy. Goldie—the real Goldie—has a sensual energy that Angela envies bitterly, even though the girl lacks any acting gift. All youth has the energy of promise.

Angela's hand is shaking when she refills her glass, and a wave of alcohol sloshes onto the carpet. "I never realized until tonight how much I wanted you," Eric groans as his porcelain pelvis hammers the girl-doll's belly. Drunk and fumbling,

Angela has trouble figuring out how the dolls' genitals fit together. Their sealed mysteries infuriate her. Her flesh-and-blood body has always been too open, like a wound. *Bang, bang, bang!* The doll flesh clashes. The lovers are fighting—no, they are only making love again. Angela leans over to pour more vodka and catches sight of her bleary reflection in the surface of a copper lamp. Crooked red snarl, warped cheekbones, asymmetrical eyes. She looks like a Picasso canvas dissolving in flame. Angela giggles and lights a cigarette. She holds the lighter to Eric's crotch. The flame scorches the porcelain. *Bitch! What did you do that for?* Because she is the director, of course. She can do what she wants. Now it is Goldie's turn to taste the fire. The flame leaps too high, catching the synthetic hair, and Angela suddenly finds herself with a plastic torch in her hand. She laughs and flings both dolls onto the carpet. Goldie's tresses are a smear of scorched nylon.

Angela crawls to the floor. Clumsy but purposeful, she makes a circle of teepees out of matchbooks. She places the lovers in the center with a twist of newspaper for kindling and strikes a match. The newspaper quickly catches fire on the vodka-soaked carpet, then one by one, the matchbooks burst into life. The flames are disappointingly tame at first, but within seconds the pyre roars high. As their bodies blacken and squirm, the dolls clutch each other like real human lovers. Angela laughs so hard that tears run in greasy rivers through her melting rouge.

. . .

The play is canceled before the first rehearsal. No one is very disappointed, though some of Angela's colleagues regret her passing and hold a memorial service at the theater. After all the exotic risks she had taken, they find her death mundane: a solitary orgy of alcohol, an apartment fire caused by a cigarette. They shake their heads and wonder what Angela would think of her own final act. Drunken carelessness. A foreseeable end for a lonely woman.

If Angela's fate is predictable, the deaths of her leading actors are not. By some grotesque coincidence the two she had chosen,

Eric and Goldie, lose their lives in a fire that same night. The promising young man had followed the stripper back to her room in a Tenderloin hotel; a freebasing crack addict had set the building on fire. The lovers were found in bed, their faces contorted into charred masks, their arms contracted in a pugilistic position as if they had not been making love, but boxing. At first it was hard to identify the corpses as male and female. The woman's hair had been scorched to stubble, and both victims' genitals were burned into unrecognizable nubs, like lumps of coal. Their tissues of their lower bodies had shrunken and sealed, joining them below the waist. They did not even look human to the firemen who first saw them, behind reeking curtains of smoke. They looked like primitive stick figures, like a pair of blackened totems after an obscene private ritual.

Mekong Medusa
by Julia Solis

S omething was cutting into her. Something inside her was pinched and cramped and smothered. Ariana tugged at the front of her dress, adjusted the wire on the left side of her bra, shifted the weight of her left foot so that it rested on her heel, thereby preventing the straps of her sandal from binding her toes. Then her mental radar pushed outward, searching for the source of the oppressive discomfort.

She was sitting on a metal chair, the table clearing her knees by several inches, giving her plenty of room to breathe. Doris sat on the other side of the table, leaning back in her seat, far from intruding on Ariana's space. The ceiling was a good ten feet above Ariana's head but when she looked up, her toes curled inward for a moment. She knew this was it: somehow, the ceiling and the walls were just too close.

Amazing, she thought. They managed to make it seem so real.

The club was designed to resemble the corroding interior of a submarine's hull. It was a cylindrical, narrow space with a metal door on each end, a small bar in the front, and a stage in the rear. The only light came from a row of dim lamps that hung like oversized drops of battery acid from the rounded ceiling. An abundance of tables and chairs crowded the space from counter to stage making it impossible to move without bumping into something.

Ariana and Doris were the only customers in the club; they sat at the table closest to the stage. The ridiculous stage curtains—blue vinyl shower curtains on which coralline fish with long eyelashes teemed in wide-eyed confusion—were still closed. Ariana, who had never been there before, had no idea what kind of show to expect. But, after recently stumbling onto the club, Doris had been very excited about bringing Ariana. Ariana needed little prodding—anything to be alone with Doris, to get away from husbands who had no idea that their wives had become more than just friends.

Doris stared at the vinyl curtains. "All those fish," she said. "I had an aquarium once when I was little. It was filled to the brim with small brown fish. There were so many fish that they had to wriggle around each other to swim. I got very tired of seeing them squirm, so I put the tank in my closet and shut the door. And sure enough, after a week, the whole thing had turned into a lumpy soup."

Doris smiled. She had a conventionally pretty face but when she smiled her mouth seemed to triple in size, her lips widening to an inordinate degree as if her cheekbones were trying to escape through the corners of her mouth. Ariana was fascinated by this orificial metamorphosis. Doris's almost skeletal hands were fascinating, too. Ariana watched Doris's thin fingers glide nervously along the frosted surface of her cocktail glass, leaving a fish-scale pattern of prints as if that part of her body was surreptitiously trying to leave evidence that could incriminate her for an heinous act committed long ago. Doris, a gaunt blonde in her late twenties, showed off her angular figure with a sheer white dress beneath a clear vinyl raincoat. Ariana preferred long, opaque dresses for her more voluptuous shape.

"Lovely," Ariana said. "And then what happened?"

"And then the lumpy soup of primordial sea parted and you emerged," Doris said. "But you had wet hair." She pulled an ice cube from her Vodka Chlorine and wrapped a strand of Ariana's black hair around it, leaning across the table until the cocktail glass squeaked against the raincoat between her breasts. She balanced several ice cubes in the mass of dark curls falling around Ariana's shoulders.

"That's better," Doris said, leaning back. "Some part of you should always be dripping." For the third time that evening, Doris quoted Shelley's *On the Medusa of Leonardo da Vinci*, this time reciting the final rhyme, "A woman's countenance, with serpent locks. Gazing in death on heaven from those wet rocks."

Ariana thought the poem was unpleasantly Goth, but perhaps the lines were just unpleasant for other reasons. She was about to respond when the pustular ceiling lights suddenly dimmed and a spotlight focused on the vinyl fish curtains shielding the stage. The fish were drawn aside, revealing a sunken pit. Ariana turned her head to look and the ice cubes slid from her shoulders into the opening of her dress, shocking her with cold.

An ornate, lion-footed bathtub stood in the center of the pit. A small, very pale girl in a rose-patterned bikini splashed around in the water. The girl had a puzzled, babyish expression on her face. Perhaps she was wondering what she was doing in a bathtub wearing a bikini, with not a bar of soap in sight. She tugged on the tight fabric of her top before sliding further into the water and kicking up her legs. She seemed to be trying to entertain herself until someone came and told her what to do.

The girl didn't notice the older woman—her mother?—approach from the upstage shadows. The woman wore a cheap housedress decorated with the same rose pattern as the girl's bikini. As the spotlight tightened like a noose around the white edge of the tub, the woman's hands descended on the girl's head.

Before the girl could move, the woman had pushed her head under the water. The small feet kicked up with a loud splash; her writhing torso glimmered beneath a curtain of iridescent beads. The girl's fists shot upward as if searching for support in the drops spraying around her, then plunged back into the water. After a minute, the older woman grabbed the struggling girl beneath the shoulders and pulled her up.

"Incredible," Ariana whispered. The girl's panicked gasps bounced back and forth between the tubular walls.

"Isn't it?" Doris said, smiling from ear to ear, as if she herself had staged the act.

"That girl is very brave!"

"And she's obedient," Doris said. "I can appreciate that."

They watched the "mother" give the "daughter's" head another push beneath the water, then pull her back up a minute later.

Ariana noticed something move across the wall behind Doris and turned her head. The dark submarine walls were now covered with portholes—no, projections—that hadn't been visible before the lights had dimmed: photos of drowning victims, screened with a circular crop as if the bodies were being observed through a periscope. Portraits of men and women in various stages of drowning; close-ups of struggling hands and death-distorted faces, but mostly images of pale bodies drifting in an open sea. Ariana noticed that even in their steady path across the walls, the pictures trembled slightly, like buoys bobbing on waves.

To her great surprise, Ariana saw her own face rotate among the floating pictures. Earlier, she had accepted the bar owner's invitation to display herself in the club's funhouse lobby where her mirror image was filtered through several glass layers adding tints and ripples. Doris had pulled Ariana's dress down from her shoulders and sprayed her hair with a water bottle provided by the house.

Standing in front of the ornate mirror, mesmerized by the morbid gaze of her own black pupils, Ariana had admired her reflection—the damp, sickly cast of her blurred but still beautiful face, her moist curls gliding like seaweed over her pale green skin.

A loud splash jerked Ariana's attention back to the tub. In the brief silence during which the girl's body turned beneath the water's surface, they heard the woman humming to herself.

The girl, rising, drew a loud breath, a large, loud gulp of air, and with that gulp, Ariana was suddenly inside the girl, stretching into her lungs, feeling them the way she might feel the interior of a fox hole or mole burrow; some narrow place, mysterious and terrible, with surfaces she did not want to explore but was forced to explore now; dark wet lung surfaces that refused to expand fast enough.

A burst of empathy filled Ariana with loathing for the older woman.

"I hate the mother," she whispered in Doris's direction.

"Then I will make you into her," Doris said. "You will be the mother. And I will be your conscience, coming to haunt you—if your daughter dies."

Ariana nodded, considering this. "But where are you going to find me?"

"There are rooms here. Rooms with bolts, locks, and safety chains. I will find you in one of those rooms."

The vinyl curtains slowly closed on the scene of the struggling girl. They caught a last glimpse of her writhing beneath her mother's hands. Ariana was relieved and disappointed simultaneously: the girl had been spared the role of a corpse. Ariana glanced at Doris, who still had a look of eager anticipation on her face, despite the way the scene had been resolved.

The sound of splashing water continued behind the closed curtains, then broke off abruptly. "Have another drink," Doris said, signaling the bartender at the far end of the room for two more Vodka Chlorines. Neither woman had been tempted by the bar's display of tequila bottles containing not the customary earthworm, but the larvae commonly used in aquatic forensics, the coelopidae, ephididrae, and the large rat-tailed maggots.

Now that the spotlight was off, the hull was illumined only by the floating projections. It was eerily silent; the air was stale, tinged with gasoline fumes and human exhaust. Again Ariana felt an immense weight bearing down on her. As soon as the bartender delivered the drinks, Ariana emptied her glass, looking for a lubricated space between her thoughts and the nearby ceiling.

A screen descended in front of the stage, accompanied by a soundtrack of boots stomping heavily through mud. The word "Vietnam" flickered on the canvas. The woman who had just played the mother appeared on screen, wearing the same housedress with the rose pattern. She had a terrified expression on her face; beads of sweat were dripping down her forehead and cheeks. When the camera zoomed out, she was shown clamped between two soldiers who were dragging her through the Vietnamese swamp.

An old-fashioned text box appeared: SHOW US WHERE YOU DISPOSED OF HER REMAINS!

"Oh," Ariana gasped.

Doris gloated. "The girl is dead!"

. . .

Ariana felt the tension crawl from her toes to her calves, settling at the bottom of her spine. Doris had secured Ariana's ankles in straps fastened to the metal table. Ariana's legs were raised, her knees spread above her waist; her wrists tied to the upper corners of the slab. She was naked, spread like a frog awaiting dissection on a metal tray. This in itself was not a new position for her. But the brace that Doris was now adjusting over the long, black curls—like an orthodontist's facebow of surgical steel that fastened behind the head so as to center a clasp above the mouth—was something Ariana had never seen before. The touch of steel on her cheeks made her whole body flush with excitement. When Doris pulled away, Ariana noticed that she could still move her head, but the brace's clasp remained secured over her mouth.

They were in the nightclub's Swamp Room. In this particular chamber the walls were camouflaged as virgin brush, trees were knotted in brackish water, the ceiling dense with foliage, Spanish moss dangling from the corners. The floor's linoleum, nearly invisible beneath a layer of mud, bore Doris's stiletto prints, tracing her steps to the corner where the tip of a coiled rubber hose had been lying in a pile of rotting leaves before she picked it up. The faucet to which the hose was attached jutted from the wall above Ariana's head.

Doris stood next to the table in the room's center, gazing at Ariana's body, especially the large, soft breasts. Ariana's nipples were nearly as dark as her scarlet mouth. Doris's hand—the one that held the hose—slipped into Ariana's limp grasp. Ariana's fingers closed gently around Doris's fist.

"Are you ready?" Doris asked. When Ariana nodded, Doris pulled away her hand.

She bent over Ariana's torso. "Here are your roses," Doris said, biting into one of the breasts, sucking the white skin, leaving a ring of toothmark blossoms unfolding on the side of the gently sloping hill. Turning the faucet just slightly, releasing a thin trickle, she splashed Ariana's face... "and here are the tears for your dead child. But—" Water dripped into the piercing black eyes, ran across the flushed cheeks and collected in the mass of curls beneath her head. "Tears are not enough," she continued. "You must show true remorse."

Ariana shook her head. The icy water dripping onto her face was running into her nostrils, but after she exhaled, she smelled the rubber and damp soil from the hose. She now saw a clasp attached to the tip that would lock the hose into the steel brace. Doris pinched Ariana's nostrils shut, waiting for the moist lips to open for the rubber kiss, fastening the hose to the brace with her free hand. The clasp around the rubber shaft was loose enough for Doris to slide the tube in and out of Ariana's mouth while leaving it attached to the metal contraption. Ariana began to writhe. When her lips finally parted, Doris pushed in the hose.

Shocked by the sudden flux of water, Ariana kicked against her restraints. She could breathe through her nose, but had to carefully alternate her inhalations with rapid swallows, forcing her to take quick, short breaths. Doris was pumping the hose in and out of Ariana's mouth, adjusting the water trickle, allowing Ariana to find a jagged rhythm of breathing; at the same time, her other hand ran along the soft, open thighs, gliding between the smooth legs. When Ariana coughed, Doris slid two fingers into the orifice glistening above the table's metal surface. There was a moment's respite, during which the sliding motion of the hose was replaced by the thrust of Doris's fingers into Ariana's increasingly inflamed body. Then Doris bent forward. As her lips fastened around the tip of one of the breasts, she shoved the hose inside Ariana's mouth and let go.

. . .

The panic travels like a wave from her toes to her thighs, up her spine toward the tips of her hair and down again. It settles between Ariana's legs, gathering into a swelling pressure point. Trembling violently, she swallows, trying to keep up with the drops collecting in her mouth, the gulps distracting her from the lack of oxygen, the vacuum between her sucking cheeks: she becomes a swallowing machine, a single-purpose valve. Doris fingers, adjusts pieces of the soft machinery, she whispers, tightens, and repairs. Ariana begins to float, her limbs crystallizing into moist, sun-kissed cliffs. At the center of the pressure, the radiant blonde lighthouse, Doris pulls her fingers to let Ariana drain.

Doris extracts the hose, puts her fingers between Ariana's lips. The room smells damp and fertile: strange, like boiling chocolate mixed with a heavy iron aftertaste. Ariana's face has turned red, even the pale skin on her breast acquiring a pink moist sheen.

"And now? You still don't feel remorse?"

Ariana shakes her head

Doris turns up the water just a notch

but now the machine sputters; Ariana inhales water and loses her balance, the panic surging downward from her spine, as if she were a crumpled marionette suddenly forced to snap her limbs. Between the paralyzing icepick tension there is only one point of release, surging and swelling between her thighs, but Ariana can't reach it, can't find her way there yet

and then the ground opens beneath her and now there's no more sun and cliffs, no lighthouse; now Ariana is face down in the swamp, chewing on a rubber serpent, she bucks and thrashes and in her thrashing opens as the mud-covered water snakes enter every orifice: and Ariana surrenders, finally, opening wide

as the hose in her mouth plunges into her, breaks through every membrane in her head, writhing inside her, multiplying, pouring deeper, breaking through her skull, rubber tentacles bursting out and squirming on her head, a tangle of rubber hose serpents—a Gorgon liquid-gorged,

    m

      e

        d

          u

            s

aaaaaaaaaaaaa

· · ·

Felice had buttoned up Ellie's dress, placed a kiss on her pink cheek and delivered her to the back entrance, where the girl's father was waiting to pick her up. Then she pulled a coat over her rose-covered housedress and entered the bar from a side door to catch the last of the Vietnam film. Even before the film was over, the club's only two customers got up and vanished down the rear hallway, the stiletto heels of the skinny blonde echoing back along the narrow corridor. Felice watched as the "soldier" on her screen persona's left pulled her by the hair and stuck her face into the mud, until she reached into the morass and pulled up her daughter's arm.

This was the first time the film was being shown. It was intended to draw customers into the swamp room, which otherwise couldn't compete with the plastic wading pool or the ornate Turkish *hammam*. The Vietnam setting didn't make much sense to Felice, but that was beside the point. She had to do it anyway.

There was a close-up of Felice, who even through the mud and fake bruises looked as if she had been crying, and it was true, she had been secretly crying while the crew was setting up for the shot—weeping because she had so much wanted to save her baby, she really had, but when the phone had rung after days of silence, she *had* to run and answer it, knowing Tomas was finally coming back to her. When she returned to the bathroom, little Bettina was face-down in the lukewarm water, a plastic shampoo bottle slowly cruising around her halo of brown curls. Nothing they had done to Felice during and after the investigation could fill that wormhole of guilt running along the walls of her intestines—until this club had opened and she could torture herself here every single night. When the screen went blank, Felice got herself a glass of water from the bar and sat down on one of the stools.

PreScylla screened the Spanish inquisition film again, since there were no customers anyway. Felice watched the drip torture, waiting for the couple in the back to leave so she could clean the room. On some nights she volunteered to do janitorial duties and after an hour of scrubbing and disinfecting, her hands finally stopped shaking and went limp.

After twenty minutes she rose, walked to the back and put on her apron. The customers rarely stayed in the rooms for more than half an hour. Just as Felice entered the corridor, the door opened in the rear and the two women emerged. Cringing, Felice realized that she had to pass them on the way to the supply closet, although she hated to be seen by anyone.

The women were silent, looking at the ground. The prettier one with the wet hair looked up for a moment as Felice walked past her. The woman's gaze, eyes black and small with loathing, shot right through Felice, as if in that brief instance the woman had seen Bettina somewhere in the back of Felice's face.

Felice caught her breath. She froze in her tracks, petrified by the venomous stare. Her hand grasped the doorknob of the room from which the women had just emerged, seeking support. But then she got hold of herself and forced herself to keep walking.

She knows nothing, Felice told herself, hands shaking.
She can't possibly know.

Beholder
by Stephen Dedman

Radcliffe, the publisher, was a collector of paintings rather than a connoisseur, and Verner rarely comments on any of his acquisitions. The nude hanging in the guest room, however, is enough to make his eyes dilate. "That's *good*," he murmurs, as he ambles toward it for a closer look, "and I'm ashamed to admit I don't recognize the style. Who did it?"

"Mark Stannard," replies Radcliffe. "He did a few fantasy covers for us about two years ago, then disappeared—went back to Montana or wherever, I think. I saw that at an auction, and didn't recognize it for his work at first, either."

Verner, who'd been one of Radcliffe's cover artists before he became famed for his portraits, nods. "The technique's pretty good," he opines. "I don't suppose you happen to know who the model was?"

"I'm afraid not. She's lovely, isn't she?"

"Beautiful," says Verner. "Possibly the most beautiful women I've ever seen."

· · ·

"Do you want me?" she asks.

"Yes," says Mark.

She smiles, and undoes another button of her scarlet silk blouse. "Good," she says. "How much do you want me?"

"What?"

"How much? Tell me how much."

He stares, feeling very much out of his depth. He'd grown up in a small town, had come to New York little more than a month ago, and was sure that he understood the city less every day. "More than any woman I've ever seen."

"And how many have you seen?" she asks, but is pleased enough to undo another button.

"I don't know, but none of them were as beautiful as you."

Her smile widens a little more, and she undoes the last button and slips out of the red silk blouse, draping it over the end of the divan. "I've always wanted someone to paint my picture," she said, "someone who thought I was beautiful. But I don't like being lied to," she says, softly.

"I'm not lying," he says. His mouth is dry, yet he feels as though he were drowning.

"You really think I'm the most beautiful woman you've ever seen?"

"Yes," he replies. She is certainly unlike any of the girls from his home town; dark-skinned, somewhere between cinnamon and caramel in color, and almond-eyed, with midnight-black ringlets cascading almost to her hips. She told him she'd been born in Bangkok; she'd never seen her father, but her mother swore he was American, dark as strong coffee or bitter chocolate. She told him her name was Jade, or it had been since she came to the U.S. a few years before. She told him she was a model and an actress. Sometimes a dancer. He wondered what she'd told other men.

He'd advertised for a model for a book cover he was painting. The publisher hadn't liked her; they wanted a blonde. He thought they were insane, but business was business. He'd asked her if she'd like to model for him anyway.

"Yes," he repeats. He's seen, and known, many attractive women before—sunny blondes, icy blondes, redheads like snow and fire, slender women, bouncy women, tall women, tiny women, women of lightning and quicksilver, women as serene as trees—and has persuaded many to model for him, but he's suddenly sure that Jade *is* the most beautiful woman he's ever seen. Her face is elfin, sharp-featured but delicate, with high cheekbones, a small mouth with sensual lips, and eyes dark as an eclipse. Even her narcissism is a turn-on to him, a mutual celebration of her beauty. "Yes."

For that, she smiles briefly, and unfastens her lacy black bra. Her breasts aren't especially large, but as high and round as a teenager's, and shaped like... Mark finds himself thinking of pomegranates, then of Persephone and Hades, then hastily derails that train of thought. Her nipples are long, surrounded by almond-shaped areolae of labyrinthine, almost Escheresque complexity. He realizes that she's never mentioned her age, and that he could never guess it unless she wanted him to.

"Say it."

"You're the most beautiful woman I've ever seen."

"You haven't seen all of me yet. You might be wrong."

He forces his head up to look into her eyes. The gravity in the studio seems to be higher than usual. He can think of nothing to say to this. She stands, so that he is once again looking at her breasts. He tries raising his head again, but she begins unbuttoning her short black skirt, and he finds himself looking down. The skirt is slowly lowered to the tops of her thighs, then falls to the ground to lie at her feet like a puddle that she then steps out of daintily. She is wearing nothing now but black leather boots, a black G-string, and her earrings. He waits for her to remove the thong, but she doesn't move. "Do you still want me?"

"Yes. Yes, of course."

Another brief smile. "I'm not doing everything myself," she says, and points to the floor before her feet. He walks towards her, as though he could see nothing else. Her eyes are on a level with his mouth, and he kisses first one, then the other. She places her hands on his shoulders, then kisses him on the lips briefly, and gently pushes down. He kisses the side of her neck, then her throat, then kneels as he kisses her breasts. Her nipples are dark and hard and delicious as (he tries not to think of pomegranates) coffee beans, and he runs his tongue around them, teasing them, then slowly sucking one in between his lips, his teeth, chewing on it gently as he rubs the other between thumb and forefinger, feeling both swell and harden further. He is not a virgin, he has seduced or been seduced by models before, has seen and tasted and known their bodies, but this seems new, and he feels as though he could kneel here forever. Jade, however, obviously has other ideas; she lets him suckle for several minutes, stroking the back of his head, before applying pressure to his shoulder again. He kisses his way down her smooth belly, pausing briefly to flick his tongue across her navel, making her giggle. He stops just above the barrier of her G-string, then reaches for the hem and lowers it. Her pubic hair is trimmed into a narrow black arrowhead, almost like an exclamation point rising from her vulva. He releases his breath in a barely audible gasp when he sees it, and Jade throws back her head and laughs loudly. "Scared of what you might find?" He shakes his head, blushing slightly, and she sits down on the divan with her legs up in the air; she peels the G-string off quickly as though it were a band-aid, then spreads her legs to give him a better view. "Stay there," she commands, and begins stroking her thighs, her belly, spiraling in toward the shadowy cleft that seemed, to Mark, to be sucking all the light in the room toward it. "Still beautiful?" she asks.

"Even more beautiful," he says, not lying. She smiles, and parts her glossy labia with her thumbs, giving him a glimpse of the nacreous pinkness inside. "Do you still want me?"

"Yes."

"Will you always want me?"

"Yes," he says, believing it. She glances down, and Mark, still on his knees, crosses the distance between them. He butterfly-kisses her breasts, then quickly descends until he is breathing in the heady female perfume of her pheromones before parting her pouting labia with his tongue. He laps up her juices while nuzzling her clit, and she twines her legs around his back, trapping him. "Beautiful?"

"Yes."

"The most beautiful woman you've ever seen?"

"Yes," he says, and circles her clit with his tongue. She leans back on the divan and lets him lick. Aroused as she is, she is slow to reach orgasm, but when she does, she laughs, shudders, flails her arms, bangs her head, and kicks hard enough to bruise him. He lifts his eyes to see her face. She is so beautiful in her afterglow that he is almost overwhelmed. He kisses her clit lightly, and her new-moon eyes snap open. "Get undressed," she commands.

He strips with more haste than grace, but she doesn't comment, doesn't even look at him except for a quick appraising glance at his erection, judging the state of his arousal by its angle and color. He takes a step toward her, but she shakes her head and stands. "Lie down," she commands.

He obeys, and she straddles him, lowering herself over his erection, but stops short of impaling herself, her labia barely kissing the crimson tip of his cock. "Will you always want me?"

"Yes," he hisses. She lowers herself half an inch, the walls of her cunt brushing against the edges of his glans. "Will you want only me?"

He hesitates, but she leans forward and writhes so that her nipples brush against his lips. "Will you?" She descends another half an inch. He gasps. "Am I the most beautiful woman you've ever seen?"

"Yes." She smiles, pushes a breast into his open mouth, and slides down his erection until his pubic hair tickles her clit, his balls bumping against her silky ass. She holds his head to her breasts as she rides him, the sound of her heartbeat loud in his ears, and his hands explore her body; his eyes close as he nears his orgasm, so that all his senses but sight are full of her. "Will you want only me?" she whispers, and he hears someone shouting yes Yes YES YES! as the darkness engulfs him completely.

It is still dark when he opens his eyes again, with only a little light seeping in through the drawn curtains. He lies there for a moment, then stands and walks to the kitchen. His mouth feels dry, and he shuffles towards the kitchen, switching lights on as he passes them. He grabs a Cherry Coke from the fridge, and looks around the room. Nothing seems to be missing, except for Jade and her clothes—and then he glances again at the Degas print on the wall, above the bookshelf. Trembling slightly, he walks over for a closer look, then stares down at the book of Jim

Burns cover art lying on top of the shelves. He leafs through it, then grabs *The History of the Nude*, Woodroffe's *Mythopoeikon*, Olivia's *Let them Eat Cheesecake*. All the same. Forgetting his nakedness, he rushes to the window, throws the curtains open, and stares outside.

All the women he sees are dark-skinned, somewhere between cinnamon and caramel in color, and almond-eyed, with mid-night-black ringlets, every one of them the most beautiful woman he's ever seen. A few look up, but none of them know him, and he knows none of them.

. . .

Radcliffe hides a smile; Verner is almost as famous a womanizer as he is a painter of nudes. "Can I take a photo of this?"

"A photo?" says Radcliffe. "Yes, of course." He doesn't ask why, but Verner obviously hears the question anyway.

"I want to show it around the modeling agencies, see who remembers her," he says. "I have to see her, and if she looks anything like her picture, I have to paint her."

"I never argue with a connoisseur, but you see beautiful women every day. Do you really think she's that beautiful?"

"If you were an artist, you'd understand," says Verner, and nods again. "Yes, quite probably, the most beautiful woman I've ever seen."

Homewrecker
by Poppy Z. Brite

My Uncle Edna killed hogs. He came home from the slaughterhouse every day smelling of shit and pig blood, and if I didn't have his bath drawn with plenty of perfume and bubble stuff, he'd whup my ass until I felt his hard-on poking me in the leg.

Like I said, he killed hogs. At night, though, you'd never have known it to see him in his satin gown. He swished around the old farmhouse like some kind of fairy godmother, swigging from a bottle of J.D. and cussing the bitch who stole his man.

"Homewrecker!" he'd shriek, pounding his fist on the table and rattling the stack of rhinestone bracelets he wore on his skinny arm. "How could he want her when he had me? How could he do it, boy?"

And you had to wonder, because even with his lipstick smeared and his chest hair poking out of his gown, there was a certain tired glamour to Uncle Edna. Thing was, the bitch hadn't even wanted his man. Uncle Jude, who'd been with Uncle Edna since he was just plain old Ed Slopes, had all of a sudden turned het and gone slobbering off after a henna-headed barfly who called herself Tina. What Tina considered a night's amusement, Uncle Jude decided was the grand passion of his life. And that was the last we saw of him. We never could understand it.

Uncle Edna was 36 when Uncle Jude left. The years and the whiskey rode him hard after that, but the man knew how to do his makeup, and I thought Uncle Jude would fall back in love with him if they could just see each other again.

I couldn't do anything about it, though, and back then I was more interested in catching frogs and snakes than in the affairs of grown-ups' hearts. But a few years later, I heard Tina was back in town.

I knew I couldn't let Uncle Edna find out. He'd want to get out his shotgun and go after her, and then he'd get cornholed to death in jail and who'd take care of me? So I talked to a certain kid at school. He made me suck his dick out behind the cafeteria, but I came home with four Xanax. I ground them up and put them in Uncle Edna's bottle of J.D. that same night. Pretty soon he was snoring like a chainsaw and drooling on his party dress. I went out to look for Tina. I didn't especially want to see her, but I thought maybe I could find out where she'd last seen Uncle Jude.

I parked my bike across the street from the only bar in town, the Silky Q. Inside, the men stood or danced in pairs. A few wore drag, but most were in jeans and flannels; this was a working man's town.

Then I saw her. She'd slid her meaty ass into a booth and was cuddled up to one of the men in it. The other man sat glaring at her, nearly in tears. I recognized them as Bob and Jim Frenchette, a couple who'd been married as long as I could remember. Tina's red-nailed hand was on Bob's thigh, stroking the worn denim.

I walked up to the table.

Jim and Bob were too far gone to pay me any mind. Tina didn't seem to recognize me. I'd been a little kid when she saw me last, and she'd hardly noticed me then, bent as she was on sucking Uncle Jude's neck. I stared into her light blue eyes. Her lashes were clumped with black mascara, her lids frosted with turquoise shadow. Her mouth was a lipstick wound. Her lips twitched in a scornful smile, then parted.

"What you want, boy?"

I couldn't think of anything to say. I didn't know what I had meant to do. I stumbled away from the table. My hands were trembling and my cheeks flaming. I was outside, unchaining my bike from the lamppost, when Tina came out of the bar.

She crossed the deserted street, pinning me where I stood with those wolf-pale eyes. I wanted to jump on my bike and speed away, or just run, but I couldn't. I wanted to look away from those slippery red lips that glistened like hog grease. But I couldn't.

"Your uncle…" she whispered. "Jules, wasn't it?"

I shook my head, but Tina kept smiling and bending closer until her lips were right against my ear.

"He was a lousy fuck," she said.

Her sharp red nails bit into my shoulder. She pushed me back against the lamppost and sank to her knees in front of me. I felt hot bile rising in my throat, but I couldn't move, even when her other hand undid my pants.

I tried to keep my dick from getting hard, I truly did. But it was like her mouth sucked the blood into it, right to the surface of the skin. I thought she might tear it out by the roots. Her tongue slithered over my balls, into my peehole. There came a sharp stinging at the base of my dick, unlike anything I'd felt when other boys sucked it. Then I was shooting my jizz into her mouth, much as I didn't want to, and she was swallowing it like she'd been starved.

Tina wiped her mouth and laughed. Then she stood, turned, and walked back to the bar like I wasn't even there. The door closed behind her, and I fell to my knees and puked until my throat was raw. But even as the rancid taste of half-digested food filled my mouth and nose, I could feel my dick getting hard again.

I had to whack off before I could get on my bike. As I came on the sidewalk, I imagined those fat shiny lips closing around me again, and I started to cry. I couldn't get the nasty thoughts out of my head, things I'd never thought about before: the smell of dank sea coves and fish markets, the soft squish of a body encased in a layer of fat, with big floppy globes of it stuck on the chest and rear like cancers. And the thoughts were like a cancer in me.

As fast as my feet could pedal, I rode home to Uncle Edna. But I had a feeling I could never really go home again.

Matchbox Screamers
by Ian Grey

A lis stood at the door naked except for a green hospital smock, a noticeable crawl of blood on her bare inner thigh. The black bag was, as always, slung over her shoulder. I'd been cutting some stereo cables and I dropped my knife, but found no words.

"Hi. You busy?" Alis slurred with disturbing perk. Blanched skin and puffy lips pulled back into a sweet opiate smile. She looked like a betrayed but still hopeful Girl Scout.

"You're bleeding, Alis."

She shrugged. "Of course I'm bleeding. I had an abortion. Wanna fuck?"

From a particular type of young woman, this would be merely a transgressive one-liner. But it was past two A.M., and this was Alis (pronounced like "Alice," but she'd changed the spelling, believing there was power in self-definition.) Our history together had been disturbing, but not far outside the range of what one encountered in West Hollywood in the early 80s, and in certain circles. I told her she should get out of the cold hallway. She tottered in, somehow navigating the dark hallway to my bedroom.

Positioned at the end of my bed, my Korg Trident synthesizer played a sawtooth melody snippet over and over, while both a radio and TV blared dumb media. Ambient-overkill, numbing, simultaneously a cocoon of sound, and a sonic spear trying to drive something … out. She leaned over, kissed me, her tongue cool with half-metabolized medication. Her eyes never shut, but appraised my reaction as she ran a hand down to her thigh, daubed it in her blood, raised it to my lips. "Taste it. Taste what's gone."

I did. Because I wanted something gone myself, wanted the taste of it, the proof. The proof of its leaving.

I have always—in general and in particular—had much invested in knowing little and remembering less. The combined auto-distractions of radio, TV, and synthesizer were part of this investment. The part of me that yearned for connection atrophied in direct proportion to the part that wanted to forget. There was something in me I feared, and hated, and so wanted gone.

I'd met Alis three years earlier at a club called the Zero Zero, cunningly dubbed by those in the know as the Double Zero. A few hundred sweaty feet of raw space, a cheap PA system blaring out Stax and industrial noise favorites. Alis, dressed in fake gold fur, red hair streaming all over the place, her shoulders cartoonishly wide and legs oddly muscled, was frowning in the direction of some bad trust-fund art. She looked like a warrior goddess on the cover of a Conan paperback.

An older man had accompanied Alis to the Double Zero. He introduced us, amused and somewhat proprietary at our obvious mutual interest. There was something both patriarchal and vaguely reptilian about this man. I swallowed sudden bile.

Close up, I saw that Alis had one green eye, the other was a deep shade of indigo. Over her shoulder was a big fake leather purse with the words "Fashion Bug" set in cheap metal letters.

I said something about her eye. Smooth work. She traced her lids with skilled, spidery fingers. "Damn. Just a minute."

She scuttled down a dark hallway and came back with both eyes green. The older man had, meanwhile, merged with the crowd as a punk version of some John Lee Hooker song tore at the walls.

"Being able to change things is important, " Alis said, blinking. "The stuff you don't like."

"You can't change things."

"I just did." A cute wink.

"I mean, real things."

"Willpower. That's how. Like how you push back what hurts."

I stared at her. The older man appeared, smiling as if he'd heard it all. "The body manifests what the mind ignores," he said with campy portent. Alis nodded, and looked down at the dirty floor. The man ambled off to investigate a photo-collage filled with shrieking tots.

"It's like when you get hard," Alis continued.

"That isn't a matter of will."

"It's mine. I had something that hurt. I had to get it outside. It's something you have to keep doing."

Eventually, she asked me home, perhaps smelling success. For all I knew, I might have been one, but self-hate's a bitch for accurate reportage. We left the club, drove to her apartment on Sycamore Street, a dark blind alley off Sunset. Any crime movie shot on a cheap backlot would provide the right visual. My skin felt like cellophane with Alis there.

Alis' apartment decor was simulated abattoir: heads of hair on wall-pegs, human faces stretched grotesquely on gilt frames, a variety of fake body parts and two complete human skeletons. Alis ignored the carnage. Absently, she remarked, "William's. He does special effects."

"Your—?"

She laughed. "William's always been there. Like my work."

I probed. "Like the pain?"

"Whatever."

My eye had already made the grue for fake, and was more attracted to what looked like thousands of match books, the old-fashioned kind. Wood-like paper, all the same brand.

Inside each was a tiny shape I couldn't make out. The matchbooks were stacked in geometric piles: a square here, a pyramid there. There was a frightening sense of compulsion to these sculptures—and that is what they turned out to be—as though the creation of one led inevitably to the creation of another until exhaustion terminated the effort.

"I get the strength from this," Alis said. "It's—reciprocal."

"What is?"

"My work. Will you hurt me?"

"Yes."

I looked closer at the matchbook pyramid. Inside each matchbook, trapped, was a tiny human figure with tiny gouges for eyes and mouth—each face painfully etched with the same expression. All were bald.

"Yes." Alis said before I could. "They're screaming,"

"Why?"

"Wouldn't you scream if you were trapped in a tiny matchbook?"

We had sex that night amid the screaming matchbook men, latex body parts and skeletons. I dimly recall trying to be tender, and Alis insisting otherwise. At one point, I felt her asshole convulse around my prick; I continued to hold her neck in the stranglehold she'd requested. The convulsion spread to the rest of her body. She screamed, the sound infecting my perception of the room itself: the skeletons, the gore—everything was an extension of Alis' orgasm, wobbling madly in sympathetic vibrato.

Later, while she slept, I took things. At the time, I was running on instinct.

. . .

I am now sitting naked, surrounded by Alis' things, a candle burning and throwing shadows over my cock, which has been painfully erect for hours, the veins dark. I hope not with blue un-oxygenated blood, but actual pitch.

Alis was absorbed into the art and music scene for three years. Rumors of heroin addiction, cult involvement, and assorted Los Angeles perversities resulted at the mention of her name. In Los Angeles, connections are rare but still cheap. Although I hooked up with Alis here and there, there was no pattern or commitment. During this time, and until her last visit two months ago, I had been in the music industry, had achieved an ethically questionable sort of success.

I remember one kid. His music redefined a tired genre, and invigorated a cynical young demographic sick of the world of the dry-fuck advert anti-life that had been left them in place of a legacy. I'll call him Kim.

Kim's band caused a considerable stir with its independently-released CDs. He came into my office after we'd signed him. He didn't want to be with a big company like the one I worked for. But the band needed money for kids, wives, and heroin.

"Just don't fuck up the music," Kim said.

"I can't. I'm a suit."

He smiled, mistaking my ineptness for irony-laced sincerity and fingered his contract. I thought of the phrase *living wills.* "It says here you have final approval about who produces us."

"Yes."

Suddenly Kim's rough-boy junkie exterior melted. "Don't fuck us up, man. This is all I have."

I told him I wouldn't fuck him up then got him a producer who'd had a string of British synth-pop hits. The press screamed sell-out. Kim's record sold 7.5 million, first month. Kim killed himself a week later by lethal injection.

To say it was the guilt of everyday tragedies like Kim's that drove me to my current state, prick in one hand, an absurdist assemblage of watchers surrounding me, would ignore what happened before Kim. My therapists had their own ideas, the stuff of TV guest-neurotic psycho-gothic melodrama. All I know is that since I was a boy, there were infernally foul tempered creatures inside of me hissing I was bad, a sham, and worse—that they would soon return me to my proper and much lower station.

Eventually, these voices gained means of expression and a form—a scream. A scream my mouth could never sound, the detritus of a lifetime of denying its existence.

I recall lying in my bed one night as a child, masturbating. Although orgasm would bring temporary relief, it also lent this coiled thing in me more energy, more … mass.

When I hit puberty, I would actually see it, floating in mid-air, mocking me like a demonic, smoke-formed Cheshire Cat, although its actual shape was far more terrible than that. It was my hope that, were I ever able to give that scream form, I could capture it. I saw a film once, *The Black Cat.* At one point, Bela Lugosi remarks: "Supernatural? Maybe. Baloney? Maybe not." I wept at that line, hearing it as an affirmation of my own experience.

One night, desperate, almost gagging with its implication, I attempted to capture the dark, floating apparition. I clawed at the air, wildly, made a sickening contact. The shape burst into a million gaseous bits, which still floated above me, as though considering their next manifestation. Suddenly, the darkness, the legion pieces of my scream crawled down from the air and surrounded my soft prick like a black glove of toxic smoke.

My orgasm was indescribable.

. . .

I had no morally-defensible rationale for letting Alis in that last night. Alis, strange, fucked-up as ever, obscenely wanting sex. Her blood on her finger, in my mouth, my dick hard as hell. She mumbled, "I walked all the way here."

"From where?"

"The hospital. Where else do you get an abortion?"

She now sat primly on the bed. One of the low-wattage pin spots I used for illumination focused on a small trickle of almost-dried blood on the inside of her left thigh. For a weirdly synchronous moment, we both studied it, although I guess for different reasons.

"Like a little river," Alis said to herself. "A little river of me."

Alis spaced out, face scary white, scarier still because that whiteness was somehow unbearably desirable to me. Familiar.

With an absent motion of one hand, the hospital green fell. The impression of some barbarian warrior was complete when I saw her naked: everything on her was soft yet defined with implied muscle.

"Man, I am so fucking horny. I'm so fucking glad that ... *thing* ... is out of me." The rage in her voice was like slow lava.

"You should be at the hospital, Alis. The blood—"

"It stopped hours ago." She smiled at the red stain on my lips. "It doesn't seem to bother you—"

"—but—"

"—it doesn't matter. Fuck me, John. Please?"

"Christ, Alis. This is all fucked up."

"So?" The girl-smile again. "I want to give you a present."

She leaned back, breasts sloping with a graceful languor that looked like slow motion photography. I already had hopes that went beyond sex. Something that would give me so much more. Even if she disappeared from my life forever. But I would have to ask. Or take.

"William loved my body," Alis said. "He especially loved to rub his dick on my breasts."

"Alis, please—"

An IV needle was still taped to her arm. Absently, she plucked it free, to the accompaniment of a small freshet of blood. "Imagine I am your sister. I just had an abortion. Our child. We came so close to creating an abomination." She unzipped me, stroked blood over my cock. "The relief. Our mutual experience. How could we *not* celebrate?"

I spread her legs, ran my cock over distended lips, felt the sweet and sour of wet labial skin and caked, dry blood. I pulled back.

"William's in special effects." A short, cursory laugh. "He made paintings of me. My body, I mean. He got his bad out. Showed me what art was for."

She reached inside herself, and fed me more old blood. Then I did what William had done, insinuating my cock between her breasts. Alis studied me, suddenly hard-edged, sober and clinical, observing. The sense of being judged harshly was intolerably exciting. When she sensed my approaching release, Alis's voice hissed, "Come, you old bastard."

I did. She watched the milky products of my orgasm spatter her breasts and neck. Whatever was in her eyes changed yet again. Concern and worry now, seeing the expression on my face.

"Don't feel bad. I like it. Really." She absently ran a finger through a pool of semen gathered above her sternum as though it were thin paint. "It's out of you for now."

I rolled over. The room was fragrant with blood, come, sweat. I turned on a CD. Droning ambient techno. I closed my eyes. The scream was there. Thinking I was asleep, she quietly reached for her bag. Small objects fell out, silently hitting the carpeted floor. Lipsticks, small tools, an Exacto blade. I recognized one familiar object.

She reached out, found a tiny metal box, like something that would hold a charm. With a weird grace, she leaned over, took the box, opened it.

"Clay," she whispered. Inside the box were perhaps three fingers of doughy material. She wiped my semen from her chest, her blood from her cunt, massaged both into the material, kneading it into a shape.

I fell to the side of the bed, trying to cry, to scream. A shadow seemed to solidify near her, mocking our efforts. I wanted to explain to Alis what was wrong, that I was sorry, that maybe someday we'd be like regular people, but I had no language for it.

The familiar object—one of Alis' matchbox screamers. "See, you fill the hole with the bad thing. It's what you do with art. To get better."

But, I thought, *I am not an artist.*

She slid her wet finger into the tiny figure's mouth, and quietly sobbed. I fell asleep staring at her immobile shape.

In the morning, she was gone. Next to the bed was a new matchbox screamer, made of her clay, blood, and my come. I kept it.

Along with the others I'd stolen that first night.

· · ·

Alis disappeared for good after that. I learned via an Internet search and some questions to the boys in market research that she'd left L.A., had moved up to Fresno. She worked as a waitress at, of all places, a Dennys. There was no report of further art activities. William ("Smith," I learned) won an Academy Award for best make-up effects for a bloated science fiction epic I'd given a miss.

The scream left its home in my isolated moments, and started to occupy more and more of my time. Nothing would stop its invasion, as I'd feel my cock filling up with old bad poison. I quit my job. The bills piled up and eviction neared; the feeling and the scream became less insistent. I stopped paying the phone bill, stopped talking, ate nothing, surviving only on protein drinks. Los Angeles is the best place in the world to dissolve into one's self.

I still own a very complex MIDI studio. Samplers, synthesizers, rhythm machines, all linked together. I scarcely have to do anything to make my own soundtrack. Perhaps an hour ago I took a tab of my latest medication, pressed "Play," listened to the machines' music and lay down.

By my bed is a black Phillipe Starck dresser, an architectural slash of metal with one drawer. I open it, remove a box of condoms, my prick filling with blood, inhumanly dark. Another box is already on the floor, emptied, the tiny figures I'd stolen from Alis arranged in a semi-circle next to it.

I stroke myself, imagining her blood running down her leg, the plastic seconds between touch and taste leading to a perfect union of expulsion. I glance at the surgical knife I'd purchased at a medical supply store, cool steel.

Then I remove the matchbook Alis had crafted for me from the box, giving it a leading position in front of the nine similar matchbook screamers, their mouths all used up, Alis' mouths. They chatter a bit anyway, which they've been doing for some time now.

The air in the room is still. One small bulb reveals my scream, floating in mid-air. Old as I am, dark as pitch, a distorted mask of a boy made black neon gas. I wait for it to scatter.

"Being able to change things is important. The stuff you don't like.... you fill the hole with the bad thing. It's what you do with art. To get better ... Willpower. Like how you push back what hurts ... Like when you get hard."

I try one last time to shout it out of existence, but my voice had been stolen so many years ago.

The main screamer, the one Alis had sculpted for me with spidery fingers, still had no eyes, but its mouth had opened days ago. The clay remains mysteriously moist.

Now, it takes on definition as I watch. Its tiny features finally match my own. The assembly chatters encouragement for us, for her, for me, for all like us. The mocking cloud-shape disperses, floating with confident purpose for my cock. Remotely amazed to find myself weeping, I come, and feed the last screaming aperture my seed. The matchbox screamers' eyes finally open, as if startled, the scream trapped there, and, pulling my cock outward from my body, I reach for the blade.

The Virgin Spring
by Lorelei Shannon

"*A*i, ai, mi Dios, ah, mi Dios …*"

Maria twists in her narrow virgin's bed. Sweat-soaked sheets cling to her like the greedy arms of a lover; her back arches as she is pierced by the holy rapture of God.

It is not yet light out. She has awakened the household with her cries and they hover at the doorway, loathe to disturb her, anxious to hear the Word. Maria, the blessed. Maria, the intended bride of Jesus.

She gasps, head thrown back, skin glistening cinnamon against the white of her cotton nightgown. Her dark eyes open. She sees Mama, Papa, *Abuelita*, *Tia* Rosa, *Tia* Juanita. She smiles at their beloved, ravaged faces, skin cracked and weathered as the desert floor, tumors and pustules like swarming anthills.

"He was inside me," she whispers. "His holy spirit. Praise Him. Praise Him."

. . .

They sit silently around the breakfast table, the five old ones, waiting for her to speak. Maria hums as she prepares eggs and tortillas and strong black coffee. It is a little indulgence of hers to make them wait; perhaps a tiny sin. But surely God will forgive her for that. She is special, she knows, and she enjoys being special. And she is determined to enjoy this, her last mortal day on Earth.

The seventh daughter of a seventh daughter, born on the hot blue morning that the Americans opened the doors of the *maquiladora*, the plastics plant, Maria first saw the Holy Virgin when she was just twelve.

The young girl had found dark, clotted blood in her panties on the morning of her birthday. Innocent, terrified, she ran from the bathroom, screaming for her mother. Then the world went away in a flash of blue fire. Her namesake appeared to her in a blaze of color and beauty, whispering her name, entreating her to listen, listen.

Not a week went by before God visited her in her sleep.

Maria was wracked with fever for three days, brown cheeks flushed and burning, eyes shiny as silver. She raved about demons and angels and holy blood as her mother wept and cooled her head with damp cloths, and her father silently prepared for his baby girl to die.

But she didn't. Her fever broke with the suddenness of a cooling rainstorm over the desert. When she awoke, Maria was no longer a little girl. She was a prophet.

God came to her often. Sometimes He spoke through her in riddles and strange, singing poetry. Sometimes He warned her of flash floods or lightning strikes. Sometimes He whispered parables, touching, pointed and true. All this she passed on to the people.

Her beloved, monstrous people.

For the townsfolk of Guadalupe had begun to change on the day Maria was born. Their skin grew thick and oily, then blossomed into tumors like globs of wet pink bubblegum. Their hair and their clothes, even their breath, carried the sharp, poisonous smell of liquid plastic. Their lungs filled with fluid, and they grew old before their time. The babies were born with no eyes, or no legs, or no brains, eyes shining like *luminaria* when the doctor held a flashlight to the back of their tiny heads.

But not Maria. Her eyes are as bright as the candles in the Church of St. Sebastian. Her skin is the rich, creamy color of fresh caramel, her hair as glossy as the wings of a raven. It is obvious to all that she is a precious, coddled favorite of God. Perhaps there would have been jealousy, were Maria not so sweet, so affectionate and giving. She loves her family, her neighbors, her little friends with their slick raw-meat faces, kissing their lumpy cheeks as if they are beautiful as porcelain dolls.

The village whispers about her, listens to her, adores her. She is touched by the hand of God.

Maria, now eighteen, smiles at the anxious faces of her family. Her laugh is like the chiming of bells. She can stand to tease them no longer.

"He spoke to me in pictures," she says. "He showed me the face of our land. The mountains. The sky. I was like a hot wind sweeping through the desert, borne aloft by His sweet breath."

"Will it flood this year?" asks *Abuelita*, her voice breathy and quavering. The fat pink mass on her tongue makes her hard to understand.

Maria pats her grandmother's hand. "He did not tell me."

"Will Corazon Ruiz's baby be a boy or a girl?" asks *Tia* Rosa, clasping her hands.

"I do not know," says Maria, eyes sparkling.

"You—you are still going to the convent this fall, aren't you?" asks Mama, touching her daughter's ebony hair.

Again, Maria laughs. "Yes, of course, Mama. I will go. It is what I want most in the world."

For the first time in her life, Maria is lying. It feels strange. She touches Mama's hair, looks into the single black eye that has not yet been covered by the spongy tumor on her forehead.

The old ones breathe a collective sigh of relief. It is not that they want to lose Maria, but she is too delicate, too pure, too precious to remain in the sinful outside world. They want to see her safe within the convent walls, where the love of God will nourish her, where she can grow like a rare and perfect flower.

"What else did he show you?" asks Papa.

Maria takes a deep breath. "He showed me—He showed me the face of William."

Mama gasps. Papa scowls. William? Why?

Maria was never any trouble growing up, of course. She did not date. She had no interest in boys, although they followed her through the streets like mongrel dogs. Then she met William.

She first saw him at the mission last winter. Like her, he was a volunteer, wrapping Christmas presents for the poor children of Guadalupe. His red hair and blue eyes made him stand out;

the only white boy Maria had ever seen. She found him strange and beautiful.

He was traveling for a year, he said, before entering seminary. He seemed to fall in love with Maria instantly.

Their relationship is the subject of much speculation and gossip. Maria and William read the Bible together, go for walks in the evenings, cook for the mission. Her family, especially Papa, does not approve.

But she is such a good girl. She is wise beyond her years. William is gentle and kind, and his devotion seems innocent. They respect her judgment. They would not dream of questioning it. William is her friend, that is all. And he seems to love the children, with their carts and crutches and wet little rubber-monster faces, as much as does Maria herself.

"What does it mean?" asks Mama, looking worried.

Maria looks up at the cracked ceiling and seems to look through it, at the vast, pale blue morning sky. "He is leaving tomorrow, Mama. It means I must say goodbye to him tonight. That is all."

Another lie.

The old ones smile and nod their approval.

. . .

Many hours later, Maria is waiting in the living room, sitting on the frayed blue couch in her white cotton dress when William comes to the door.

Her heart is suddenly filled with strong emotion. She hugs her family, one by one, telling them good-bye. They are not surprised. She is such an affectionate child. She gazes into their faces for a long time, knowing she will not see them again. William shifts from foot to foot and studies the ancient gray carpet.

"Are you ready?" he asks, in his strange, flat American accent. He smiles at her. Maria nods, and slips her arm through his. She smiles up at him, and for a brief, shameful, flickering moment, she thinks that God's will is harsh.

The night is blood-warm. The acrid, chemical breeze that strokes Maria's cheek is as soft as a sleeping baby's breath. The night is moonless, and the stars are so very bright.

Arm in arm, Maria and William stroll through the narrow dirt streets of Guadalupe. Dogs playfully dance alongside them, wagging their twisted, lumpen tails. People wave and smile from their front porches. Somewhere, someone is playing a guitar and singing a song of love lost.

They don't speak, William and Maria, but she wraps both of her arms around his wiry bicep. She rests her head on his shoulder. His eyes glow with quiet joy.

They walk past the grocery store, the *botanica*, the mission with its white, gleaming steeple made luminous in the starlight.

As they leave Guadalupe behind and walk out into the desert, Maria looks over her shoulder at the *maquiladora*, the massive, hulking factory that looms at the far end of town, breathing invisible poisons into the air both night and day. Giving families the money to feed their children. Turning their children into monsters. She sighs, and wonders at the unknowable ways of her God.

But she does not wish to think of such things now. William's gaze is like the sun on her face. Of course, she knows he loves her. Of course. And though she has never spoken it, she loves him too.

He slips his arm around her slender waist as they walk. Her hand slides along his slim, muscular back, around to his lean ribs, then down until it rests on the waistband of his bluejeans. The movement of the muscles of his hip is strangely exciting, in a way she doesn't fully understand.

They walk past green *mesquite* trees, granite boulders, treacherous, jumping *cholla* cactus, *ocotillo* plants like eight-foot thorny weeds. The whisper of the breeze blends with the songs of nightbirds and crickets. The hard dirt crunches beneath Maria's sandals. William glances down at her tiny bare toes anxiously from time to time. But she does not fear snakes or scorpions. They have never come near her. They would not dare.

She feels his breath quicken as they walk. They are moving purposefully now, heading for a place they will know when they see it. William's heart has begun to pound. Maria can feel it thumping against his ribs as if it would leap from his chest and into hers.

They come to the place, and they stop. A granite boulder juts up from the ground. Next to it, a smooth, shallow dip in the desert floor, as if some huge creature has been sleeping there for years.

"Would you like to rest?" William whispers in Maria's ear. She nods. His breath on her face makes her shiver pleasantly.

William takes the plaid shirt he has tied around his waist and spreads it on the ground, in the hollow. He smiles and gestures for Maria to sit, then lowers himself down next to her. He takes her hand.

Now, she thinks. It begins and ends now.

"Maria." His voice is shaking. "I—I'm not going to seminary." He looks at her as if he has just confessed to murder, but she smiles, and nods her encouragement.

William looks up at the starfilled sky. "I love you, Maria. I want you to marry me."

"I know," she whispers. She is filled with sudden, poignant sadness.

He looks at her, half hoping, half afraid.

"I love you too," she says, taking his face in her hands. "I love you, William."

He kisses her. His lips are sweet and warm. Maria slides her hands into his soft, wavy hair, drawing him closer.

His arms are around her, one hand cupping the back of her neck, the other moving up and down her back in long, smooth strokes. He kisses her.

Maria's heart begins to beat faster. She feels William's tongue run along her upper lip, soft as a rose petal. She moves her hands over the front of his white T-shirt, feeling the slim, hard muscles of his chest.

William draws Maria close, pressing her tightly against him. He kisses her neck, then starts to nibble.

She gasps. A warmth is spreading between her legs. William licks the hollow of her throat, and his hand slides up to cup her small breast. His thumb moves gently back and forth over her tiny nipple, sending little shocks of pleasure through her, making her back arch all by itself.

The warmth becomes heat, and wetness, and then a soft, maddening throb as he begins to unbutton her dress.

Maria's breath becomes ragged. She wants something, wants it desperately, although she isn't exactly sure what it could be.

Her dress is open to the waist. William lowers his head and nuzzles between her breasts, kissing, licking the fine sheen of sweat that has formed on her body. Maria strokes his hair, kisses the crown of his head. He smells of American shampoo, and the noonday sun, and deadly, pungent toxins.

He is suckling now, tongue flicking over Maria's nipple like the wing of a moth. She throws her head back. A little moan slips from her mouth as a nighthawk glides silently overhead on midnight wings.

Maria is suddenly greedy for William's pale skin, for the taste of his flesh. She starts to lift his T-shirt over his head.

He grasps her hands. He looks away, down, as if embarrassed.

Maria smiles, turning his face to her with delicate hands. She touches her forehead to his, telling him without words that he has nothing to be ashamed of, that she will find him beautiful, no matter what. He still won't look at her as she pulls the T-shirt off.

He has only been in Guadalupe for a few months, but the town has begun to make him its own. There is a raised, sticky tumor the size of a quarter in the center of his chest, like a third nipple.

Tenderly, with infinite love, Maria kisses it. When she touches William's face, she finds he is weeping.

William slips the flannel shirt out from under Maria, spreads it on the ground behind her, where her head would rest if she were lying down. She smiles at him, nods.

"Are you sure?" he whispers. "Is this what you really want?"

"Yes, my love." But is it? She thinks briefly, wistfully, of life with William, of a home and children they will never have.

But it is God's will.

"Yes," as he eases her down to the ground.

He finishes unbuttoning her dress, and spreads its halves open, like the white wings of a butterfly. Maria feels the soft, now cool breeze on her bare skin. She shivers with pleasure as her nipples grow erect.

William runs his hand along the delicate curve of her belly, tracing the edge of her panties with his finger. "You are so beautiful," he breathes. "I've loved you since the first day I saw you."

She kisses his hand, then places it over her breast. "I am yours."

He pulls her panties down slowly, so slowly it nearly drives her mad. She wants him to see her. She wants nothing between them.

William rubs his cheek against her soft, black, curling fur. He presses his lips to her, sending a jolt of pleasure up her spine. He breathes in her scent, and lingers. His warm breath on her vulva makes her whimper with want.

He kisses her again, more deeply. She feels his tongue slip between her folds, and she cries out. Slowly, worshipfully, he begins to lick her.

Maria had never in her short life guessed that such a thing occurred between people. It is shocking. It is unbelievably delicious. Her breath comes in high-pitched sobs, chest heaving, hips writhing. I cannot bear it, she thinks, trying at once to twist away, and to open herself wider for him.

He slides his hands beneath her, gripping her slender hips. He will not let her go. His tongue is moving faster, rhythmically, as fast as the pounding of her heart.

It hits her suddenly, with the force of a lightening bolt in the midst of a summer storm. Wave upon wave of pleasure, unlike anything she has ever felt before. Maria's back bends; she rises up from the earth as if she would take flight. She cries out again and again, calling upon God, thanking him for the time she has with William, knowing even through her ecstasy that it will end soon now, very soon.

She sinks back to the ground as the feeling fades, still gasping. Her limbs are weak, her thighs trembling. William is over her, on top of her, kissing her lips. She tastes the honeymusk flavor of herself on his mouth, and finds it beautiful.

"Are you ready?" he asks.

"Yes," she replies, not knowing for what.

He unbuttons his jeans, slides them down over his narrow hips. Again, he is on top of her. She feels him pressing against her, and, just for a moment, feels a flicker of fear.

She is very wet, and he is pushing harder now. She feels resistance, momentary pain. He is breathing hard, mouth against her ear. She kisses his cheek, gasps as he enters her.

They are one. It is as if someone has switched on a light in a darkened room. Maria sees everything. She senses the ground squirrels in their holes, the coyotes with their golden, trickster eyes, the cactus wrens asleep in the tall saguaros. She feels the burn of the stars a million miles above her. She feels the cool gurgle of water in layers of rock below.

"Are you all right?" William whispers. Maria nods, unable to speak, presses her lips to his forehead. There is no turning back.

"Does it hurt?" he asks, brushing the hair from her eyes. She smiles at him, and shakes her head, for she is far beyond feeling pain.

He begins to move inside her. He rocks his hips gently, like waves on a quiet sea. It feels so very, very good. Maria rests her hands on his rounded, muscular backside, moving her hips in rhythm with his.

Maria moans as William thrusts a little deeper. She moans as the ground beneath her warms, liquefies, reaches up to meet her flesh. She cries out as the flesh of her back reaches down to join the earth.

She holds him tightly, rocking, thrusting. She does not want to leave him, although she knows she must. She digs her fingertips into the sweatslick muscles of his lower back as her feet sink into the ground.

William cries out, arching up and away from Maria. She touches the sharp angle of his jaw as he empties himself into her. She shudders all over, the mortal part of her gripped with intense pleasure. She feels his seed flow deep inside, touching her now-molten core.

"William," she cries. "William, William."

He lies on top of her for a time, whispering her name, kissing her, swearing his undying love. Tears of scarlet slip down Maria's temples as she strokes his hair.

At last, he pulls out of her. Maria feels a sorrow that is sister to grief, knowing she will never feel him again.

She sees through his eyes the crimson poppy that is spreading between her thighs, staining the white of her dress.

"You're bleeding," says William, frightened.

"Yes." She smiles at him. She would take his face in her hands, but she cannot reach him. Her back has fused with the earth.

"Maria—you're bleeding a lot." His voice is shaking. He reaches down between her legs, touches the trickle of red that flows freely now.

Maria drops her head to the ground, unable to support it any longer. The back of her skull immediately begins to grow into the rock. Her hair spreads out around her, becoming black basalt.

"I—you need a doctor! Oh, God, what have I done?" William is sobbing now, sobbing as the trickle becomes a gush, sobbing as Maria's parted legs begin to sink into the earth.

"You have done nothing but love me," she whispers, voice rough as her throat begins to calcify. "This is the will of God, my darling, my only, only love ..."

Maria smiles, one last time. She feels her lips harden and crack as they become glittering mica-laced granite.

William howls. He plunges his hands into the gushing, gurgling stream of blood that bursts forth from the petals of a flawless pink rose quartz. He rubs it into his face, as if he could keep Maria with him that way.

He splashes his body with her blood, covering his chest and belly. He screams her name over and over again. Maria's heart breaks as she watches him through her shiny obsidian eyes, but she can no longer speak, or even cry.

William's chin drops to his chest. He kneels between the granite formations that once were strong young legs, letting the blood wash over him. He lets out a miserable howl, then another.

Look, my love, thinks Maria. See what I have done for you.

He may have heard her. He may have, for he pauses, touches his bloodslicked chest with his fingers. He gasps as the tumor melts from his flesh like sugar.

You are the first, thinks Maria. Only the first.

William stops crying. He raises his bloodslicked head, and gazes at the facelike stone formation on the desert floor. He touches the gentle rise and curve of the glittering granite below it. He stretches himself out over the hard stone, feeling it bruise his chest, his groin. He lies down, listening to the gurgle of the spring, feeling its warmth as it gushes against his thigh. After awhile, he sleeps.

Learn At Home! Your Career In Evil!
by John Shirley

It was while his wife slept: that's when it was easiest for Kander to think about killing her. Just the fact of her being awake, Elias Kander had learned, troubled him with doubts about the project. It was as if her movements about the house, her prattle, spoke of her as a living, suffering reality, and underlined the deepest meanings in the word murder.

But as she slept ...

On those nights when he'd been working late in the lab, Kander would come home to find her soundly asleep, resentfully dosed with sedatives. Sedated, she was reduced to something like a hapless infant, clutching the quilt her grandmother had made. A time when he should feel pangs of conscience at her profound vulnerability, was just the time he felt safest thinking about her annihilation. Vistas of freedom opened up, in her hypothetical absence ...

But what if there really were hell to pay?

What if evil were objectively real and not relative? And what about the thing in the lab?

. . .

A sleepy Tuesday night, the city hugging itself against moody Chicago winds off the Lake; but it was warm by the gas fire in the steak house. Kander and Berryman came here after an afternoon's research, as it was across the street from the university's library.

Waiting for Kander to return from the men's room, Berryman sipped his merlot and looked at his companion's empty plate across the table. How thoroughly Kander ate everything; not a shred of beef left, every pea vanished.

Berryman considered his own peculiar ambivalence to their monthly dinners; their boys' nights out. He'd felt the usual frisson on seeing Kander's almost piratical grin, the glitter in his eyes that presaged the ideas, in every philosophical menu, they'd feast on along with the prime rib; and a moment later, also as usual, a kind of chill dread took him. Kander had a gift for taking him to the frontiers of the thinkable, and then into the disorienting wilderness beyond. But maybe that was the natural consequence of a humanistic journalist—Berryman—locking horns with a scientist. And sometimes Berryman thought Kander was more a scientist than a human being.

"I've been thinking about journalists, Larry," Kander said, sitting down. He was a stocky, bulletheaded man with amazingly thick forearms, blunt fingers; more like a football coach than a physicist who'd minored in behavioral science. He wore the same threadbare sweater the last time they'd suppered together, and the time before that; his greying black hair—an inch past the collar only because he rarely remembered the barber—brushed straight back from his forehead. Berryman was constrastingly tall, gangly, had trouble folding his long legs under the restaurant's elegantly tiny tables. Long hair on purpose, tied in a greying ponytail. They'd been roommates at the university across the street where Kander now had research tenure.

Berryman scratched in his short, curly brown beard. "You're thinking about journalists? I'm thinking about leaving, then. You'll be doing experiments on me next."

"How do you know for sure I haven't been?" Kander grinned and patted his coat for a cigarette.

"Amy made you give up the cigarettes, Kander, remember? Or have you started again?"

"Oh that's right, damn her, no smokes, well—anyway …" He poured some more red wine, drank half the glass off in one gulp and said, "My thinking is that journalists are by nature dilettantes. They have to be. I don't mean a scholar who writes a ten volume biography of Jefferson. I mean—"

"Guys like me who write for *Rolling Stone* and the *Trib* and, on a good day, *The New Yorker*. Yes, I'm well aware of your contempt for—"

"No, not at all, not at all. I'm not contemptuous of your trade, merely indifferent to it. But you must admit, journalists can't get into a thing too deeply because the next piece is always calling, and the next paycheck."

"Often the case, yes. But some specialize. And you get a feel for what's under the surface, though you can't spend long looking for it. Sometimes, though, you're with it longer than you'd like …"

"Yes: your war correspondence. I daresay you learned a great deal about South America. Peru, and, oh my yes, Chile—"

"Sometimes more than I'd like to know. What's your point, implying that journalists are shallow? You going to have a bumper sticker made up—'physicists do it deeper'?"

"Given the chance, we do! Unless we make the mistake of getting married. But my dear fellow—" Kander was American, but he'd gone to a boarding school in England for eight years, as a boy, and it had left its mark. "—I'm talking about getting to essences. What are the essences of things? Of human events? To get to them you must first wade through all the details of a study. Now, journalists think they dabble, and knock off an essence. But they can't; more often than not they get it wrong. A scientist though—he may work through mountains of detail, rivers of i-dotting and oceans of calculation, but ultimately he is after essences—the big picture and the defining laws that underlie things. Now take your upsetting sojourn in what was it, Peru or Chile? Where you discovered that during 'the dirty war' whole families of dissidents were disappeared—"

"It doesn't seem to matter to you what country it was, Kander. Sometimes they weren't even really dissidents. They seem to pick them at random, some sort of quota."

"Just so. And they murdered the men, used some of the women for sex slaves, and when they abducted women who were pregnant, they often kept them alive just long enough to bear the children, whereupon the children were taken from them, for sale to childless officers—"

"And the women were then thrown alive out of airplanes over the Pacific. What's your point?" Berryman knew he was being snappish, but Kander was being altogether too gleeful over a recollection that never failed to make Berryman's guts churn.

"When you write about it, you write—and very well, yes— about the political and social histories that made such brutality possible. As if it were explainable with mere history! There's where you made your error. It wasn't history, my boy. It wasn't a shattering of modern ethics with a loss of faith in the rules of the Holy Roman Empire; it wasn't brutalizing by military juntas and a century of crushing the 'Indios'."

"You're not going to say Eugenics, are you? Korzybski-ism? Because if you are—"

"Not at all! I'm no crypto-Nazi, my friend. No—if you look at the essence of the thing, it was as if a sort of disease was passed from one man to another. A disease that killed empathy, that allowed dehumanization—and extreme brutality."

"It is a kind of disease—but it has a social ontology."

"Not as you mean it. That kind of brutality goes deeper. It is contrary to the human spirit—and yet it was very widespread, in that South American hell-hole, just as it was among the Germans in World War Two. And the secret? It may be … that evil is *communicable*. That evil is communicable almost like a virus."

"You mean … there's some unknown physical factor, a microorganism that passes from one man to another affecting the brain and—"

"No! That is just what I don't mean. I mean that evil as a thing in itself is passed from one man to the next. Not through the example of brutality, or through coarsening from abuse— but as a kind of living, sentient substance—and this is what underlies such things. This is the essence that a journalist does not look deep enough to see."

Berryman stared at him; then he laughed. "You're fucking with me again. You had me going there."

"Am I?" Shutters closed in Kander's face; suddenly he seemed remote. "Well. We'll talk about it another time. Perhaps."

Just then the Mexican busboy came along. "You feenish?" he asked.

"Yes, yes," Kander muttered impatiently. And he could not be induced to say much more that night, except to ask what Berryman, an associate at the university, thought of the new coeds, especially the latest crop of blondes.

. . .

It took only six weeks for the toxic-metals compound to do its work on Kander's wife. It was not a poison that killed, not directly: at this dosage it was a poison no one could see, or even infer: it was just despair. A little lead, a little mercury, a few select trace elements, a compound selected for its effect on the nervous system.

They were watching *The Wonderful World of Disney* when he was sure it was working on her.

It was a repeat of the Disney adaptation of *The Ransom of Red Chief*. She liked O. Henry stories. He had found that watching TV with her was often enough to satisfy her need for him to act like a husband. It was close enough to their "doing something together." It wasn't really necessary for him to watch the television; it was sufficient for him to rest his gaze on the screen. Now and then he would focus on it, mutter a comment, and then go back into his ruminations again. She didn't seem to mind if he kept a pad by the chair and scribbled the occasional note to himself; a patching equation, some new slant to the miniature particle accelerator he'd designed. How the world would beat a path to his door, he thought, as the little boy on Disney yowled and chased Christopher ... what was his name, the guy who'd played the professor on *Back to the Future* ... Christopher Lloyd? How the world of physics would genuflect to him when he unveiled his micro-accelerator. A twenty-foot machine that could do what miles of tunnel in Texas only approached. The excellences of quantum computing—only he had tapped them. The implications ...

But it was best that *she* disappear before all that take place. If he were to get rid of her when the cold light of fame shone on him—well, someone would look too close at her death. And if he divorced her ... her lawyer would turn up the funds he'd misappropriated from her senile mother's bank account; an account only his wife was supposed to be able to access. Her lawyer would not care that those funds had paid for his work after the grant had run out.

He glanced at her appraisingly. Was it working? She was a short Austrian woman, his wife, with thick ankles, narrow shoulders; she was curled, now, in the other easy chair, wearing only her nightgown. She'd complained of feeling weak and tired for days, but it was the psychological sickness he needed from her ...

"You know," she said, her voice curiously flat, "we shouldn't have ... I mean, it seemed right, philosophically, for you to get a vasectomy. But we could have had one child without adding to the overpopulation much, to any, you know, real ..."

"It was your health too, my dear. Your tipped uterus. The risk."

"Yes. We could have adopted—we still could. But—" She shook her head. Her eyes glistened with unshed tears and the image of the running child on the TV screen duplicated twistedly in them. "This world is ... it seems so hopeless. There'll be twelve billion people in a few decades. Terrorism, global warming, famine, the privileged part of the world all ... all one ugly mall ... the cruelty, the mindless, mindless cruelty ... and then what happens? You begin to age terribly and it's as if the sickness in the world goes right into your body ... like your body ... with its sagging and decay and senility ... it is like it is mocking the world's sickness and ..."

It's working, he thought. The medical journals were right on target. She was deeply, profoundly depressed.

"I know exactly what you mean," he said.

"It wouldn't matter so much if I had ... something. Anything in my life besides ... But I'm just ... I mean I'm not creative, and I'm not a scientist like you, I'm not ... if I had a child. That'd be meaning. But it's too late for that."

"I'm surprised that watching *The Ransom of Red Chief* makes you want a child. Considering how the child behaves ... They're all Red Chief a lot of the time ..."

"Oh I don't mind that—wanting a child without that is like wanting wild animals all to be tame. They *should be* wild ... But my life is already ... it's caged."

"Yes. I feel that way too. For both of us."

She looked at him, a little disappointed. She'd had some faint hope he might rescue her from this down-spiraling plunge.

For a moment, it occurred to him that he could. He could stop putting the incremental doses of toxins in her food. He could take her to a toxicologist. They'd assume she'd gotten some bad water somewhere ...

But he heard himself say—almost as if it were someone else saying it—

"I'm a failure as a scientist. And I don't want to live in this world ... if you don't."

. . .

It took five more tedious, wheedling days to break her down completely. He upped the dose, and he deprived her of sleep when he could, pretending migraines that made him howl in the night. He drove her closer and closer to the reach of that depression that had its own mind, its own will, its own agenda.

At last, at three-thirty in the morning, after insisting that she watch the Shopping Channel with him for hours—a channel anyone not stupid, stupefied, or mad would find nightmarish, after a few minutes—she said, "Yes, let's do it." Her voice dry as a desert skull. "Yes."

He wasted no time. He got the capsules, long since prepared. Hers the powerful sleeping agent she sometimes used. His appearing to be exactly the same—except that he'd secretly emptied out each pill in his own bottle, and put flour in his capsules. They each took a whole bottle of the prescription sedative. Only his would produce nothing but constipation.

She was asleep in ten minutes, holding his hand. He nearly fell asleep himself, waiting beside her. What woke him was something cold, touching him. The coldness of her fingers, gripping his. Fingers cold as death.

. . .

"I said, I've come to ... to give you condolences," Berryman said, grimacing. "What a stupid phrase that is. I never know what to say when someone dies and I have to ... but you know how I feel."

"Yes, yes I do," Kander said. Wanting Berryman to go away. He stood in front of his microaccelerator, blinking at Berryman. How had the man gotten in?

But he'd been sleeping so badly, drinking so much, he'd probably forgotten to lock the lab door. Probably hadn't heard the knocking over the whine of the machinery.

"If there's anything I can do ..."

"No, no, my friend she's ... well, I almost feel her with me, you know. I used to make fun of such sentiments but, ah ..."

It occurred to him—why not Berryman? Why not let Berryman be the one to break it to the world? Why wait till the papers were published, the results duplicated? There would be scoffing at first—a particle accelerator that could do more than the big ones could do, that could unlock the secrets of the sub-atomic universe, the unknown essences, consciousness itself, in a small university laboratory? They wouldn't condescend to jeering. They'd merely quirk their mouths and arch a brow. But let them—he'd demonstrate it first hand, once the public's interest was aroused. Let them come and see for themselves. The government boys would come around because the possibilities for applying this technology to a particle beam weapon were obvious ... yes, yes, he'd mention it during the interview.

"Where would you like to do the interview, Berryman?"

"What?"

"Oh, I'm sorry—I'm getting to be an eccentric professor here, getting ahead of myself. Not enough sleep you know—ah, I want you to be the one to ... to break the news ..."

. . .

"Still, it's all theoretical," Berryman was saying, so *very* annoyingly, "at least to the public—unless there's something you can demonstrate ..."

They were drinking Irish whisky, tasting of smoke and peat, in Kander's little cubicle of an office.

"I mean, Kander, I'll write it up, but if you want to get all the government agencies and the big corporations pounding on your door—"

"Well, then. Well, now," Kander took another long pull and suddenly it seemed plausible. "Why not? Come along then ..."

They went weaving into the laboratory, Berryman knocking over a beaker as he went. "Oh, hell—"

"Never mind, forget it, it's just acid, it's nothing." He had brought the whisky with him and he drank from it as he went through the door to the inner lab, amber liquid curling from the corners of his mouth, spattering the floor. "Ahhh, yes. Come along, come along. Now, look through here, through this smoked glass viewer while I fire 'er up here ... and consider, consider that there is a recognizably conscious component to quantum measurements: what is consciously perceived is thereby changed only by the perception. There's argument about how literally this should be taken—but I've taken it very literally, I've taken that plunge, and I've found something wonderful. Quantum computing makes possible fine adjustments of a scanning tunneling microscope, turning it into, well, a powerful particle accelerator, effectively ... and since we're passing through this lens of sheer quantum consciousness in effecting this, we open a door into the possibilities for consciousness to be found in so-called 'matter' itself."

"I see nothing through this window, Kander, except, uh, a kind of squirming smoke—"

"It's a living 'smoke' my friend. Listen—look at me now and listen—What characterizes raw consciousness? Not just awareness—but reaction. Response. Feeling. Yes, yes it turns out that suffering is something inherent in consciousness, along with pleasurable feelings—and that it's there even in the consciousness found in raw inorganic matter."

"You're saying a brick can feel?"

"Not at all! But within a brick, or anything else, is the *potential* for feeling. Now, this can be used, enslaved so to speak, to investigate matter from within and report to us its truest nature; can even be sent on waves of light to other solar systems, to report to us what it finds there—this process of enslavement you see, that's the difficulty, so, ah, you've got to get involved in the training of this background consciousness once you've quantified a bit of it—bottled up a workable unit of it as I have—and that training is done with suffering. But how to make it suffer? It turns out, my friend, that while evil is, yes, relative, it is also, from the *point of view of any given entity or aligned group of entities,* a real essence. And this so-called 'evil' can be extracted from quantum sub-probability essences and used to train this consciousness to obey us—"

"You're torturing raw consciousness to make it your slave?"

"Oh stop with the theatrical tone of horrified judgment! Do you eat animals? They have some smattering of consciousness. And now would you get a horse to carry you over a wasteland? You whip it, you force it to your will. Don't be childish about this. Clamp down on your journalistic shallowness and look deep into the truths of life! For, my friend, life is comprised of intertwined essences! And once liberated those heretofore unknown essences are unbelievably powerful! The essence of evil ... in order to use it I had to isolate it—"

"You've got the essence of evil in there?"

"Yes. Well, it's what people think of an evil ... I envision a day when it's but a pure tool in our hands—just a tool, completely in our command and therefore never again our master— and we'll train people ... train them in schools to use evil to—"

Berryman vaguely remembered an old Blue Öyster Cult lyric: *I'll make it a career of Evil ...*

He chuckled, "I think this is where I say, 'You're mad, professor'. Only I don't think you're mad, I think you're drunk."

"Am I now? Listen, the stuff ... just looking at it for awhile—it affects you. I spent an hour one night looking into that squirming mass and I—"

He almost said, and *I decided, when I stepped away from the instrument, to murder my wife.* "And I'd rather not discuss it! Well, Berryman, did it not affect you, just now? Looking at the squirming smoke? No odd thoughts entered your head?"

"Um—perhaps." He blushed. Sex. Forbidden sex. "But—it could be just psychological suggestion, it could be a microwave or something hitting some part of my brain—to say it's the essence of evil—"

"Have another drink. You're going to need it. I'm going to open this chamber, and I'm going to introduce one of these ... one of these cats here ... And you'll see it transformed, remarkably changed, into pure energy, an energy that is pure catness, you see ... Come here, cat, dammit ... You know we hire people to steal cats from the suburbs, for the lab? We often have to take off their collars ... Muffy here hasn't had her collar taken off ... Ow! The little bitch scratched me!"

"Out-smarted you. You should be ashamed, stealing people's cats, Kander. There she goes, she's run under the ... You left the little door ... the hatch on that thing ... you left it open ... the smoke ... oh God, Kander. Oh God."

. . .

It wasn't Kander he was running from. The sight of Kander on all fours, clothes in tatters, knees bloody from the broken glass, running in circles on hands and knees chasing an imaginary tail like a maddened cat. Kander yowling like a cat.

Nor was it the fact that Muffy the cat was watching Kander do this from under the table and *was laughing in Kander's own voice.*

No, it was the squirming smoke, and what Berryman saw in it: A hall of liquid mirrors, one mirror reflecting into the next so the reflection replicated into an apparent infinity; and what was reflected in the mirror, was despair. Despair replicated unto infinity. A hungry, predatory despair. Berryman saw the bloody drain in the floor of that South American prison where all those women had been tortured, tortured for no political reason, no practical application, to no purpose at all.

He felt the thing that had escaped from Kander's lab—felt it sniff the back of his neck as he ran out into the partly-cloudy campus afternoon—

But its inverted joy was so fulsome, so thunderously resonant, it could not be satisfied with merely Berryman. It reared up like a swollen dick big as a genii. It married the clouds overhead and joined them, crushed them to it, so that electricity sizzled free of them and communicated with the ground in a forest of quivering arcs and darkness fell over all like the smells of a concentration camp, and students, between classes, wailed in a chorus of despondency so uniform it could almost have come from a single throat; and yet some of them gave out, immediately afterward, a yell of unbridled exultation, free at last from the cruelty of self respect, and they set about fulfilling all that they'd held so long in quivering check …

. . .

… the very bricks …

The very bricks had gone soft, like blocks of cheese, and softer yet, and they ground unctuously together, the bricks of the building humping one another …

And the buildings sagged in on themselves, top floor falling lumpishly onto the next down, and those two floors on the next, and the whole thing spreading, wallowing, and people crushed, some of them, but others crawling to one another in the glutinous debris …

But it wasn't these he was drawn to It was just one girl.

He was long past resisting; the thing was on them like a hurricane-force Santa Ana wind, parching out all restraint, leaving only the unstoppable drive to merge and to bang, one on the other, like two people on the opposite sides of a door, each banging on it at the same time, loud as they could, each demanding that the other open it—

That's how they fucked.

He had seen the girl, no more than twenty years old, earlier that morning, in the cafeteria. He'd stopped in, on the way to see Kander, for a bagel and coffee. Her hair in raven ringlets falling with springy lushness over bared shoulders; one of those clinging tank tops; tight jeans; sandals that showed small feet, scarlet nails; when she'd turned, feeling his hot gaze, her face amazingly open, full of maybes, possibilities in her full lips and Amer-Asian eyes. Golden skin. Part Japanese, part black, part Caucasian, and something else—Indian? Her cheekbones were high. They led to her eyes and down to her lips.

Her smile had been impossibly open. Not an invitation, just ... open.

But, panicky with his rapture, he had said nothing; and she had turned away, and picked out a chocolate pudding.

Now ... the center of the quad, under the sky ...

The very center of the campus quadrangle. Brick, it was, with pebble paths from the four corners meeting at a concrete star in the middle. But the bricks and pebbles and concrete had all gone soft, and were alive: he could feel them returning his touch as he and the girl rolled on them, as he banged himself into her ...

Some part of him struggled for objectivity, struggled for freedom from the overwhelming energies boiling around him ... Boiling around the hundreds and hundreds of copulating couples and threesomes and foursomes across the campus square ...

He had been running from the lab, he'd seen her, and she had shouted something joyfully to him as she ran up to him, tearing off her top, and he hadn't been able to make it out because of the thudding, the inarticulate music coming from everywhere and nowhere, sounding like five radio stations turned on full blast over loudspeakers, five different rock-songs all played at once, a chaos of conflicting sounds merging into a mass of exuberant noise—except for no clear reason all the songs had the same percussion, the same beat ... THUD THUD THUD THUD ... maybe just his pulse ... THUD THUD THUD THUD ... White noise, red noise and black ...

And he hadn't been able to hear her over this but she'd grabbed his hands and pressed them to her breasts—

Her breasts were songs of Solomon, were each like a dove, fitting perfectly under his hands, each one upturned and nuzzling his palm with a stiff nipple.

Run, he told himself. Get away from here.

Her belly was soft but muscular, moving in a bellydance she'd never learned in life, and he was peeling off her jeans … and their clothes, they found, fell away from them like wet ashes, in the magic that was rampant about them, and you could scrape the fabric away with your nails. In moments they were nude and rolling on the impossibly soft bricks, with the white noise, the red noise, the black noise; rolled by the golden waves of godsized sound and he had only a few glimpses of the others, copulating ludicrously to all sides and with frenetic energy. The obese, unpleasantly naked sixty-year-old Dean of Mathematical Studies was slamming it to the rippling-buff thirty year old lesbian volleyball coach, and the fifty-five-year-old lady with the mustache who was in charge of the cafeteria had stripped away most of her white uniform and was straddling the quarterback of the football team and he was digging at her flapping breasts till they bled and he was mouthing *I love you baby* at her; and the Gay Men's Glee Club was copulating not only with one another but with the girls from the Young Republican Women's Sorority Association, and the black campus mailman was fucking wildly with the blond woman who taught jazz dancing—but it wasn't the first time; and biology classes were copulating with physics classes …

And they fucked faster, he and the golden skinned raven haired girl, her eyes flashing like onyx under a laser, and he could feel her cervix pressing against the end of his dick as he ground into her, feel the dimple in the middle of her cervix that led to her uterus, could feel the spongy tissue of the inner vagina with almost unbearable detail as she chewed at his tongue, only making it bleed a little, as close by the president of the Students for Christ screamed, "FUCK ME PLEASE UNTIL IT KILLS ME!" to the wrestling coach until the doddering head of the philosophy department shoved his improbably engorged dick so deep into the student's throat he gagged and choked, the old man, his wattles shimmering with his humping, singing "I got my cock in my pocket and it's shovin' out through my pants, just wanna fuck, don't want no romance!" Or *was* he singing that? Was that in Berryman's mind? Some part of Berryman was becoming increasingly detached as he fucked harder, driving bleedingly hard into the gorgeous Asian student; something in him trying to crawl out from under this slavery ... The old man jamming himself into the student's throat clawed at the air and fell over the other two in the threesome, shaking in death ... Others, mostly the older ones, were beginning to die but even those not breaking under the strain were showing haunted eyes, amping desperation, and the Dean of Comparative Religion grabbed a gun from the fallen holster of a cop and blew out his own brains and the man next to him took the gun from the Dean's limp hand and shot himself in the throat and the woman beside *him* took up the gun ...

While overhead the black thunderclouds still shed their lightnings, sent eager arcs into the receptive cunt of the Earth itself ...

For a while now Berryman had been coming, ejaculating in the girl but the coming wouldn't stop, went achingly on and on and on, he was quite empty but still his urethra convulsed as it tried to pump something into her, and all that came up now was blood in place of come, and he screamed with the pain and she tried to push away from him with her hands but her legs, locked behind his back, disobeyed her, pulled him closer to her yet—

Berryman made a supreme internal effort—arising from an experience of self observation, of mindfulness, of an experience of the possibility of freedom in detached consciousness, something he'd learned from an old man in the Andes ...

And never before had he really succeeded in it; never before had it quite crystallized in him. But now under these unspeakable pressures it came together and he was whole, and he was free—

His body was still caught, but some essence ...

An essence! Another essence ...

Some essence was hovering over the humping, screaming figures, and calling out … Calling out like to like. To another essence, its own kind.

Then the other essence came; the other end of the spectrum, closing the circuit, closing the gap: the blue light, and the silence …

How Screwtape hated silence …

The silence came rolling across them in a wave of release, of icy purity, of relaxing, of forgiving, and they fell away from one another, those who'd survived, and lay gasping, falling into a deep state of rest, and the lightnings stopped, the squirming smoke dissipated in the sudden drenching downpour of rain. The bricks became hard and his dick became soft and …

And the cat, Muffy, ran past him, carrying one of Kander's eyes in its jaws.

About the Writers

Poppy Z. Brite is the author of four novels, *Lost Souls, Drawing Blood, Exquisite Corpse,* and *The Lazarus Heart;* two short story collections, *Wormwood* (also published as *Swamp Foetus*) and *Are You Loathsome Tonight?* (published in the UK as *Self-Made Man*); and a biography of rock diva Courtney Love. She recently wrote and illustrated the novella *Plastic Jesus* for Subterranean Press, and is at work on a new novel. She lives in New Orleans with her husband, Christopher, and many beasts. She has, as far as we know, no Uncle Edna.

Dominick Cancilla is a regular guy who just happens to like writing about fear and dismemberment. He lives in Santa Monica, CA, with his wife, author Deborah Markus, and his son Markus. Dominick's work has appeared in *Robert Bloch's Psychos, Bending the Landscape: Fantasy, The Best of Cemetery Dance, Whispered from the Grave,* and other anthologies, as well as in a good fistful of magazines. When not writing, Dominick is Webmaster for www.cemeterydance.com and www.subterraneanpress.com.

M. Christian has published over 100 stories, and has appeared in such anthologies as *Best American Erotica, Best Gay Erotica, Skull Full of Spurs, Graven Images, Song of Cthulhu, Mondo Zombie, Viscera,* and magazines like *Talebones, Wetbones, XX Magazine, Gothic.Net* (www.gothic.net), *Errata* (www.errata.com), *Night Terrors,* and many others. He is also the editor of *Eros Ex Machina, Midsummer Night's Dreams, Guilty Pleasures, Rough Stuff* (with Simon Sheppard), and *The Burning Pen.* A collection of his short fiction, *Dirty Words,* is forthcoming. The only thing that scares him more than having too much to do—is not having enough.

J.R. Corcorrhan is a tattoo artist living in Colorado. He's also been an insurance investigator, a drug counselor, and a high school English teacher. Corcorrhan writes whenever he's not cruising mountain roads on his '76 Harley or trading stocks on the Net. "Seeing Things" is his first publication. He writes: "I have this thing about eyeballs. They're mushy and stiff; dry and wet; beautiful and disgusting. They're the inside-out parts that we don't clothe. I write about them all the time. So all I can say about this one is, 'Here's looking at you, kid!'"

Samuel Cross is the alter ego of JenLynn Sweet, the author who recently worked at a Nevada brothel to cover a story on porn stars in legal prostitution. She has since been featured on Fox, A&E, Extra, Black Entertainment Television and numerous talk shows and adult films. She writes regularly for adult Web sites, books and magazines while completing her first novel, *Happy Trails*.

Stephen Dedman is a hairy, lecherous polyamorist, and the author of the novels *The Art of Arrow Cutting* and *Foreign Bodies*. His short stories have appeared in an eclectic range of anthologies and magazines, including *Little Deaths, The Year's Best Fantasy and Horror, Eros Ex Machina,* and *Midsummer Nights' Dreams*. His first short fiction collection, *The Lady of Situations*, was published in 1999. Would you believe they let him write children's books, too? Stephen, his wife, and her wife all live in Western Australia.

Robert Devereaux is the author of *Deadweight, Walking Wounded,* and two dozen published short stories. His pious little morality play about God, moptops, mistimed sneezes, and simultaneous orgasm is a prequel to *Santa Steps Out* (Dark Highway Press/Leisure Books), which chronicles the erotic misadventures of Santa Claus, the Tooth Fairy, and the Easter

Bunny. Nowadays he delves into Dickens, glories in the wonders of northern Colorado, and putters away at one novel about world-saving do-gooders who do good and save the world, and another about what it feels like to carry logs for some short-fused old ex-duke with a starry-eyed daughter, a book of magic spells, and the power to rouse and quell tempests.

Ian Grey's work has appeared in *Time Out, Icon, Fangoria, Gothic.Net, Link* and many other periodicals. He has also written site-specific texts for The American Museum of the Moving Image, Franklin Furnace, PS 122, and Thread Waxing Space. He covers music and film for the alternative weekly, *City Paper.* His nonfiction book *Sex, Stupidity and Greed: Inside the American Movie Industry* was published in 1998. Mr. Grey is now at work on an epic docu-novel dealing with sex, pop music, mass murder, family and a property called *Serum V,* which is based upon two lines from a Depeche Mode song. Mr. Grey likes to think he will be among the very first to do this.

Rob Hardin is a writer and studio musician whose last book, *Distorture,* won the Firecracker Award for Best Fiction. Currently at work on a novel that bears little resemblance to the *fin de siecle* forties flick in this anthology, Hardin (or Bachelor Number Twelve, as he is referred to by estranged acquaintances) is also in pre-production on an album of original chamber music with some of the finest tufted titmice in the Lower East Side. His manly hobbies include writing about himself in third person and leering on a budget. (Bartender: "Madam, this glass of water is from the grinning gent in tails.")

The versatile and prolific **Nancy Holder** (her more than two dozen novels and eighty-plus short stories include romance, sf, fantasy, and erotica, and she is the recipient of four Bram Stoker Awards for horror) has lately been having a lot of fun writing *Buffy the Vampire Slayer* and *Sabrina the Teenage Witch* books. She's been known to frequent health clubs and work out, but is definitely not allergic to her husband.

Charlee Jacob had just been rear-ended for the third time when Paula Guran asked for a story. Suffering injuries, spaced out on medication, and running in her sleep (as she sometimes does without the other influences), she half-remembered a dream of being in a basement where people were being flayed alive. Seemed like a good idea. Jacob's debut novel *This Symbiotic Fascination* was a nominee for both the Stoker International Horror Guild Awards. Her first collection, *Dread In The Beast* was released in 1999 and her second, *Up, Out Of Cities That Blow Hot And Cold*, is due out this year. Aother novel, *Silk Bones*, will soon be published in eBook form and chapbook of poetry *Flowers From A Dark Star* will also be out in 2000.

San Francisco writer, editor, and performer **Thomas S. Roche** stayed up too late one Christmas Eve, drank a six-pack of Rolling Rock and watched *Reform School Girls* twice while alphabetizing his porn. The result, written between midnight and six A.M. to the sound of gunfire outside Roche's window on the happiest day of the year, was the tragicomic morality play "Payback's a Bitch." His horror, crime, and erotica stories have appeared in over 100 anthologies and magazines and in his collection, *Dark Matter*. Subscribe to Roche's newsletter by sending email to thomasroche-announce-subscribe@onelist.com or visiting www.thomasroche.com.

Jay Russell lives in London and writes stuff that no one knows where to shelve. His books include the novels *Celestial Dogs, Blood,* and *Burning Bright,* and a short story collection, *Waltzes and Whispers.* Two new novels, *Greed & Stuff* (a "Marty Burns" book) and *Brown Harvest*, are coming soon. Curious readers can find out more at www.sff.net/people/jrussell. Jay Russell loves his mother. But only within reason.

David J. Schow writes movies, short stories, nonfiction, TV, and novels, in roughly that order. Triage generally leaves film work as the "day job" and short stories as the passion. Sometimes elements of both combine, hence, "Saturnalia," which began as a teleplay idea which needed to be shorn of the strictures of TV in order to bloom. With any luck, you'll see the following books, in 2000: *Lost Angels* (new edition of 1990 short story collection), *Wild Hairs* (nonfiction), *The Lost Bloch, Volume Two: Hell On Earth* (as editor), and a new, yet-untitled short story collection, circa Hallowe'en.

Lorelei Shannon grew up in the Arizona desert and learned to walk holding on to the tail of a coyote. She spent her childhood reading Edgar Allan Poe and feeding flies to a big praying mantis in her mother's rose garden. She is now a writer, computer game designer, artist, and punk belly dancer. While making fajitas one night, she saw the face of Clive Barker in a tortilla, and wrote "The Virgin Spring" the very next day.

John Shirley is the author of fourteen novels as well as a screenwriter. His most recent collections are *Black Butterflies* and *Really, Really, Really, Really Weird Stories*. This year has seen the re-release of his classic cyberpunk trilogy of *Eclipse, Eclipse Penumbra,* and *Eclipse Corona,* and a new novella, *Demons* from Cemetery Dance. He wrote the lyrics for the Blue Öyster Cult tune he quotes in his story for this anthology. Shirley's never considered murdering his current wife—although he admits the thought has entered his mind concerning some of his *ex*-wives. His Web site is www.darkecho.com/JohnShirley/.

Julia Solis—corpse model, translator and fiction writer— collects pictures of shipwrecks and drowning women. Her literary magazine, *The Spitting Image,* can be found at www.seatopia.com

Steve Rasnic Tem has published 250 plus short stories to date. His recent publications include a short story collection, *City Fishing,* from Silver Salamander, and a chapbook collaboration with his wife Melanie Tem, *The Man On The Ceiling,* from American Fantasy. He has four children and two grandchildren, all of whom would be shocked to hear that he knows anything at all about sex.

Anne Tourney is a sweet, soft-spoken creature who grew up in the Bible Belt, where she served multiple sentences locked in her bedroom for decapitating her dolls and encouraging them to fornicate. Her erotic fiction has appeared in *Paramour*, *Fishnet*, *The Best American Erotica 1994* and *1999*, and *The Unmade Bed: Twentieth-Century Erotica*. She leads a life of clandestine perversion in the San Francisco Bay Area.

Connie Wilkins lives in western Massachusetts, where she co-owns two stores supplying the non-essential necessities of college life. When let loose in the big city, she roams the aisles of mega-bookstores turning anthologies containing her stories face-out. On the last foray, these included two of Bruce Coville's sf books for children, Daw Books' *Prom Night*, and (pseudonymously) the *Best Lesbian Erotica* anthologies for 1999 and 2000.

About the Editor

Paula Guran edits *Horror Garage*, a punk-psychotronic-21st-century sort of horror fiction magazine. A contributing editor to Universal Studios' HorrorOnline (www.horroronline.com), she also edits, publishes, and writes most of *DarkEcho*, the Bram Stoker and International Horror Guild award-winning weekly electronic newsletter for horror writers and others and its related Web site (www.darkecho.com). She also writes, edits, works, and instructs for Writers On the Net (www.writers.com). Contact her at darkecho@aol.com.

Vol V Nation "Forsaken" = Vocal version